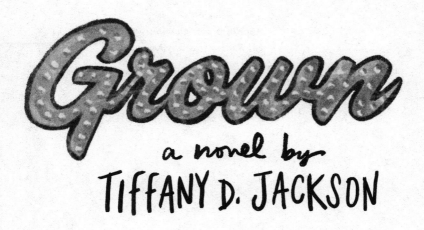

# Grown

a novel by
## TIFFANY D. JACKSON

KATHERINE TEGEN BOOKS
*An Imprint of HarperCollins Publishers*

**Also by Tiffany D. Jackson**

*Allegedly*
*Monday's Not Coming*
*Let Me Hear a Rhyme*

"All water has a perfect memory and is forever
trying to get back to where it was."
—Toni Morrison

To the victims, to the survivors, to the bravehearted,
to the girls who grew up too fast . . .
we believe you.

Katherine Tegen Books is an imprint of HarperCollins Publishers.

Grown
Copyright © 2020 by Tiffany D. Jackson
All rights reserved. Printed in the United States of America.
No part of this book may be used or reproduced in any manner
whatsoever without written permission except in the case of brief quotations
embodied in critical articles and reviews. For information
address HarperCollins Children's Books, a division of
HarperCollins Publishers, 195 Broadway, New York, NY 10007.
www.epicreads.com

ISBN 978-0-06-284035-6

Typography by Erin Fitzsimmons
20 21 22 23 24   PC/LSCH   10 9 8 7 6 5 4 3 2 1

First Edition

# Part One

# *Chapter 1*
## BEET JUICE

*NOW*

When I awake, I am eye-level with a puddle of beet juice soaked into the carpet, soft fibers cushioning my cheek. The beet juice is dark, thin, dried sticky between my fingers.

Damn, I have to pee.

I roll over, spine unforgiving, and struggle to my feet, knees wobbling, pain shooting stars through my skull. Out of the one eye that isn't swollen, everything is a bright blur. The blinding sun shines through dozens of floor-to-ceiling windows overlooking the city. My jaw is an unhinged door. I lick blood off my bottom lip, relish the metal taste and take in the room.

There's blood everywhere.

No, not blood. Beet juice. Or maybe cranberry. Thinned

barbecue sauce. But no, not blood. Blood means more than I can comprehend.

The beet-juice stains are all around his penthouse—on the cream sofa, the satin curtains, the ivory dining table, splatters on the ceiling . . . I even managed to spill some beet juice down my tank top and jeans. A hectic painting on what was once a pure white canvas.

A breeze glides up my bald head, the tips of my ears icy as I'm attacked by shivers. It's not the beet juice or my position on the floor that unnerves me; it's the silence. No music, no television, no voices . . . damn, I'm a mess and he's going to be so mad when he sees all these stains. The thought of his inevitable reaction produces more terror than the blood surrounding me.

Sorry, not blood. Beet juice.

I step over Melissa, cast aside like a dead dog, wrapping arms around myself. Where are my shoes? I didn't walk in here barefoot.

Wait . . . why am I still here? Didn't I leave last night?

A bloody handprint glides across the wall toward the bedroom, the door wide open.

Korey is slumped facedown, hanging off the bed . . . body covered in beet juice. Flaming words are stuck in my esophagus, but my body is frozen, rooted to the floor. If I move . . . if he catches me . . . he'll kill me.

Three pounds on the front door. A voice booms.

"Police! Open up!"

Piss runs down my leg, soaking my sock.

# Chapter 2

## SWIM GOOD

*THEN*

In my past life, I was a mermaid.

I lived deep in the ocean, swimming free, eating crustaceans, and singing five-octave ballads. My notes caused ripples in the sea—whales, turtles, and seahorses alike gathered for my daily concerts.

But on land, I struggle to breathe. Humans don't understand my pescatarian diet, and singing is a concept, not an aspiration.

Sitting a few feet away from a near-Olympic-size racing pool, I warm up my quads. Pool water is nothing but fake water. Swimming in it feels unnatural. But it's the closest substitute I can manage to find.

Whitney Houston hums through my headphones: "Where Do Broken Hearts Go."

The stretching playlist has some of my favorite classics—Mariah Carey, Aretha Franklin, Diana Ross, Chaka Khan, Nina Simone. Wish I could hook it up to a waterproof speaker and drop it into the pool. Synchronized swimmers listen to music underwater all the time. Maybe I should try out next year. Be a tour de force—an underwater ballerina who can sing.

Arms extended up with a graceful bow, I stretch and hum and stretch and hum . . .

"All right, Enchanted. Would you just sing already!" Mackenzie Miller stuffs her long blond hair into a swim cap.

"Huh?"

"Go ahead, sing," she says, her pink lips in a sly smirk. "You know you want to."

"Might as well," Hannah Tavano says next to her, slipping out of her track pants. "You're humming loud enough."

The entire swim team nods in agreement.

"Well, I'm always willing to give the people what they want," I say, stripping out of my sweats. I step to the edge of the pool, grabbing hold of my invisible mic.

*"Where do broken hearts go?*
*Can they find their way home?*
*Back to the open arms*
*of a love that's waiting there."*

The thing about singing near the pool is the acoustics. My voice carries, notes bouncing off the tiles, the dome roof, then skipping across the water like a pebble before boomeranging back. Every word pulses and echoes through my bloodstream, but then the song ends. The adrenaline leaves me breathless.

Applause shakes me out of a trance, and I glimpse down at my fans, a group of eight pale faces in matching navy swimsuits.

"Wow. It's like . . . you can really sing," Hannah says in disbelief. "You sound just like Beyoncé!"

The other teammates nod in agreement.

My heart deflates a bit. I love Beyoncé, but they use that comparison because that's the only black singer they know.

"Ladies," a voice shouts behind us. Coach Wilson leans against the doorframe of her office, pushing her red glasses back up her thin nose.

"If you're done with your concert, can you kindly get your butts in the water? Now! Ten laps. Let's go!"

The whistle blows and I dive in, slipping under the surface like sliding into a freshly made bed.

In the lanes to the right and left of me, Mackenzie and Hannah practice their breaststroke. My goggles are tight, but on purpose. I hate when chlorine slips through the crevices and I end up with red eyes like I've been smoking a blunt. Not that I'd know what that's like. But being one of ten black students in the entire school . . . the stupid assumption would be too easy.

After a warm-up, coach talks us through a few practice drills.

I hit the wall at the end of the pool on my last lap and power back. On land, Coach Wilson clicks her stopwatch, her face unreadable.

"Few seconds off. Not bad. Could be better."

I sniff, wiping my face dry. "You are full of compliments."

"Compliments don't help you improve," she chuckles. "All right, ladies! Showers. Then class. And I better not hear about any of you being late to homeroom. Jones, a word?"

Dripping wet, I skip into her office. "Yes, Coach?"

She tips her glasses. "You're spilling out of your uniform there."

I give myself a once-over. "I . . . am?"

"Butts and boobs need to be fully covered. Might be time to move up a size."

The locker room smells of chlorine and musty wet socks as a blow-dryer churns in the background. Glad I don't have problems like long hair to deal with anymore. In and out the shower, I can be ready for school in less than ten minutes.

Parkwood High School is the only private one in the county that doesn't have a strict dress code, but the student handbook specifically says no hats, no short skirts, no "distracting" hairstyles.

Yeah, I can read between the words unsaid there too.

I solved that problem by shaving off my locs. But somehow, my presence is still distracting.

At the mirror, I glide a hand over my baldy, the short hair

prickling my fingertips. The cutest shirt I own looks plain in the dingy locker-room light. I didn't want to do too much . . . it would set off alarms and I'm already nervous enough about today as it is. Maybe later, with Gab's gold hoops and some bright pink lipstick, I'll look . . . hot.

Hot? This is going to be a disaster.

Mackenzie slams her locker shut with a smirk. "Kyle Bacon."

I press my lips together to compose myself before feigning ignorance. "Who?"

"Kyle Bacon? He's a senior. Tall . . . um, dark eyes . . ."

Black, I want to say, help fill in the blank she's trying to avoid.

"What about him?" I sigh, knowing where this is going.

"Well . . . he doesn't have a date to the dance. You should go with him."

"Why? I don't even know him."

"You can get to know each other. Like a blind date."

"I'm not taking a blind date to homecoming."

"Come on! You'll look so good together in pictures."

"How do you know?"

Mackenzie's cheeks burn pink, her freckles on fire.

"Just . . . well, he's cute! And you're, like, really pretty."

I snort. "I can't believe you're quoting *Mean Girls* right now."

"All I'm saying is, you need a date. He's available. It's not like you're strangers. He saw you at the talent showcase last year. Actually, everyone saw you at the talent showcase, but he remembers you."

"Really?"

"Yeah! I mean, he liked the video I posted." She pulls out her phone and scrolls through Instagram, turning up the sound. There I am, singing Aretha's "Ain't No Way." Bet seventy-five percent of my classmates had never even heard of the song before.

I swallow back the memory. The last thing I need today is a reminder of the stage fright that hit me minutes beforehand. But like Gab says . . . wasn't ready then, but I'm ready now.

I shrug. "Well. Maybe. Since we'll look good together and all."

"Cool! Study sesh after school? If I fail bio, my mom will kill me. Or take my phone. I don't know which is worse."

I slip on my book bag. "Um, nah. I got something to do."

Despite Coach's lateness warning, I wait until the coast is clear before popping out of my hiding spot, sneakers squeaking against the wet tile. I pull back the curtains and set up my phone. Ten-minute vocal warm-up video on YouTube.

"La la la la la la la la laaaaaaa."

Pool acoustics are great, but showers are really where it's at! The only sound booth I've ever known.

I rehearse my song for later over and over. It has to be perfect, flawless.

Who knows when I'll have this chance again.

# *Chapter 3*

## CAGED BIRDS MUST SING

Mom is predictably twenty minutes late for pickup. Daddy says LaToya Jones will be late to her own funeral. It's why he refused to have a traditional wedding and went straight to the courthouse a few months before I came into this world.

So I'm used to working in my songbook on the outside steps of school, waiting for her arrival . . .

*In your heart, it's a start.*
*And we can't grow when we're this far apart.*
*Let's take it to another level*
*I'll be a sunrise in your meadow . . .*

Two honks snap me out of a groove. *Beep! Beep!*

"Heyyyy, Chanty!" Mom says, still in her hospital scrubs, her brown locs tied up into a neat bun. "Sorry I'm late. Where's your sister?"

"Here I am," Shea says, skipping behind me as we climb into the truck. "Bye, Becky. Bye, Anna. Bye, Lindsey!"

"Bye, Shea Shea," a group of her fellow freshmen sing with a wave.

Shea bounces into the middle of the back seat, her little chocolate face nudging Mom's forearm. "Mom, can I go over Lindsey Gray's house this weekend?"

"Chores first, white girls second. Buckle up!"

"Mom," she groans. "The window is open. People can hear you."

Mom rolls up the window as we drive off, Shea babbling about her day. She's adjusted well to high school, easier to do with an established group of friends from middle school rather than as a transfer student like me, fitting in like a little brown chameleon in every circle. I'm the blowfish out of water next to my little sister.

"Don't forget to fold the laundry. And take the salmon out the freezer," Mom says as we drop Shea off at home.

"I won't! Geez!"

"Don't let the twins pick all the veggies off their slices," I remind her. "And Destiny likes her pizza cut into squares or she won't eat it. Also new *Love and Hip Hop* tonight!"

"I know, Chanty, I know," she laughs. "Becky and I are gonna watch it together on FaceTime."

Mom backs out the driveway. "OK, you got the address to this swim meet?"

"Yup," I say, nervously typing it into the GPS.

Mom frowns. "Oh. It's in Manhattan?"

"Um, yeah."

"Dang. Didn't think it was going to be all the way in the city. And so late on a school night!"

"Bigger pool, I guess." I try to make my lies sound believable, smooth as untouched water.

"OK. But text Daddy and tell him we'll be home late."

On the way, Mom conducts the home orchestra from her speakerphone.

"Shea, what temp is that oven on? You put it up too high and the pizza's gonna burn. And did you take out fish like I told you?"

"Yes, Mom!" Shea sighs. "Geez!"

It's rare that Shea watches the Littles alone. I still consider her one of them.

"Daddy's picking up baby girl from day care before his shift. Where's the twins?"

"They're Kung Fu Panda-ing in the living room."

"Hi, Mommy!" they scream in the background.

"Hi, babies! How are my munchkins? What's the best thing that happened to you today?"

Mom is always multitasking, her mind working like several browser tabs opened at once. She gives Shea her last set of directions before hanging up.

"So what is this? A special meet or something?"

"Um, yes. Coach recommended me. College recruiters are going to be there and everything."

"Really?" She brightens, a grin growing across her face, and presses the gas a little harder. I turn up the volume on 107.5 WBLS, an oldies R&B station. Whitney Houston's "Saving All My Love for You" plays, and I hum along.

It's good practice.

"I don't understand how she got the times mixed up." Mom huffs as we scuffle across campus.

"Honest mistake," I say, checking the time just as a text from Gab pops up.

**What up! How's it going?**

                                        **Not there yet.**

**Girl! The line closes in thirty
minutes. Move ur ass!**

"A whole week early, though?" Mom carries on. "Doesn't she know some of us have jobs? Why are you walking so fast? Slow down!"

As she drags behind me, digging in her giant purse for her keys, I casually stroke into the next phase of my plan.

"Hey, Mom. Since we have some time, I mean, while we're here . . . can we stop at another tryout?"

"What kind of swim meet would be this late?"

"Well, it's actually a singing competition. A friend told me about it . . . today. It's just a little thing."

Mom's head pops up, eyes narrow. "Oh, really now?"

Torn between coming clean and pressing on, I dive deeper.

"Please! It'll be real quick. It's only fifteen minutes from here."

"Oh, and how would you know that?"

"I, uh, googled it on the way. I thought maybe if we finished up early, we could stop by. Not that I expected to, just, you know, being . . . proactive. Like you always tell me, right? Looks good for college recommendations."

Mom blows out some air. "Chanty, we talked about this. School, then activities, then homework, then housework, and *then* singing. That's what's going to get you into college!"

She's been beating this horse to death for years.

"I know! And we did, see? School, check. Activities, check. I did my homework during lunch. Shea has us covered at home, so . . ."

Mom shakes her head. "Oh, all right. You got one hour."

I smile. That's all I need.

A roar of applause bursts from inside the auditorium, bombarding the hectic lobby of the Beacon Theatre.

"I thought you said this was a small competition," Mom exclaims behind me, gaping at the massive MUSIC LIVE: AUDITIONS banner.

"Um, yeah, I thought so too," I mutter, noting the LIVE taping sign and camera lights.

"Wait, Chanty . . . is this *Music LIVE*? The one on BET?"

I pretend not to hear her as we make our way to the registration table with minutes to spare.

"Hi. Enchanted Jones," I say out of breath. "I'm here for the auditions."

"You're lucky. We were just about to shut it down. Are you registered?"

"Yes, I . . . uh, did it online."

Mom grunts behind me as the lady slides her finger down the chart.

"Got you! OK. Here's your number. You have your track ready?"

"Yup, right here," I say, waving my iPhone.

"Cool. Now, when they call your name, hand your ballot to the judges and take the stage. Go ahead. Good luck!"

"Thanks," I say, turning to Mom, her arms crossed. I know I'm busted, but I ignore her eye daggers. At the end of the night, it'll all be worth it; I know it.

Inside, the theater is jammed with people. The purple and white stage lights swim across a wave of faces. Music beats through my chest. I grab Mom's hand, surveying the scene and finding two empty red velvet seats in the back.

Onstage, a girl with long extensions is singing—really, slaughtering—Destiny's Child's "Cater 2 U," the crowd booing her. A camera projects her face on massive screens as she struggles to maintain a brave smile.

*Music LIVE* is BET's version of *American Idol*. A three-round singing competition. The grand prize: ten thousand dollars. If I win, it'll be enough to pay for real studio time to record my album. Even if I don't win, it's an opportunity to be noticed by record labels, managers, and A&R reps. All a big *if*, but better than nothing.

What I didn't know was that the auditions were open to the public. Gab left out that crucial detail.

Everyone, including other contestants, is dressed in an array of party clothes and heels. I gulp.

"Be right back," I say to Mom, running off before she can ask questions.

In the bathroom, I struggle with Gab's mascara and eyeliner, thread her gold bamboo hoop earrings, add a touch of pink to my lips, and glide a shaky hand down my scalp. I take a quick selfie and send it to Gab.

**This pink looks horrible on me.**

**It's camera-ready pink! You cute!**

Back at my seat, Mom looks me over.

"Um, did they call me yet?"

"No," Mom says, tone clipped, and I try not to wish Grandma was here instead.

I recognize the profile of Richie Price at the table facing the stage. He's a big-time music producer–turned–TV director, or something. I read his bio on the website. Beside him, Melissa Short, a music executive from RCA. Beside her, Don Michael, singer.

"OK. Next up, Amber B. Come on down, Amber!"

The crowd cheers as a girl who looks about my age makes her way to the stage. She waves at the judges and struts center stage.

"Hi, sweetheart," Richie says.

"Hi!" she chirps, lush golden curls bouncing around her heart-shaped face.

"What are you singing for us tonight?"

"Beyoncé's 'Halo.'"

"OK, ma, let's hear it!"

Amber nods at the soundman, and the beat thumps into the speakers. The crowd claps along. Amber grabs the mic, closing her eyes.

*"Remember those walls I built*
*Well, baby, they tumbling down . . ."*

Her voice is . . . majestic. A blend of sweet with sharp edges. A voice made for the stage. I slump lower in my seat, nerves firing into my stomach.

"Mom," I squeak. "Mom, we should go."

But Mom can't hear me, too hypnotized by Amber's skin sparkling like moondust under the stage lights. I'm never going to sound as good as her. Or look as good as her. I slip on my hoodie and grab my book bag. If I leave now, Mom can just meet me at the car.

I rise to my feet as chaos erupts by the door. A cloud of burly linemen dressed in black piles in, surrounding something . . . or someone. The person, dressed in a white hooded sweat suit, stops in the middle of the aisle.

As the stranger pulls back his hoodie, a shriek erupts from the crowd. "Oh my GOD! Korey Fields!"

Korey Fields's megawatt smile lights up the room. He walks with a slight bop in his step down to the judges' table. He gives

Richie a pound, and they exchange a few words, oblivious to the excitement that has taken over the theater. Onstage, Amber finishes her song but stands shell-shocked.

"Wow, Chanty," Mom shouts, clapping. "Korey Fields!"

I'm speechless. This was supposed to be a simple audition. First the crowd, now Korey Freaking Fields . . . all here to see me make a fool out of myself.

"Mom, let's go before . . ."

"Next up . . . Enchanted Jones!"

# Chapter 4
## HEART SONG

My name booms over the loudspeaker. Too loud to ignore.

"OK, Chanty, you're up! Good luck, baby!"

Mom kisses my cheek and pats me on the butt. The entire theater turns in my direction. I swallow and head for the stage.

Korey sits behind Richie, surrounded by his entourage, at least a dozen people, while the audience elbows over each other to grab pictures. They don't even notice me take the stage. I'm invisible—how I always feel.

"Hi, sweetheart," Richie says.

"Hello," I croak out, and the mic delivers feedback. "Um. I'm . . . uh, my name is Enchanted."

"Yes, we already know your name. What are you singing for us today?"

"Oh! Um, 'If I Were Your Woman' by Gladys Knight."

Korey's eyes lock on me. He's like a large moon in a starless sky.

Richie frowns. "Hmm?" The judges look at one another, unsure, then shrug. "OK, let's see what you got!"

I nod at the soundman.

The chords ring in, the crowd silent. I start to sing, keeping a running checklist of all the performance notes I learned on YouTube:

Chin up.

Hold the mic firm.

Eye contact with the audience.

But the only person I seem to see is Korey, who hasn't taken his eyes off me.

*"You're a part of me*

Korey leans forward in his chair. And somehow, seeing him, the one person I can make out in a room full of nameless faces, soothes my nerves. So I sing to him, just him. The way I used to sing to Grandma during my living room concerts when I was a kid.

*And you don't even know it*

*I'm what you need*

*But I'm too afraid to show it . . .*

When I'm done, the room bursts into applause. Korey's mouth hangs open, staring up in awe.

• • •

Judge #1-Melissa: "You have a great voice. But a little shaky. Need a few more rounds of singing lessons."

Judge #2-Don: "Eh, I don't like the song. Too old-school. Not something of today."

Judge #3-Richie: "You two are crazy. You hear all that untamed talent? But I'm outnumbered here. Better luck next year, sweetheart. I'm sure we'll see you again. Soon."

# Chapter 5

## BRIGHT EYES

Backstage is dark enough to mask the oncoming tears. The perfect place to hide when you need a moment or two. Or ten. Or fifteen.

I need a few before rejoining Mom, before spending the forty-five-minute drive home in awkward silence. I tricked her into taking me to this audition, all for nothing. I don't understand. I know I nailed that song. Did way better than others. But maybe it wasn't the song choice. Maybe it was the whole package that turned them away. My skin, my clothes, my crooked smile, my nonexistent hair . . .

"Nice song."

His breath touches the back of my neck, and I whip around. Korey Fields.

My tongue plays dead in my mouth, lips parting. When did he come back here? And how . . . wait, I'm talking to Korey Fields. Well, no, I'm not talking. He's talking to me. *Say something, dummy!*

"Um . . . thanks."

His smile lights up the dark space. Up close, he smells rich, like honey and musky tanning oil. His outfit is crisp, not a speck of dirt on him. Not even on his kicks.

"Interesting pick," he says, nodding as if impressed.

"Interesting?" I repeat.

"I'm just surprised someone your age would choose such a . . . classic."

I don't know how to take that, so I shrug and offer honesty.

"It was one of my grandma's favorites."

He pauses, a stunned look in his eyes before chuckling. "Yeah, mine too."

We stand in silence, staring at each other. The next contestant is already onstage, singing Beyoncé. Guess I missed the memo that I should've gone with any song from her catalog.

Korey seems much taller in his music videos, towering over every girl he dances on. But in person, he's regular. Not that he's short or nothing, just not the LeBron James I thought he'd be. More Steph Curry.

"You have a voice," he says. "You take lessons?"

"Kinda." I don't think YouTube counts. "But I practice all the time! And write my own songs."

"Hm. Well, you should take some. Professional ones."

I blink. "Ouch. Was I that bad?"

"Oh, nah. Not like that!" He chuckles. "But even naturals need some coaching. Like sports. You get better the more you train. You feel me?"

I think of Coach Wilson and smile. "Yeah, I think I know exactly what you mean."

Korey searches my face.

"Here, let me show you something real quick."

I gasp as he steps toward me, laying one hand flat on my stomach, then the other on the middle of my back. I tense up, frantically searching the room.

Does ANYONE see this? Korey Fields . . . is touching ME!

But there's only bodyguards. And they all seem to be standing away from us, backs turned, pretending they're invisible.

"Relax, ma, it's OK. You're safe with me," he says with a wink, voice raspy. "See, you gotta breathe from your diaphragm. Do it with me, ready?"

I breathe in deep, my belly expanding as he caresses my back.

"Now release a note as you exhale."

I do as he says, and the note comes out smooth and effortless.

"See? Better?"

"Yeah." I giggle. "Better."

I look up into his eyes and . . . I can't look away . . . so I don't because he doesn't either. His lips, pressed into a hard line, part.

"Damn. You got some beautiful eyes."

My heart beats hard against my ribs, hands rested on his like they've always belonged there, rubbing the rough patches on his knuckles. Then it hits me . . . I'm touching Korey Fields. THE Korey Fields . . . and Mom could come back here any moment. It'd be sixth grade all over again, when I got caught in the closet kissing Jose Torres.

Except Korey isn't a regular boy like Jose. He's . . . so much more.

"I, um, I gotta go. My . . . mom is probably wondering where I'm at."

A flash of confusion sweeps across his face. He hesitates before unattaching himself.

"How old are you?"

I gulp. "Seventeen."

For a long moment, his face is expressionless. Then he offers a smile.

"You're gonna come to my show next Saturday," he says. "I'll hook you and your parents up with some VIP tickets."

The last contestant jogs backstage with a face-splitting smile. She was picked. Of course.

"Um, OK," I say.

"Your name will be at the box office," he says whipping out his phone before winking at me. "See you later, Bright Eyes."

He taps one of his bodyguards, who gives me a once-over before exiting.

Butterflies tickle the inside of my chest. Maybe I'm hallucinating. Because there's absolutely no way Korey Fields would ever be into me.

# Chapter 6

## A STAR IS BORN

According to Wikipedia, Korey Fields is twenty-eight years old.

Korey was a protégé. A child superstar at thirteen, he was discovered on YouTube, singing Stevie Wonder songs.

Raised by his grandmother, he could play several instruments, including drums, piano, guitar, and even trumpet. All self-taught while spending hours at his local Baptist church.

They called him the second coming of Michael Jackson, with such hit singles as "Invincible," "I Remember You," "Work It," and "Love Is a Verb."

My parents loved dancing to his song "A Lifetime of Love."

Fifteen top Billboard hits. Triple-platinum albums. Back-to-back sold-out concerts and tours.

He won his first Grammy at age fifteen.

He's an *E* shy of being an EGOT (Emmy Grammy Oscar Tony).

The shirtless photo on the cover of his latest album is like an oil painting of a Greek god. He's the color of earth. Dark eyes, sharp chin, perfect nose, a chest chiseled out of amber stone, muscles forming a V right above his jeans waistband . . .

Korey Fields is twenty-eight years old.

He's young. But not that young.

# Chapter 7
## FRIENDS TO THE END

Gabriela dips her fish stick in a cup of ketchup that sits on top of her biology textbook.

"So, our evil plan worked," she says with a grin.

"Yeah. Even though LaToya Jones almost killed me."

Like most lunch periods, we find ourselves chilling in the dark gym alcove near the school's trophy display, skin drenched in fluorescent lighting. I dip my fish sticks in tartar sauce, stealing some of her ketchup for my fries.

"And the lipstick? Earrings?"

"Perfect. But none of that matters . . . because I met *Korey Fields*." I try to hold in my swoon. "He gave me a nickname. Did I mention that yet?"

"Yes." She sighs, flipping open her notebook. "For the fourth time now."

"Yeah, but it's *how* he said it."

Rolling her eyes, she chuckles. "I'm sure he was just being nice."

"No way. It's wasn't like how Daddy's friends call me sweetheart. No, this seemed . . . specific. Just for me."

"Ew, girl, are you double dipping? Stop mixing your pickled mayo with my pureed tomatoes."

"It tastes better this way! OK, listen to this. 'Soul eyes, souls rise. Be it a day or a lifetime. When the beauty comes alive. Would you be mine?' Then the hook would sort of be this hum melody."

Gab's smile stretches wide. "Whoa. That's fire! You came up with that today? You're such a beast!"

From the outside, our friendship seems understandable: same height, weight, and pedigree, except Gab is a year older, and instead of a baldy, she has a head of thick, straight, dark brown hair she keeps in a sloppy high bun. But any word you'd think to describe me, think of her as the antonym. Where I'm clumsy and awkward, Gab is modelesque and confident. Where I'm anxious and frantic, Gab is calm, wise beyond her years. Nothing tips her scale.

Yet we're two of the few girls of color in a field of lilies. She's the only girl in the entire school I can talk to without overexplaining my existence. That brings a level of sisterly comfort. For both of us.

Comfort enough to admit my deepest emotion. "He said he liked my singing."

Gab smiles. "Of course he did. Because you're good, and the world needs to know that. This is just a start. Soon you'll be performing in sold-out concerts!"

I shrug. "Maybe. Maybe even with him."

She plucks a thought from my head and frowns. "He's too old for you."

"Well. Y-y-yeah, obviously," I mumble, my cheeks on fire. "But a girl can dream, right?"

Her face contorts. "Why the hell would you want to dream about that old-ass uncle?"

"Uncle? He ain't that old! He's not even thirty! He's only, what, seven years older than Jay?"

Gab's eyes squint over her can of Sprite. "That's completely different, and you know it."

"OK, OK! Easy, killer," I laugh. "I can't believe you still get in your feelings about that."

Jay. Gab's boyfriend. Gab's *college* boyfriend.

She squirms. "It's just . . . gross, what people say about us."

OK, so it's not the same thing. Jay is twenty-one and has been with Gab for three years.

Footsteps down the hall make me swallow back my response. Two freshmen pass the alcove, stopping to stare at us.

"What?" Gab snaps. "Can I help y'all with something? If not, then beat it!"

The two kids exchange a look then glance back at us, their eyes wide. Gab slams her notebook shut.

"Did I stutter? I said fuck off!" Her voice a whip snap. They jump, scurrying away, mumbling.

"Damn, Gab. Take it easy."

"I hate how people stare at us like we're some damn aliens, like they've never seen a black or Latina in their life!"

After almost two years, I'm used to the stares. The blue, green, and hazel eyes are part of the decor. Gab doesn't have that problem; she could pass for a white girl, blending into the field. But she'd never acknowledge that.

"Why you always want to hang out over here?" I ask.

Gab's face is tinted mint under the fluorescents, her jawline reflecting off a hockey trophy won back in the nineties, covered in dust.

She shrugs, returning to her textbook. "It's easier to talk to you here. Too many nosey people. Plus, I can actually get some homework done instead of waiting until I'm off the clock. Oh! I got you this cute hoodie! It was buy one, get one fifty percent off. Twinning!"

Gab works at Old Navy in the White Plains Galleria. That's when she's not driving down to Fordham University to visit Jay. In the car she owns, paid for with her own money. She doesn't have much time for trivial nonsense like homework. She's a senior going on fifty.

But at least she has a boyfriend. All I have is swimming, music, and dreams of Korey.

"I wish you could come to the concert with us."

"That fresh shipment of Rockstar jeans isn't going to fold

itself," she jokes. "Besides, this is your time to shine!" She carries a note as far as her lungs will allow, singing the lines I just shared with her. Why she refuses to share the stage with me, I'll never know.

I think of Korey again. His hand on my stomach, palm pressing into my belly button, imprinting on me. Wonder what it would be like to really BE with him, having the type of love he always sings about.

"He was . . . sweet."

Gab pretends not to hear me and continues copying the lesson on cell units.

# *Chapter 8*
## WILL AND WILLOW MEETING NOTES

Between moving to Hartsdale with its limited diversity and attending an elite private school, Mom thought the best way for the Littles and me to connect with the black people in our area was to join Will and Willow Incorporated. The objective of Will and Willow as stated on their website: "to create a medium of contact for African American mothers to bring their children together in social and cultural environments to be strengthened through leadership development, volunteer service, and civic duty."

My cousin says it's for bougie black moms to show off their equally bougie black kids. And he isn't exactly wrong.

There are chapters all over the country, divided into groups by age. We, the Westchester Teen chapter, have a once-a-month meeting, directed by our teen government board:

**Malika Evens:** President

**Sean Patrick Jr.:** Vice President

**Creighton Stevens:** Treasurer

**Aisha Woods:** Secretary

**Enchanted Jones:** just a regular ol' member

**Shea Jones:** her little sister, newest member of the teen Group Five.

We all live about ten miles from each other but these kids' parents have money. Surgeons, lawyers, architects, politicians—one is even related to Denzel Washington. Meanwhile, my family is making it by the skin of our teeth, and it shows.

Our meetings go a little something like this:

**Creighton:** Where's Emery?

**Enchanted:** Think he had to work.

**Malika:** Of course. OK, everyone, let's get started. Now, as you all know, next month is the Eastern Regional Teen Cluster. Our room block at the Marriott has been confirmed. Creighton, has everyone paid their dues?

**Creighton:** Everyone except the Jones sisters.

**Shea:** Chant?

**Enchanted:** My mom is dropping the money off on Friday.

**Malika:** Right. Well, until then, we'll assume you won't be attending.

**Enchanted:** Or . . . you can assume we *are* going since I just told you my mom will drop off the money on Friday.

**Malika:** Which is six days away.

**Sean:** Damn girl, can't you borrow some dough from . . . somebody? I was looking forward to us dancing.

**Enchanted:** Why borrow when we have it?

**Malika:** But you don't.

**Aisha:** We can't go too guy heavy. We need more girls!

**Creighton:** Hey, don't worry about it, Enchanted. I've added y'all to the count and I'll square up with your mom on Friday.

**Shea:** Thanks, Creighton.

**Malika:** Anyways, like I was saying . . . the rental van to New Jersey will leave at seven thirty a.m. sharp from the town shopping center. No CP time. My mother, Mrs. Woods, and Mr. Stevens will be our chaperones. Enchanted, Mrs. Woods volunteered you to sing the black national anthem. You need the words?

**Enchanted:** Nah, I'm good.

**Malika:** Good at what?

**Sean:** Nah, she means she *good* like she cool. Straight. Gucci. She got it covered. You keep forgetting she didn't grow up in the 'burbs like us.

**Malika:** Whatever. Here, everybody. This is your packing list and the schedule. We need to wear business suits on the last day.

**Shea:** Chant . . .

**Enchanted:** Relax, you can fit into my old one. I'm wearing Mom's.

**Sean:** Y'all! First night, party in my room! I already talked to my boys from the Brooklyn and Philly chapters and they'll be—

**Aisha:** I don't think Warren will like that.

**Sean:** Who's Warren?

**Malika:** Aisha's boyfriend.

**Sean:** Yo, that clown that dropped you off in that hoopty?

**Aisha:** Shut up, Sean! We all ain't lucky enough for our daddy to buy us a BMW after he crashed the first one.

**Sean:** Man, whatever. So, what y'all drinking? I can have my boy from the Danbury chapter bring some bottles from his brother's army base.

**Malika:** Look. I'm not trying to sound like . . . well, like a mom or something. But everyone has to be on their best behavior this year.

**Creighton:** Meaning?

**Malika:** No sneaking off to girls' rooms or partying. No getting drunk at the teen social.

**Aisha:** Our chapter already has a scarlet letter

on our backs. Let's just not give them . . .
anything else to talk about.

**Sean:** So we gotta be mad basic? That's wack.

**Enchanted:** Is there anything else? I have to head
out early.

**Sean:** What for?

**Malika:** We haven't even gone over the schedule
yet. We have a presentation to prepare!

**Enchanted:** Going to see Korey Fields tonight.

**Sean:** Oh, dope! I heard that joint was sold out.
How'd you get tickets?

**Shea:** He gave—

**Enchanted:** Parents lucked up on tickets! That's
all.

**Malika:** Well. Have fun in the nosebleed section.

# *Chapter 9*

## VIP STANDS FOR . . .

VIP stands for Very Important Person. I looked that up on Wikipedia.

When we picked up our tickets from will call at Madison Square Garden, the attendant gave us bright green VIP badges, with the words *Backstage Access*.

Mom, Daddy, and I wore them proudly to our seats in the front row. I've never felt more important or more seen. I want this feeling for the rest of my life.

The moment he stepped onstage and uttered that first note, screams echoed through the building.

Korey Fields is a giant shirtless god.

I try to keep my chin off the floor, to keep from drooling

down my pink sweater.

And for a split second, I think he notices me in the crowd and winks at me. But no, I must be imagining things. I do that every now and then.

Except I wish it was real.

After the show ends, we make our way to the backstage entrance, nearly swallowed by a crowd trying to finagle their way in. But they don't have badges like we do. We're VIP. An attendant waves us on.

"Guest of K's? This way."

We're led through the maze of hallways to a door with a sign that says *Greenroom*, which really isn't green but dressed in black curtains wrapped around the walls. Chilled champagne bottles and trays of hors d'oeuvres sit on tables while white leather sofas cradle music stars.

"Wow," Daddy whispers to Mom. "Can you believe this?"

"Oh my God," Mom says, slapping Daddy's arm. "Terry, look! Don't *look* look, but look. That's Usher!"

Celebrities spill in, all wearing the same VIP badge. We're as important as the celebrities!

This could be my greenroom someday. Maybe someday soon.

"Enchanted, when Mr. Fields come back here, remember to thank him for the tickets!"

The thought of seeing him again, really seeing him, makes me bounce on the balls of my feet. But it's dark back here. What if he doesn't see me? Chill, I tell myself. Gab wouldn't act this . . . silly. She would be effortlessly cool. Need to draw from that power.

"Pull down your shirt, baby," Mom mumbles, yanking my top. "Don't want these grown men looking at what you got."

There's a flurry of activity before Korey steps inside, surrounded by a swarm of cameras, security, and . . . women. Gorgeous model types, the kind you'd see on Instagram with over a million followers, in tight bodycon dresses, weaves down to their snatched waists. I step back, nauseous and ready to leave, when he spots me from across the room. Without hesitation, he charges right over, his swarm following. Madison Square falls silent.

"Hey," he says, his voice sultry, extending his hand. Soft, just like I remember, his fingertips tickle my palm ever so slight and I'm tangled up in his eyes.

And he still doesn't have his shirt on.

After a beat, he turns to Daddy.

"You must be the father. Korey," he says. "No offense, sir, but your daughter definitely favors her pretty momma."

"Aight now, don't be trying to steal my wife," Daddy laughs, shaking his hand. "I've heard stories about you!"

"All lies, I swear!"

Mom nudges my arm and I remember my one duty.

"Um, thank you for the tickets."

"Anytime."

"Your show was amazing," Mom gushes, clapping her hands. "Our little girl here thinks the world of you."

Mortified, I wince at the word *little*. Korey notices, offering a sympathetic grin.

"Well, I think your daughter has an amazing voice," he says with a wink. "Hey, have y'all met Charlie Wilson yet?"

Mom's and Daddy's eyes light up.

"Charlie Wilson?" Daddy gasps. "THE Charlie Wilson?"

"Yeah, he's right over there. Hey, Tony? Take these good folks to meet Uncle Charlie."

The bodyguard I saw the night I Korey him gives a silent nod. I start to trail behind Mom before Korey catches my hand.

"Hey," he coos. "Where you going, Bright Eyes?"

My heart does that fluttering thing again. He called me by my name.

"Um, nice show," I squeak.

"So, you approve?"

"I mean, I don't think you need my approval."

"No. It matters what you think of me, though."

Still starstruck, I say the first thing that comes to mind.

"Your show was . . . breathtaking."

His smile cracks into a laugh. "Breathtaking?"

In an instant, I want the earth to swallow me whole.

"OMG. OMG. I'm so . . . that was so . . . OMG. I didn't mean it like that!"

"Yes. Yes, you did. And I like it."

For a moment, it feels like we're the only ones in the room. Maybe on the planet.

"So, anymore shows for you?" he asks.

"No, just singing to the Littles."

"The Littles?"

"Oh yeah, that's what I call my sibs. I have three sisters and one brother. I'm the oldest."

"Daaaamn, that's a lot of y'all! Your folks were busy."

"Ew! I don't want to think of my parents that way!"

"My bad," he laughs. "Man, I always wanted a big family. This only-kid thing ain't all that."

"It's . . . uh, crowded. Plus, it's different. By my age, you were already touring all over the world." I wince at the age difference slipup but carry on. "I mean, it must have been amazing, doing the thing you love most. No one saying you can't, or you have to babysit this kid or clean that."

He chuckles. "Well, I got a feeling I'll be seeing you behind the mic real soon. You got this . . . hunger about you. I can sense it."

"It's . . . all I've ever wanted to do," I say, my chest seeming lighter.

Korey leans back with an admiring glow. "Damn. I feel that."

Across the room, my parents are gushing in front of their favorite artist. Tony is somehow blocking my view of them. Or maybe he's blocking their view of me.

"Here," Korey says, stepping closer. "Give me your phone."

He glances around, lowering my phone to his hip, and programs in a number, before sending himself a text.

"There. Now I got you," he says, slipping it in my jacket pocket with a light pat to my hip. "Just . . . don't tell anyone, aight? It'll be our thang, Bright Eyes."

My breath hitches in my throat. We have a *thang*.

Mom is at my side again, her face flushed. She loops arms with me.

"Wow, he's just as amazing in person!"

"Yeah, he's really been a mentor to me, all these years. Which is what I want to be for your daughter. Like I said before, she definitely has something special."

# Chapter 10
## BEACH BUMS

We were once beach bums before moving to this thickened forest. We were a family that played in the sand, swam in rough waters, shoulders kissed by the sun.

Mommy and Daddy grew up on a beach in Far Rockaway, Queens, and called themselves the first fish of our family. Daddy says we evolved from fish, which is why we are so drawn to water. It's a part of our genetic memory. That made sense to him, while the idea of God did not.

During the summer, we'd pack up coolers and stay at the beach from sunup to sundown.

We lived in a three-bedroom apartment with my grandma, my mom's mom, facing the ocean. In mornings before school,

I'd step on the balcony, filling my nose with the sea breeze. Grandma would join me, gazing out at the choppy water in longing.

"It sure is busy out there today. How about a song?"

Grandma called me her very own Little Mermaid, since I never wanted to get out of the water. I wanted to live in the sea and sing at the shore, even in the winter when the waves were a frozen ice sculpture. She said my voice was from another world that filled our home with the soulful melodies of Aretha Franklin, Patti LaBelle, and Whitney Houston.

But our home was a tiny aquarium, and we, a school of fish, bumped into each other at every turn, muddling the water with tension, Mom and Grandma biting hunks out of each other like starving piranhas.

Fish die quick in a tank, Daddy said. We needed room, to flourish, to grow, to go to college, to dive deep and go where they never could.

We, meaning my four siblings and me.

We couldn't afford to live on our own, but drowning in Grandma's swelling quirks made Mom and Daddy map out a plan. Daddy took extra shifts for the cable company, and Mom went to nursing school. Three years, they saved for this house that smells like wet moss, its dampness leaving our skin chilled, the billowy high trees blocking all traces of the sun. No soft waves or sweeping winds, just a chorus of bugs and angrily chirping birds. We're now a school of fish surrounded by white fishermen.

Daddy is always tired—that's if I see him, which is rare. He joined an electrical union, takes double shifts repairing cable wires, all to pay the mortgage and private-school tuition. He doesn't bring up going to the beach anymore or how we were fish. Mom became our personal driver. When they're both at work, I'm the only parent for miles. Yes, we have more room to swim but without a car, we float in a suburban aquarium, rather than an ocean.

In the mornings, before I make breakfast for the Littles, I hold a seashell to my ear and listen to the sounds of home.

# Chapter 11

## SHOP TALK

In the narrow bathroom, I straddle the toilet seat, a smock buttoned around my neck, watching hair rain down around me, a buzzing near my left ear. I flinch.

"Hold still, now," Daddy says, gripping my head. "Almost done."

Daddy bought a new clipper kit when I decided to shave my head. Before, he only used a razor on his beard but decided his daughter deserved the finer things. Plus, it saves us eighteen dollars and weekly trips to the barbershop.

"Hey, watch the neck," I say with a wince.

"I've got this. Chill. Damn, kid. Your mom's hair don't grow like this. Must be from my side of the family."

"You say that about everything." I snicker. "Singing, swimming, height, weight, feet . . . all from your side of the family."

He laughs. "Well, that's the truth, Ruth!"

"Really? Dad jokes? You've been in the 'burbs too long. We gotta get you back to Queens."

"You know all this extra hair . . . is gonna cost you."

"How much?"

"Fifty dollars. Same as last week."

I smirk. "You can add it to my tab."

"Daddy!" a voice shrieks.

We turn to the open bathroom door, into the immediate kitchen, at Destiny in her booster seat, her mouth full of mashed potatoes.

Daddy turns off the clippers. "Yes, baby girl."

"Mo' fish stick?"

"Finish what's on your plate first. Eyes bigger than your stomach."

Pearl hops up from the table, running by, her mini locs flopping.

"Aye," he calls. "Where do you think you're going?"

She shrugs. "I'm done."

"You ain't done if your plate still on the table. Ain't no maid service around these parts."

"It's your turn to do the dishes anyway," Phoenix adds from, well, somewhere close.

"Is not!"

"How about you both do them," Daddy says.

Pearl and Phoenix groan together the way only twins can before they start clearing the table.

"Daddy, I need more juice," Destiny says, waving her empty cup at him.

With Mom working late and Daddy having a rare Friday off, I'm sure he's not used to hearing his name so much. He rubs his head.

"Lawd," he grumbles. "Shea, can you pour your sister some juice, please?"

Shea nods, busy FaceTiming with a friend from school, gossiping about some boy.

"Is this what y'all do in high school now? FaceTime with each other even though you see each other all day?" He chuckles, clicking on the clippers. "Don't remember you ever doing that."

I stare at him in the mirror, his eyes focused as he lines me up.

"Daddy," I say with a measured voice. "Can I have a car? Please?"

Daddy's head snaps up, returning my stare.

"I've done the research," I continue before he can fix his mouth to say no. "We can lease a car for two hundred and twenty-eight dollars a month. I'll be able to help with the Littles. Take Shea and me to school."

Daddy sighs and shuts off the clippers. The walls of the bathroom shrink.

"It's just not something we can swing right now. With tuition, Will and Willow dues, summer camp next year . . . we're stretched thin. Plus, the union might be striking soon.

Which would mean . . . a lot of changes around here."

I've heard Mommy and Daddy talk about it. A union strike would mean no pay, and strikes can go on for months, maybe years. Shea and I would have to drop out of Parkwood. Worst case, we could lose the house.

"But I wanna get a job."

Daddy's lips press together. "You have your entire life to work. For now, we just want you to be a normal teenager."

There's nothing normal about being trapped in the house, taking care of kids you didn't birth.

"OK . . . well then, can you help me pay for singing lessons?"

His shoulders sag. "That'd be another activity and we really need you here to watch the Littles."

"But you heard what Korey Fields said. I have real potential. Singing lessons can help me find my voice. This could be my shot!"

"Baby, we talked about this. Singing is . . . a big risk. Doesn't work out for everybody. There's thousands of singers out there, and only the lucky ones really make it."

I look down at my hair scattered on the floor.

Daddy wipes his mouth, fidgets with his tools, then uses a brush to dust the stray hairs off my shoulders.

"So, what's up next for the Disney club?" he says, hope in his voice. "What are you guys watching tonight?"

I rip the smock off me.

"*The Little Mermaid*," I mutter, tossing it in the tub.

Ariel's father didn't let her do anything either.

# *Chapter 12*

## A WHOLE NEW WORLD

"All right, guys, we ready?"

"Yeah!" the room cheers.

It's been two weeks since the concert, and I've followed Korey Fields's every move on Instagram. He's had back-to-back appearances. Between his video recaps, Insta-stories, and thirst-trap photos of his bare chest, I spent every evening in bed scrolling, ogling, and analyzing each post like a private eye.

But tonight, I needed to send Korey to the back of my thoughts and focus on our weekly tradition—Disney club.

After a dinner of fish sticks and broccoli, I make popcorn and fresh limeade as Shea sets up pillows in the living room.

"Tonight, Littles, we introduce you to *Aladdin*!"

"It's stupid. How did she not recognize him?" Shea asks, plopping into her seat, pulling Destiny onto her lap. "It's not like he got a nose job or something."

"Who recognize who?" Phoenix asks, snuggling into the rocking chair.

"Hey! Stop ruining it for the rest of them! This is an important rite of passage. Genie is up there with Sebastian as far as sidekicks go. OK, any questions?"

Pearl shoots her hand up. "Can you make fish tacos tomorrow?"

"As long as you eat a salad with it."

The twins gag, Shea rolls her eyes. They all complain but I don't care. It's my job to take care of them, just like Grandma would.

Fifteen minutes into the movie, my phone vibrates. I expect it to be Mom or Daddy telling us they'll be home late as usual. Instead, it's a message from someone named Pips.

**WYD**

Pips? Who the hell is Pips and what . . .

I drop the phone with a gasp.

Shea turns. "What's up?"

The truth lodges in my throat and I swallow it back.

"Um . . . nothing."

Shea raises an eyebrow then returns to the movie.

Korey Fields is in my phone. He is in MY phone. He's texting me. What do I say? Should I play it cool? No, I'll never pull it off. So maybe . . . the truth.

**Watching Aladdin with the Littles.**

Which one? Remake or the original?

**Original.**

Of course. You're a classic type of girl. 😊

"Who are you texting?" Shea asks.

"Um, Mackenzie. Mind your business and watch the movie."

**Ever seen it?**

Of course. It's one of my Disney favorites.

It's like he said the magic word.

**Well, that's actually what we're doing. Every Friday, we watch one Disney movie, introducing the babies to the classics.**

Dope! What's on the list so far?

**Snow White**
**Sleeping Beauty**
**Cinderella**
**Alice in Wonderland**
**Peter Pan**
**The Jungle Book**
**The Little Mermaid**
**Aladdin**
**Beauty and the Beast**
**The Lion King**

The Princess and the Frog

What about Pocahontas?

No way am I exposing them to
that colonizer version of what
actually happened!

LMAO! Damn Ma! What about
Mary Poppins?

Sticking to cartoons for now.

What? What about The
Mighty Ducks? Classic!!

That's a Disney movie?

Girl, you kidding? You ever
been to Disneyland?

Nah, too expensive for all us to
go. Always wanted to tho!

They got this part that shows
how they made all their
movies. You see Swiss Family
Robinson?

No but maybe we can watch that
one together someday.

There's an air bubble, like he's thumbing a response then
stopped midthought.

Silence.

"Shit." I gasp, heart plunging into my stomach.

The Littles yelp. "Oooo! Bad word!"

"Sorry, guys."

Shea arches an eyebrow. "You OK?"

"Uh . . . yeah. Forgot I have practice in the morning."

Shea doesn't buy it but doesn't push. She grabs the remote out my lap, and rewinds a few beats. Genie is singing, *"You ain't never had a friend like me."*

I try to ease back into the movie, but I can't focus. Did I say too much? Come off too strong? *Too strong? He's Korey Fields, dummy! He's not into you! Get that through your head.*

After the movie, I change the Littles for bed, sing them a song, and shower. As soon as my head hits the pillow, my phone vibrates with a text.

**Maybe** 😘

Burying myself under blankets, I let out a gleeful shriek, eyes glued to the message.

Maybe! With a kissing emoji!

I stay up studying the message, interpreting the various layers of its meaning. Body buzzing, I may never sleep again.

On Instagram, Korey posts a video of him in a studio, singing Luther Vandross. I like the video.

Within minutes . . . he follows me back.

# Chapter 13
## BIOLOGY

"You look how I feel," Gab says, yawning into her sleeve as we enter biology. "Busy weekend?"

"Just didn't get much sleep." I once again spent most of the night scouring Korey Fields's social media. Then I went down a rabbit hole of his old home videos, playing drums in his church band. Even as a young teen, he was hot.

My phone buzzes. Korey.

**How's ur day?**

The question is a loaded gun, shot in broad daylight for all to see. I want to duck and hide, pull the invisible covers over my head. How can such a simple question feel so . . . complicated? I'm so many things. Mostly, I'm the definition of

Aretha Franklin's "Day Dreaming." Grandma loved that song. *Daydreamin' and I'm thinking of you . . .*

"All right, class," Mr. Amato says. "Let's begin. Take out your assignments."

What would happen . . . if I text him that very thought. Slice myself open so he knows how I really feel? Before I can overthink it, I do a quick search and send him the song via a YouTube link.

The link sits in our chat, a ticking time bomb as a wave of nausea hits me sideways. *This isn't right*, my gut whispers. But I'm in a room full of people, and there's no one here to tell me it's wrong.

Except maybe him. But he says nothing.

"Miss Jones, phones away please," Mr. Amato says.

*He's the kind of guy that you give your everything.*
*You trust your heart, share all of your love.*
*Till death do you part . . .*

The lyrics dance through my head as I listen with one ear for my phone. Nothing. After bio is lunch, and I can't just check messages in front of Gab.

It's a grueling forty-five minutes before the bell. I scoop up my books and rush into the hall, hoping for a spare minute alone.

"Hey, slow down, girl," Gab says, jogging after me. "What's the rush? It's not taco Tuesday."

"Oh, I . . . gotta go to the bathroom."

Gab follows me, talking about Jay's college roommates, how they all look at her like she's something to eat. In the stall, I check my phone. No response. My stomach hits the floor.

Did I read this all wrong? Was it too thirsty, too pressed? *Stupid, stupid, stupid!*

Gab and I grab trays and head to our spot. As soon as I sit, my phone vibrates and I nearly knock over my plate to check.

One message.

A link in response:

**Al Green, "Simply Beautiful"**

"Who you texting?"

I snap the phone to my chest.

"Um, Creighton."

"Ew, what does he want?"

"Nothing, just talking about the bus for Cluster. Not everyone is as lucky as you to have a car."

Gab sticks her tongue out at me. "Yeah, and I'm paying for it with my youth. I'm exhausted."

I've never lied to Gab. Ever.

# Chapter 14

## WHEN SOULS COLLIDE

I feel like summer.

I feel like crashing waves, hot sand, sticky ice-cream cones, smoky charcoal, and fireworks, all wrapped up in skin.

Korey and I volley songs for four days straight . . .

**Donny Hathaway, "A Song for You"**

**Billie Holiday, "The Very Thought of You"**

**Etta James, "A Sunday Kind of Love"**

**Minnie Riperton, "Lovin' You"**

Each song more dreamy, more magical, more bright. We're speaking our own coded language. Dancing without touching. It's hard to concentrate. Even in the mornings, when I dive into the water at practice, my laps are in slow motion as I hum, notes bubbling to the surface.

After school, I wait for Mom on the steps while Shea heads to a friend's house to study for midterms.

**WYD? At swim practice or reading?** 😊

I smile. I love the way he remembers all the little details about me.

**Reading. WYD?**

**Sound check. Want to see?**

He sends a selfie of him in a massive, empty stadium. There's a little gray in his stubble.

**Are you about to fill all those seats?**

**And then some Ma!**

He makes it sound like a walk in the park.

**What U reading?**

**I can't tell you. *Hides face***

**What? LOL! I thought we told each other everything?**

We *do?*

**OK. It's called Eclipse. From the Twilight series.**

**Bella and Edward right?**

**Yup.**

**I read that.**

**Really?????**

> Yeah. Why all the ?? U don't
> think I can read?

No! Of course you can read. You
just seem so busy.

> Lots of time on the road.

And . . . I'm surprised you'd like
that kind of book.

> It's a good story.

I guess.

> Guess?

Idk. Bella seems kinda like . . .
like she doesn't have a backbone.

> Hm. What do you mean?

It's like . . . she lets this super-old
creepy vampire come stalking into her
life. Purposely puts herself in danger,
risks her life for a guy who should
know better and leave her alone.

> LOL! Well when u put it like that.
> So why are u reading it?

Who doesn't like a good love
story?

> I know I do 😊

Korey Fields and I share the same taste in music and in
books. I want to somersault through the air.

> Yo, you ever read 50 Shades of
> Grey?

My stomach clenches. Something that always happens when he asks questions that feel outside my box.

**No. I've heard of it though.**

> **It's a good story. You should read it.**

**Isn't there . . . some crazy sex stuff in it?**

> **LOL! Think of it more like Twilight fan fiction. I want you to read it. It'll give us something to talk about next time I see you.**

He already is planning to see me again. My heart spins like a top inside my chest.

**OK.**

> **Take notes. Think you'll have it done by this weekend?**

**Probably not. I have a Will and Willow event this weekend.**

> **You're in Will and Willow? LMAO! I should've known!**

**I'm nothing like them! Really, I only joined when we moved to Westchester.**

> **I've heard some wild things about those Will and Willow girls.**

**Like what?**

**Like they into freaky shit.**
**Shit they don't want they rich**
**parents knowing about.**

That's not true.

At least I don't think so. I can't imagine Aisha or Malika being like that at all. Especially Malika—she's allergic to fun. If . . . that qualifies as fun.

**So what's this event u got**
**going on?**

It's a conference at this hotel in
Jersey City. We have meetings
and stuff, then there's a big
dance.

**U like dancing?**

Sometimes.

**U don't sound excited about it.**

Whoa. Can he really tell . . . just from a text message?

I guess I get a little . . .
uncomfortable, around all these
rich kids.

**I feel u. Well, if u need**
**someone to talk to, u know I'm**
**always here.**

# *Chapter 15*
## W&W CLUSTER

The DJ's hectic lights twirl across Shea's face as she sways on the dance floor. She hand-altered that red top herself, letting her belly button wink at the boys circling her like prey. Even the little makeup she wears appears expertly applied, thanks to the countless YouTube beauty-bloggers she and her friends worship.

Shea's first Will and Willow teen event. She is in her element, chameleoned with little effort. It's baffling how she can melt into a picture yet somehow I'm cast aside, the unwanted piece of furniture in the room.

It's not that I didn't want to dance, but no one asked. Those thoughts start swimming against the current. If my hair was longer, if I was skinnier, if I had better clothes . . . they wouldn't ignore me.

Wish Gab was here. Really, I wish Korey was here.

I check my phone for the tenth time. No new messages from Korey. And no new activity on Instagram or Twitter. His distance pinches like a bruise on the inside of my forearm. A bruise no one can see but I feel with every move.

"Yo, Enchanted," Creighton says, bumping my hip. "What's up?"

"Nothing."

"Why you ain't out there with everybody else? Your sister is having a good time."

I glance at Shea, the brightest spot of joy in the room.

"She deserves it," I mumble.

"What was that?"

"I said I'm just not into this DJ. His set is all over the place."

Creighton laughs, tugging at my arm toward the dance floor. "Man, you hard to please! Come on!"

Go along to get along, I tell my muscles so they'll loosen their gripping hold.

He waddles behind me, arms wrapping around my waist. I want to squirm away, but Shea is watching, and I want her to think I'm OK. I want her to look up to me; I'm supposed to be the older sister, the cool one.

"You know, I've been meaning to tell you, you been looking good lately."

His sweaty scent and clammy hands are distracting. He pulls me to a wall in the shadows where other kids are dancing. Or

I shouldn't say dancing—more like boys leaning back and girls grinding on them like they're trying to find a seat in the dark.

Creighton doesn't think I'm going to do that, right?

But he does. He assumes the position, backing me into him. His hands feel like raw chicken cutlets rubbing my arms.

"Um, nah," I mutter, trying to pull away, but his grip is tight. His cutlet hands reach down my dress to my bare thighs. I slap his hands away the first time. Then again.

"Cut it out," I say.

"What? Girl, come on." He yanks me hard, my head whiplashes.

"Are you stupid?" I pop at him, then storm out the ballroom, fuming, not caring who sees.

I'm at the elevators when I hear his hard-bottom shoes stumble behind me.

"Oh God, what do you want?"

The elevator door opens and he follows me in.

"Yo, where you going?" he asks.

Without the dizzy lights and music, I can hear the slur in his voice and smell the whiskey on his tongue.

"Just leave me alone," I hiss, slapping his grabby hands away.

"Chill, Chant! Why are you being like that?"

The elevator dings on my floor.

"Night, Creighton," I say hard while exiting.

He stumbles behind me.

"Yo, stop following me!"

"I'm not, but I mean, can we talk?"

"Go back to the party! We'll 'talk' later or whatever."

I take another step, he does too.

"Boy, I'm not playing with you! Leave me alone!"

"But . . . can . . . can we just talk?"

I sprint down the hall, hoping he's drunk enough to lose him, and step inside my room. But he pushes himself in, slamming the door behind him.

"Yo, stop playing with me!" he barks. "I said I wanna talk!"

In that moment, my heart hits the panic button. I'm alone with this drunk asshole. Did anyone see us leave the party? Does anyone even know we're up here? What if Shea comes looking for me?

He looks at the bed then back at me. My blood stiffens.

"Creighton . . ." I quiver. "Don't."

He tries to curl around me, kissing my neck.

"I ain't trying to do nothing. I just wanna talk."

Standing bone straight, I make my voice like steel as something unfurls inside me. I won't let this asshole attack me. I won't let my little sister see this.

"If you don't get the fuck out of here, I will scream."

Creighton's head jerks back, his eyes widening.

"No. No, don't scream!"

"Then GET OUT!"

Realization coats his face. He reels back, biting his fist.

"Shit. Shitshitshitshit. Are you . . . um, gonna tell?"

"OUT!"

Creighton mumbles more apologies before leaving. I check the peephole, watch him walk away, and take my first real breath.

"Shit," I exhale.

All the fear I should have felt comes flooding into the room in a current too fast for me to handle. I swim to my phone. It's late. Gab is probably with Jay and won't answer. Shea is downstairs and I don't want to ruin her first party, plus Mom would drive all the way here to grab us then light the building on fire.

So I call him.

"Bright Eyes," Korey sings. "I was just thinking about you."

"You were? Really?"

"Hey, what's wrong with your voice?"

"Nothing."

"Are . . . are you crying?"

"No, I . . ."

"Don't lie to me."

I sniffle then laugh. "It's stupid. Kid stuff."

"Nothing you tell me is stupid. Where are you?"

"In Jersey City. At a Marriott."

"I'm at the W Hotel. I'm sending Tony to come pick you up. Don't tell anyone."

"Why?"

"You know, I got to keep my location on the low. Remember, baby, I'm not your average dude."

# *Chapter 16*

## WHAT'S YOUR EMERGENCY?

*NOW*

**Dispatch:** 9-1-1, what's your emergency?

**Caller X:** Hello? Yes, I think someone is
screaming next door.

**Dispatch:** You hear screaming?

**Caller X:** I was in the hallway when I heard it. A
man screaming. But not normal screams,
like . . . screaming for his life.

**Dispatch:** OK. Sir, are you able to provide a
location for first responders?

**Caller X:** I knocked on the door. No one answered.

**Dispatch:** Sir, I need to you step away from the
door.

**Caller X:** I share a floor with Korey Fields. The singer. It sounded like him!

**Caller X:** Sir, I need an address to send first responders.

# Chapter 17
## SAVE ME

*THEN*

I shouldn't have listened to him. I shouldn't have been so eager to sneak out the back of the hotel into a Suburban, with the same security guard I saw with him the night we met. I should have at least changed out of my party dress. Mind on autopilot, body numb.

Until I reach room 1015.

Korey snatches the door back as if he has been waiting near it since our call. His face softens as he pulls me in.

"Damn. Are you OK?"

He yokes me into a hug. Not just any hug, the type of hug that feels like metal and magnets slamming together, desperate for each other.

"What are you doing in Jersey?" It's the only thing I can think to ask.

"You're in shock," he says, leading me to the sofa. "Come. Sit. Drink this."

He eases a glass of clear liquid into my hand that doesn't smell a thing like water. I don't resist, even though I know I shouldn't be drinking. But there are lots of things I shouldn't be doing right now.

I take a sip, then another.

"Thanks," I mumble, glancing around.

His suite is massive. A giant, plush cream living room with a balcony facing the New York skyline across the Hudson River.

Korey is dressed in heather-gray sweats and a white T-shirt. Casual and comfortable, yet somehow sexy. Yes, that's the word I want to use. Feels funny to even think it.

"What happened?"

I tell him about Creighton, my hands shaking, reliving the moment, an out-of-body experience. Korey listens, pensive but calm. Calmer than Daddy would've been if I told him some boy pushed up on me. But I guess that's the difference— Korey doesn't treat me like a kid. He treats me . . . regular, I guess.

"It's aight. You're safe now," he says, rubbing my shoulder. "Boys be like that, you know? Be mad thirsty to get some buns."

"You . . . you think he wanted to . . ."

"Oh, no doubt! That's all them little knuckleheads be thinking about. They never take the time to get to know you.

To ask how your day was. To talk about your favorite Disney movie." He chuckles. "Can't believe you be hating on *Pocahontas* like that."

I let out a laugh, my chest feeling lighter.

"And I didn't lead him on or nothing, if that's what you're thinking."

"Why would I think that?"

"Sometimes . . . that's what people think. That a girl *wanted* it."

Korey shakes his head. "That ain't your style, Bright Eyes. Trust me, one day you'll realize it ain't you and it got everything to do with the other person."

I try to relax with that fact, thumbing the edges of my glass.

"Besides, don't see what dudes get out of drugging and forcing themselves on chicks. I like my ladies awake and enjoying themselves. I don't know—maybe I'm different."

I hold my breath. "Or just a good person."

He blinks at me then shakes the ice around in his glass.

"Yeah. Maybe."

We sit there, drinking each other in, his hand resting on my knee. When did that get there? Chimes burst out of the Bluetooth speaker beside me, the start of Donny Hathaway and Roberta Flack's "The Closer I Get to You."

"Mmm," I say. "I love this song!"

"Oh, word? What you know about this?"

He reaches over me to turn up the volume and I sneak a sniff of his neck. Don't know if it's cologne or just his natural scent, but the butterflies in my stomach go bananas.

He leans back and starts singing along.

*"The closer I get to you*
*The more you make me see"*

The alcohol's making me brave. Bold. I clear my throat and join him.

*"Over and over again*
*I tried to tell myself that we*
*Could never be more than friends . . ."*

Korey's eyes sparkle as he lets out a laugh. "Damn, so you really *are* into the classics. Your parents put you on?"

My phone buzzes. A text message from Shea.

**Where are you?**

I don't want to lie to her, but I don't want her looking for me either.

**With Creighton.**

"Hey, why you all in your phone?" Korey snarls, seeming almost annoyed. "Only person you need to talk to right now is right here."

Quickly, I put the phone away.

"S-sorry. I'm sorry," I babble. "Um . . . so my granny used to take care of me and the Littles. She used to play all this music from back in the day, then make me perform it. Had to hit all them notes just like Whitney. I guess you can say she was my first teacher. My only teacher."

He smiles. "My grandma used to play her records like that. Helped her get through the day. That and Father God."

We keep singing. I hit a note and Korey whistles.

"Damn, girl, them pipes of yours! Yo, we gotta get you in the studio for real for real."

"You think . . . I mean, studio time, that's a lot of money."

"Prff! Man, not when you own it."

# Chapter 18

## LESSON PLAN

Don't know how he convinced Mom of the idea, but the next Saturday, I'm in Korey Fields's penthouse music studio on the Upper West Side.

"And we're well secured," Korey says to Mom during our tour of the facility. "Cameras around the perimeter, and my assistant Jessica works the front desk."

Korey offered to give me free private singing lessons. An offer impossible to turn down, but my parents insisted upon being within the vicinity.

"I know he's a superstar, but he's still a stranger," Daddy said. I brought up all the swim meets I'd gone to solo and the countless hours I've watched the Littles by myself, but there was no convincing them I could go alone.

"Be respectful," Mom warns before taking the elevator back down to the car. "Act like a lady, like you got some home training. Listen to everything he tells you."

Mom goes to wait in the car. An invisible hourglass flips.

We have three hours. Just us two.

I've dreamed of the day I'd enter a real studio. The day I'd be able to touch the soundboards, the mics, rub my fingers along the booth foam. But I never ever thought it would be with Korey Fields. I take a quiet moment to relish it all, like a delicious piece of cake you want to savor with every last bite. My songbook sits heavy in my bag, itching to be released.

Korey leans against the wall by the various instruments—guitars, congas, drum set—face glowing, eyes following my every step. Not watching me like a kid about to break something, but more cherishing the moment as well.

"I built this after my third album went triple platinum," Korey says, hinting at the plaques on the wall. "I wanted a place where I could create and not be on anyone's time. A place to just . . . be myself."

There's a sadness in his eyes, something left unsaid between his words.

"Must be nice, so much room to . . . breathe."

He nods then tickles his keyboard, the notes ringing out of the overhead speakers.

"You know how to play?"

"Not enough to say I really can," I laugh. "I've always wanted to play that duet that everybody does. You know that 'Dun dun DUN DUN dun dun . . .'"

He laughs. "'Heart and Soul'? Come here. I'll teach you. It ain't as complicated as it looks."

"Easy for you to say. You're the musical genius."

"Ha, 'genius' got a nice ring to it, don't it?"

He stands behind me, laying my fingers on the board, guiding me, and it almost feels like he's caressing my hand, but I could be imagining it.

"You play this note and I'll play the other."

With a few strokes, I'm playing. But the way his chest lies against my back, sandwiching me into the keyboard, my fingers trip up.

"Oh, um sorry," I mumble at the floor.

"That's OK."

He stares down at me, fireflies sizzling in his eyes.

"Um, shouldn't we be recording or something?"

He shrugs. "In a minute. You can't walk up in a studio and expect to lay down a hit! You have to ease into the vibe. Melt into it."

He picks up his guitar and plops down on the black leather sofa, stringing a couple of notes. I want to sit with him, to crawl into that space under his arm, rest my head on his chest . . . but nerves keep me frozen. *Be respectful. Act like a lady*, Mom said.

"So how do we melt?"

"Aight, rules for the studio. One, no one can know what goes down in here. This is where the magic happens, and you can't be giving away our secrets, you feel me? So you can't tell no one, not even your moms."

I start to question how I'd go about doing that, but even the thought seems childish and he's already trusting me with so much. I nod.

"Two, we don't just make music in here. We make love, you feel me? So all that uptight shit, you gotta leave at the door and free yourself."

"OK."

"And you gotta start by shedding some of them layers."

I glance down at my sweater. He couldn't mean . . .

He laughs. "Get loose. Get comfortable. See me? I don't even walk in here with shoes on."

*Listen to him. Be respectful*, I think again, and unzip my hoodie, tossing it on the sofa. I stressed all morning on what to wear, but the simple white V-neck T-shirt that snugs my frame seemed like the best option. Less is more.

"OK. Any other rules?"

Korey's mouth hangs open, eyes wide, sweeping over me.

"Wow. You are . . . so beautiful."

The blushing hurts my cheeks as the room spins and he cracks a bashful smile.

"I'm sorry. I shouldn't have said that. It's just that . . . I mean, you're mad gorgeous! Them eyes . . . every time you look at me, I forget myself."

I lace my fingers together.

"Um, thanks."

No one has ever called me beautiful. Pretty, sure. But beautiful . . . that word transcends.

Next, Korey is all business. We go over vocal warm-ups, how to sing in the booth, how to use the mic and headsets, and how music is recorded. Every passing minute feels unreal. Like at any moment I'm going to wake up from this dream and go back to facing my overcrowded home.

There's a light knock at the door before it swings open. A fair-skinned woman with long dark hair combed with a side part walks in, her eyes down.

"Her mother will be here in forty-five minutes."

"Thanks, Jess," he says, with an approving nod.

Jessica's almond-shaped eyes flicker up to mine, before she leaves as quick as she had come.

"Aight, since you love the classics so much, thinking we sing some oldies tunes together," Korey says from behind an audio board. "You know, like we did in Jersey."

"Can we do that same song?"

He grins. "Aight, Bright Eyes. Whatever you want."

I bite my lip until I can't hold it in any longer.

"You know I know that song, right?" I burst, voice cracking.

He cocks his head to the side. "Huh?"

I sing, "Turn around, bright eyes."

Korey cackles. That smile . . . how have I lived so long without it?

"Oh, word! Look at you, knowing even the white-folk

classics!" He muses to himself for a moment. "My grandma loved white-folk music."

"Mine did too," I gush. We have even more in common.

Korey leans back in his chair. "Yo, real talk, if I could have my way, I'd do like a whole cover album of all the great white hits. But . . . that'll never happen. They'd never let me sing that shit."

"They?"

"My label."

"Oh. Right, sorry," I mumble. "But this is your space. Thought you could do what you want here."

Korey has a pensiveness about him that I wouldn't expect from such a superstar. There's so much warmth in his eyes under those long lashes.

"Yo, you right," he says. "Man, I don't know, Enchanted, there's something about you. You just . . . different. Real mature."

He sits behind the keyboard, plays a few notes and sings.

I giggle and join him.

*"Turn around, bright eyes.*
*Every now and then I fall apart."*

When we sing, our voices make love in the air.

*"Your love is like a shadow on me all of the time."*

# Chapter 19

## CRADLE ROBBER

"Thanks again for the ride," I say, jumping into Gabriela's car.

"It's cool," she says, reversing out of my driveway. "Don't have to be at work till six today, but check this out!"

Gab passes me her phone, screen on an ad listing—*FOR RENT: One-bedroom apartment. $1100/month.*

"You're moving?"

"Yeah! Well, not until graduation. But look at that spot, it's perfect for me and Jay! And it's close to Fordham. Jay's been introducing me to some of the professors in the education department. Think I'm gonna like it there."

One thing about Gab: she has her life figured out and is fearless about it. I so badly wanted to tell her I had good news of my own. But . . . Korey said it was "our thang." Not like Gab tells me everything.

Gab raps along to a Bad Bunny song, tapping her steering wheel.

"Hey, why don't you want to be a singer?" I ask, suddenly curious. "You have a nice voice."

She shrugs. "I like to sing, but I don't want to BE a singer. That's your job." She snorts to herself. "Except, Jay and I write these goofy-ass songs together. It be so hilarious sometimes! We need our own comedy special on Netflix."

It's something like a fairy tale, the way Jay and Gabriela first met. Three years ago, while attending her cousin's high school graduation party, Gab stepped into her tía's backyard and noticed a light-brown boy with a dimpled smile. Jay met her eyes, watched her click down the patio steps in a pink Forever 21 dress, hair hanging nearly to her butt . . . and the stars devoured him whole. It was love at first sight.

Gab was fourteen, and Jay had just turned seventeen.

After a year-long friendship, they couldn't deny it: they were in love, fitting together like peanut butter and jelly. Bonding over reggaeton and sneakers, Jay encouraged Gab to embrace her Latin roots, and Gab encouraged him to apply for college.

But the moment he turned eighteen, everything seemed to change. Folks threw around words like "fresh meat," called him a cradle robber and a pedophile.

Even though they'd met when they were both still in high school and built off a friendship, the comments made Gab feel dirty. But Jay didn't care what people had to say, and continues to be the doting, patient, supportive boyfriend of her dreams. I've never met him, but the way Gab talks about him, he sounds . . . like everything I've ever wanted. Someone to be silly with, to sing with, to share dreams with, to have your own "thang" with. That one person who is really YOURS.

I'd give anything to have that.

"Besides, you got them pipes that's about to blow these basic bitches out the water," Gab laughs. "And while you're off being rich and famous, I'll be here, with Jay, teaching the babies how to read."

I shrug. "I don't want to be rich and famous. I just want to be rich and . . . known."

Gab smiles. "That sounds just like you."

"Nice of you to join us, Jones," Coach grumbles as I sprint across the parking lot.

"Sorry," I gasp, out of breath, jumping into the van before we peel out for our swim meet.

"Hey, where were you?" Mackenzie asked.

"Left my new suit and Gab gave me a ride home."

"Who? Wait—ahhh! Hannah, turn that up!"

Hannah grins at the back seat, then turns up the Ariana Grande song on her playlist.

The van shrieks with glee, girls wiggling in their seats.

"OMG! She totally slays." Mackenzie grins, bumping my shoulder.

"Totally," Hannah says. "OMG, Enchanted! You HAVE to sing this!"

"Yeah! Next talent competition."

Do they know ANY other singers besides Beyoncé and Ariana?

I wince a smile as a text buzzes. Korey.

**Can't wait to see that pretty ass smile of yours tomorrow. Wear something that shows them curves** 😏

# *Chapter 20*

## YOUR EYES

"Don't take off your coat. We're taking a class trip," Korey says, slipping on a leather jacket. "Tony's already in the car downstairs."

"Where are we going?" I ask, catching up to him. Mom just dropped me off. She'll have no idea we're going somewhere . . . alone.

He smirks. "You'll see."

We enter the Beacon Theatre, way different while empty and the houselights on.

"The place where we first met," he says with a dimpled grin.

"What are we doing here?"

Despite meeting Korey, I don't have good memories of this place. The wounds from the audition are still raw, and I'm itching to run back home.

"You have to get used to performing. Only place to do that is onstage. We have an hour. Let's get to work."

We pick a song from my favorite Whitney Houston album. A song I've sung a million times over. As I sing, Korey circles me, hand on his chin, deep in thought. Meanwhile, I'm loving the change in scenery. My voice seems to carry farther onstage than in the studio or my bathroom. Without the audience, my nerves aren't a tangled web. Still, Korey is here. Korey Fields! Every few seconds I want to pinch myself to check if I'm dreaming.

I'm knee-deep in the song when Korey pauses the music.

"What's up?" I ask, winded.

"You're . . . stiff."

"Huh? No, I'm not! I'm singing from my diaphragm," I say, poking my stomach. "See? Like you taught me."

He shakes his head. "This song. The way you sing it, is different than the others."

I shrug. "It's just a song."

"It's more than that. Your smile . . . this song *means* something to you."

I swallow but hold a straight face. "OK . . . so what exercises you got for that?"

"Simple," he says. "You gotta sing from your heart, Bright Eyes."

I huff. "And how you expect me to do that?"

He pauses, as if considering his next move, and pushes hesitation aside to take my hand. For a split second, his fingers thread between mine before he places my hand on my chest and holds it there. I gulp at the fire sizzling in his eyes. He feels larger than the theater, maybe the entire city.

"Aight, your heart is nothing but a muscle. It contracts and expands, working just as hard as any other muscle. The difference is, the blood pumping through it pumps through your entire body. That blood holds memories. Things you try to forget but it won't let you. You have to use those memories, use that blood to fuel you. But that blood can't move through you unless you relax. Release your hand, Bright Eyes."

I look down at the fist I formed over my heart, nails digging into my palms ready to fight, almost daring him to touch it.

"Close your eyes," he says. "And envision the moment this song first entered your heart."

"I . . . don't want to talk about it," I whimper.

He frowns. "You afraid of me?"

"No."

"Good. Then trust me."

I close my eyes and hear the sea. Waves crashing against the shore. I smell Grandma's sage and suntan lotion as the record skips . . . skipping again.

"We've worn this out, Chanty. How about you just sing it for us?"

A smile creeps on my face as I open my eyes. I take a step back, shaking my hands free.

"Aight. I'm ready."

Korey restarts the song and gives me space, letting me take the stage alone. A wave of joy replaces the numbness, and my whole body comes alive.

"Arch your neck back," Korey says over the music. "Relax the muscles trying to tighten your throat. The notes you need are stuck in there."

I roll my neck around, feeling the weight of my head fall off my shoulders. My back arches, blood racing, smile widening. This is my favorite album, one of my favorite songs, why shouldn't I smile?

*"Where do broken hearts go?*
*Can they find their way home?"*

"Use your arms," he instructs. "You are begging for answers. Where *do* broken hearts go?"

I reach out to the ceiling lights, pretending I'm singing to Grandma again. I spin around and sing to Korey, watching in awe as he circles me. He moves closer, no longer hesitating. The notes I haven't hit since I was a child come rumbling through me, shrieking like the trains through a tunnel. I pump my arms, a surge of victory taking over.

"Yes! Yes!" Korey cheers from beside me and I feel the need to sing to him and only him, inching closer.

*"I look in your eyes,*
*and I know that you still care for me."*

The song ends and I gasp at the lightning that has replaced my veins. All this time, my heart has been beating, but this is the first time I've felt fully alive.

"Again?" Korey asks, breathless.

"Again!"

# Chapter 21

## 432,000

432,000. That's how many seconds have to pass before I can see Korey again.

Our back-and-forth texts are not enough. Our song volleying is not enough. Even stalking him on social media is not enough. Every second that passes without him—without singing—feels like I'm swimming through a swamp, the mud sticking to my skin, consuming me, pulling me under.

**Send me a pic** 😊

"Who are you texting?"

I drop the phone on the floor, the carpet breaking its fall.

"Huh? What?"

Mom snickers from the sink, peeling carrots; Shea chopping onions for dinner.

"You always on that phone. Wondering who got you texting like crazy."

I clutch the phone to my chest, sinking deeper into the crook of the L-shaped sofa. Just the thought of Mom knowing makes my stomach twist into a cramp.

"J . . . just Mackenzie."

Mom smirks. "Oh, I see."

"I . . . I left my textbook in my room," I say, sprinting down the hall. "Be right back!"

Behind me, Mom whispers with a giggle to Shea, "I think your sister has a little boyfriend."

Korey Fields asked me to send him a photo . . . the one thing I'm not good at. I hate taking pictures of myself; I never do. I'm not even big on sharing pics. Another thing Gab and I have in common. She hates social media and doesn't want her face on the internet. Most of my Instagram pics are of me and the Littles.

But . . . Korey Fields wants a picture. And I can't just tell him no.

I shut my bedroom door, using it as my backdrop, and try a few different angles, the same way I've seen Shea take selfies.

**Hey! Where's my pic?**

The seconds tick louder. I'm taking too long. More attempts. Smiling, not smiling. Posing. Duck lips. Pull my T-shirt off one shoulder. Ugh!

"Chanted!" Mom calls. "Come help with dinner!"

"Just a second," I scream back, my voice shaky.

Another twenty shots. Maybe I should try some of Shea's makeup. Or a filter. Maybe black and white. Or a new shirt . . .

Or . . . maybe he's just being nice. Maybe I'm doing the most and overthinking all of this.

But . . . he called you beautiful. And he loves your eyes.

With a deep breath, I take one last selfie with my regular smile and send it before I can stop myself.

Typing bubble . . .

**You always cut your hair short?**

I give in to the instinct to glide a hand down the back of my neck.

**Yeah. It's easier for swim meets.**

Within seconds I regret the answer.

*Stupid! You sound like a kid and . . . this is Korey Fields!* He's used to dealing with women. Real women. He dated a Kardashian.

**You ever think about growing it out?**

A twitch of . . . something scratches at my stomach, mouth dry.

**No. Why?**

There's a long pause. My heart drops so low it sits next to my heel.

Footsteps down the hall. Mom's footsteps. I frantically search for a book to keep up with my lie when my phone rings. Different from my regular ring . . . it's a FaceTime.

Korey Fields . . . is FaceTiming ME.

"Holy shit," I gasp.

Mom's footsteps inch closer. I snatch my biology book out my bag and stare at the phone. Do I answer it? Tell him I'll call him back? What if he never calls again? But how will I explain this to Mom? I'm not even supposed to have his number.

It took 432,000 tiny paper cuts to press decline . . . just as Mom swings open the door.

"Found it!" I yelp, wiping the sweat off my neck.

# Chapter 22

## FEELS LIKE HOME

Saturday comes and I can't decide what to wear. I try on everything, even some of Shea's outfits. I settle on a tight green top and jeans with a denim jacket.

Daddy is taking me to the studio today but doesn't plan to stay.

"I have to go to Far Rock," he says, resisting a grimace. "Make sure the place is all right. Might run into some traffic, so just wait for me at the Starbucks on the corner when you're done. And remember to behave, Korey's doing you a big favor. He's big time!"

I tell Korey we have an extra two hours, and his smile could light up the world.

"That's just what we need."

We sing "Best Part" by H.E.R. and Daniel Caesar (one of my parents' favorite songs). Then we sing "Shallow" by Lady Gaga and Bradley Cooper (Korey loves playing the guitar), followed by a Whitney Houston solo (he loves my voice).

I don't fit in at school or in Will and Willow. And I can't fully be myself at home because, well, no one really wants me to sing. The only place I've ever felt comfortable letting loose was at Grandma's. But here, with Korey, feels like it's the first time I've been myself in a long while. If I could stay here forever, I would.

"Ready to write a little something?" Korey says, waving a notebook.

"For real?" Been bringing my songbook with me, waiting for the right moment to share. I could just burst as I slip it out of my bag.

"Yep," he laughs, pulling me over to the sofa. "Well, first, we gotta talk about making love."

I freeze. "What?"

"Making love," he says, matter-of-factly. "We gotta talk about it so we can write a song about it, Bright Eyes."

I close my songbook, full of childish words. "Um. OK."

His head cocks to the side. "Hold up, you ever been with a guy before?"

"Like . . . sexually?"

He laughs. "Damn, you make it sound mad . . . formal. But yeah. *Sexually* or whatever."

I shake my head.

"Ever been kissed?"

I shrug, since it feels like that sloppy, wet kiss with Jose Torres shouldn't count.

"Damn, Bright Eyes, you really don't know nothing. That's good, though. It's better to learn that type of stuff from someone you . . . trust."

I gulp, my heart thumping, heat rising through my chest.

"And you know," he starts, eyes on his paper, "maybe you can teach me something."

"Something like what?"

He gives me a shy grin. "Aight, don't tell nobody this . . . but . . . I'm a little scared of water."

"Really? How come?"

"Man, I don't know. Never really learned. Scared of drowning."

"I mean, we're all scared of drowning. Everybody trying to keep afloat. You just have to keep swimming. Like in *Finding Nemo*!"

"Ha, word! I like that." He pauses to stare at me, his face seeming like he's searching for something. "Well, maybe one day, you can, like, teach me how to swim. You know, since you a pro and all that. It can just be our thang, feel me?"

It's warm. Or maybe it's the way he's looking at me, that it feels like my skin is on fire yet I'm comfortable in the blaze.

"I'd love to teach you how to swim."

There's a knock on the door. Jessica enters, her face a mix of concern and fear.

"Jessica, what the—"

"Excuse me . . . sir. Enchanted's father is here."

Korey shoots me an annoyed glance. "Thought you said we had two more hours," he snaps.

My mouth opens but nothing comes out.

"So you lied to me," he hisses, walking toward me, just as Daddy enters the room, gazing at all the plaques and awards.

"Aye, what's up, man! Sorry, I'm a little early," he says, beaming at me. "Traffic was just too crazy, so I decided to turn around, pop back in. I, uh, didn't mean to, uh, wreck y'all flow or nothing. I know how y'all artists can be sensitive about y'all ish."

Korey, composing himself, winces a smile.

"Nah, it's all good," he says through clenched teeth. "We were just about to record. Enchanted, why don't you jump in the booth and show your father what we've been working on?"

# Chapter 23

## HISTORY

In fourth-period US history, I'm busy doing math.

Korey is twenty-eight. I'm seventeen. That's only . . . an eleven-year difference. When I'm eighteen, he'll be twenty-nine.

Gabriela is three years younger than Jay.

Kylie Jenner was eight years younger than Tyga.

Beyoncé was eighteen when she met thirty-year-old Jay-Z.

Mom is seven years younger than Daddy.

It's not that uncommon.

Mr. Thomas is talking about the Civil War. But there's a different kind of war going on inside me, the kind that will take an infinite number of battles to win.

On one hand, I shouldn't want Korey as much as I do.

On the other, I've never known anyone like him. We have so much in common. What if he's my soul mate? My destiny?

Age ain't nothing but a number, Korey once told me, and he's right. People always say how mature I am for my age. Even Mom.

Still, it won't look right. Hard to explain, how two souls swam across the universe and found each other.

Maybe I should wait, until I'm eighteen.

But . . . what if he finds someone else before then?

"Are you sure this is right? This doesn't . . . hello? Earth to Enchanted!"

Gab copies my biology homework with a carrot stick hanging out her mouth.

"Huh? What?"

"Yo, what's with you lately?"

"Nothing." I choke out a laugh.

I haven't told Gab yet. She has a way of asking questions that hit so sharp it could cut me open. Then she'd know.

"Whatever. So, I'm off this Saturday, and Jay is out of town. Want to hang out and do something fun and irresponsible?"

"Thought you said it's your dad's weekend?"

She rolls her eyes. "Yeah, well, he's not speaking to me at the moment."

"Still? Is it about Jay?"

She shrugs. "So do you want to chill or what?"

I want to pry, but Gab is a wall when it comes to her dad.

"Um, I can't. I have . . . something."

"Swim meet?"

"Um, yeah."

"Cool. Well, your loss. Guess I'll just Netflix and chill."

I swallow, building up the courage. "I'm going to skip school tomorrow."

Gab raises an eyebrow. "Really? For what?"

"There's an audition. In the city. Mom isn't going to take me so . . . I'm gonna go. Alone. Cover for me?"

Gab leans back with a smirk, impressed. "Well, look at you! This is a whole new Enchanted. Aight, I got you. Kill it!"

# *Chapter 24*
## SWIM LESSONS

**Don't forget your bathing suit.** 😊

Korey is waiting in a black-tinted Mercedes one block from the Harlem Metro-North train stop. Inside, it's like nightfall. His hoodie is pulled up over dark sunglasses that almost take up his entire face. He reaches across the console and wraps me in a tight hug. His smell engulfs me and my body hums with the engine.

"You ready?" he asks.

I nod, afraid my voice will come out as a quiver.

He speeds off, threading his fingers through mine, and I snuggle into the warmth of his heated butter-leather seats, the radio playing Marvin Gaye. I'm in Korey Fields's car! He picked me up from the station. I've never had a boy pick me up before.

Told Gab I was skipping school. Told Mom I had a swim meet in the evening. With all bases covered, we have at least twelve glorious hours to spend together.

Alone.

There's a slight hint of fear in Korey's eyes as he stands in the shallow end of his building's indoor pool, waist-deep.

"You sure you know what you doing?"

Korey's shirt is off. I can marvel at every groove of his chest and six-pack in person.

"Huh?" I mumble, drooling.

He smirks, splashing some water at me.

"Girl, you ain't paying attention."

"Trust me! I taught the Littles how to swim. I can teach you."

"Damn, now you comparing me to the kiddies? Way to make me feel like a man."

I laugh. "I swear I won't let you drown."

He nods. "OK."

We practice holding our breath and blowing bubbles before I teach him a few kicks. I try to be just as gentle as he is with me in the studio. But here, he's staring through my swimsuit, eyes swiping over my body.

"So you're just going to doggy-paddle over to me. You got this! Ready?"

He nods.

"GO!"

He kicks and wiggles through the water, his splashes like tidal waves.

"That's it. You're doing it!"

Then, his arms are around me, not like he's trying to feel me up, but in desperation, clinging to life.

"It's OK," I say. "You're OK!"

He stands, wiping his face, his eyes hard for a split second.

"Yo, that's enough," he hisses.

I back away, shivers crawling up my arms.

"Um, OK."

We sit on the edge of the pool in silence, our legs dangling in the water, my stomach tying itself in knots. I pushed him too hard. He's scared of the water. He's never going to forgive me. Stupid, so stupid!

"My grandma hated the water," he says, his voice cold. "She heard about all these kids drowning in the public pool and never let me near it. She was like that, scared of things she heard of but didn't see with her own eyes. Now she's gone, and she won't see this either." He turns with a slight smile. "But this was . . . cool. Can we do this again on Saturday?"

I bite my lip. "I can't. It's my homecoming dance."

His face contorts. "Oh. Oh, OK."

The disappointment swallows up all the chlorine-drenched air.

"I mean, I can . . . not go."

"Nah, nah, I want you to go," he says, placing a gentle hand on my bare thigh. "I never went to a homecoming dance."

"Really?"

"Nope. No dances or prom in homeschool."

"What was that like?"

"Homeschool?" He chuckles.

"Yeah, but homeschool while touring all over the world? I mean, that must have been lit!"

His jaw tightens, eyes growing distant as he stares into the water.

"It was . . . lonely." He takes a deep breath and slides back into the pool. "Come on, time to go."

I pout right before he grabs my waist, lifts me off the edge, and drops me in.

"Eek!" I giggle.

"Shhh." He laughs, arms wrapping around me. He looks over his shoulder at the door and I'm glad to see the smile back on his face. His eyes are on me now. He cups my face with both hands, pulling us inches apart, my bones thrumming.

Then he kisses me.

The pool becomes a hot tub, sweat beading around my neck, and I forget how to breathe.

"Thank you for teaching me how to swim." He exhales, our foreheads touching.

Combust. That's what will happen if I stay this close to him for too long. I'll be a girl wrapped in a blanket of flames, floating on water.

After we dry off and change back into our clothes, we return to the studio. I feel lighter, my chest an egg cracked open, sunny yolk spilling out, leaking love all over the room. I can't wipe the smile off my face and my lips are sore from kissing.

Kissing. I was kissing Korey Fields.

"So you got a date to this dance?"

The question rips me out of my daydreaming.

"Um, no."

He nods, busying himself with some music sheets.

"You not lying, are you?"

My stomach tenses. Korey has a weird look in his eyes. Is he jealous?

"N-n-no. No."

He shrugs and sits behind his keyboard. "So, what's tomorrow's movie?"

"*Beauty and the Beast.*"

"Ha! Tale as old as time . . ."

I spin around and sing with him. "*True as it can be* . . . wow, I *love* that song! I mean, the Disney version is beautiful, but that Peabo Bryson with Celine Dion . . . that hits!"

Korey snaps his fingers, jumping from behind his board.

"Bet. Let's do it!"

"Really?"

"Yeah." He digs in a leather bag sitting by the door and takes out a camera. "Mind if I record?"

I twist my fingers, watching him set up a tripod.

"Why?"

He grins. "What? You camera shy?"

"No . . . but . . ."

"Please, baby? It'll make me really happy."

My heart squeezes. He called me baby. I'm *his* baby.

"Yeah, of course."

# Chapter 25
## YOUTUBE

We don't spend nearly enough hours in the day thinking about kissing.

My body was in the water, but my head was in the clouds. I glide through the chlorine, my strokes soft, but not as soft as Korey's lips.

Ariel was sixteen when she married Eric in *The Little Mermaid*. When she gave up her tail for a pair of legs. Maybe that's what it's like to be in love. I couldn't imagine anything I'd give up my tail for . . . other than Korey.

Somewhere on earth, I hear my name.

"Jones! Jones!" Coach growls.

"Yes?" I cough, slipping off my goggles.

Her hands are on her hips. "You feel like joining us today?"

I look around and realize I'm the only one left in the pool. My teammates are on the sideline.

"Sorry," I mutter, scrambling out.

Coach shakes her head.


"Dude, what's gotten into you lately?"

Mackenzie flips back her fresh blow-dried hair, scraping it into a ponytail.

"What do you mean?" I feign innocence.

"You've been skipping practice. You haven't returned Kyle Bacon's calls. You barely make homeroom, and—"

Hannah screams. We both turn.

"What!"

Hannah, straddling the bench, stares at her phone. "OMG. OMG!"

"What is it?"

"Enchanted! This is you! This is you singing with Korey Fields!"

My stomach drops. "What?"

Mackenzie jumps up to join Hannah, her eyes bulging. "OMG!"

There I am. In my low-cut tank top, singing "Beauty and the Beast" with Korey.

My eyes are closed, my smile is bright. And Korey looks . . . close. Too close. We're damn near singing into each other's mouths.

"You know Korey Fields?" Hannah yells. "Why didn't you tell us?"

My tongue dries out. "I . . ."

"Enchanted, you sound amazing." Mackenzie beams.

I want to say thanks, but I'm too stunned by how our private moment was there for the entire world to see. He told me it was just for him, not for YouTube.

Suddenly, I no longer want to be a fish. I want to be a crab, roll up inside my shell and stay there forever.

A wave of buzzing phones hits each row of the locker room, the text messages an incoming swarm of locusts.

By homeroom, the entire school knows.

# *Chapter 26*
## GROUP TEXT

*W&W Squad Chat (w/o the Jones sisters)*

Sean: **Yo! You see that video of Enchanted singing with Korey Fields?? HOLY SHIT!**

Aisha: **It has like 5 million views.**

Malika: **Yeah. It's cool, I guess.**

Sean: **Man, the gossip blogs are blowing it up. Seen clips all over Instagram.**

Aisha: **Everyone at my school is talking about it.**

Malika: **Y'all don't think it's weird, the way they were eye-fucking?**

Sean: **They were just performing. Chill.**

Malika: **Nah. It looked real to me.**

Sean: **Damn, Malika! You a hater!**

Aisha: **My mom talked to Mrs. Jones and she's BIG mad. Said she didn't give permission for him to record anything!**

Sean: **Bruh! It's Korey Fields! He's like a trillionaire. He ain't asking nobody permission for nothing!**

Malika: **They got bigger things to worry about now that her dad is on strike. Still, creepy tho.**

# Chapter 27

## HOMECOMING DANCE

**What are you wearing?**

**Black dress. Just like you told me!**

The Homecoming committee decked out the gym with gold streamers, a million navy-blue balloons, and twinkling red lights. The DJ is positioned on a platformed stage framed in flashing disco lights and speakers.

Hannah and Mackenzie are on the floor, dancing off beat. Shea is near the stage, flirting with some white boy. We catch eyes, and hers flutter away.

Mom only let me come to the dance because of Shea. Mom's still mad about the video, and Shea seems almost embarrassed by the attention. I'd thought she'd be happy with a semicool sister.

I check my phone. No new messages from Korey.

I text Gab. She's also had an attitude with me since the video dropped. Which is now at twenty million views. No surprise she couldn't take off for the dance. I'm used to doing almost everything at school alone since she's always working, but tonight, I need my wing woman. The stares and murmuring whispers are suffocating. I fidget in my too-tight black dress. Korey told me to buy a size down, to stop hiding my curves.

I check my phone again. Maybe he's mad at me, too. Mad that I went to the dance, that I didn't come to the studio instead. Not that Mom would let me near him. If she had her way, I'd never see him again.

The homecoming committee takes the stage. The king and queen are crowned. I yawn, ready to call Mom for a ride home when the DJ scratches in a familiar beat.

"And tonight . . . we have a special guest!"

A voice sings into another mic, somewhere offstage.

My mouth drops and the beat drops with it. A shaded figure strolls onto the platform before light floods the stage. Cheers cascade as students rush past me onto the dance floor.

It's Korey.

"How y'all doing tonight? Special friend of mine thought y'all could use a little entertainment!"

My breath hitches. I can't move. I'm a rock in the middle of a sea of screaming fans.

Korey performs a few lines from his song, shaking hands,

slapping fives, taking selfies. The entire school is enamored by his charm, even the teachers. But his eyes are only on me.

When the song is over, he hops offstage and pulls me into a hug. Dozens of phones surround us, the room full of flashing lights.

"Meet me out back," he whispers, lips grazing my ear.

# Chapter 28
## PRIVACY

My hands are sweating as I rush into the bathroom, hoping to find a way to compose myself. I need a distraction, a way to slip out undetected.

Korey Fields. Here, at my school.

I rush straight for the largest stall, and Gab follows me in.

"OMG! What are you doing here?"

"Me?" she snaps. "I just got here. What the hell is HE doing here?"

Gab has on a plum dress and heels, her hair down, draping over her shoulders like a shawl.

"I . . . don't know."

"Don't bullshit me, Chant! I get off work early and find you like *this*!"

I reel back. "Damn, Gab. What's wrong with you?"

"You know damn well what's wrong. You've been lying to me this whole time! Is that where you snuck off to the other day? Did you lie to me so you could sneak around with *him*?"

I bite my lip, feeling like a cornered animal.

Gab's eyes widen. "Oh God, did you fuck him?"

"No!"

"Chant . . . this is so wrong. He's a grown-ass man. He got no business popping up at a girl's school like this."

"Hey! I'm not a little kid. I'll be eighteen in six months."

"Yeah, but clearly he can't seem to wait that long! Which is disgusting."

"Back off, Gab. I know what I'm doing!"

She folds her arms. "Doesn't look like it."

"What? Are you jealous?"

"Of you and Korey? Girl, please. I got a man!"

"A broke college student. He's older than you, too. Hypocrite!"

Gab blinks. "You know damn well that's different."

"Well, whatever. We're not dating. He just . . . gets me. He thinks I'm talented. Unlike some people."

"What? I'm always hyping you up. I'm the reason you even met that asshole since I was the one who pushed you to do that audition."

"Well, he really believes I'll make it. That I have range like Beyoncé."

Gab scoffs. "Beyoncé? That woman is a damn unicorn! You can never be her!"

I pull the knife out of my back and take a deep breath. "Ouch, Gab."

She winces. "I don't mean it like that. It's just . . . boys will say anything to get some ass."

"He's not a boy!"

"You right about that!"

We've never fought like this. The unbalanced anger makes me nauseous. My phone buzzes. A text from Korey.

**Come outside.**

"Tell him you're not coming! I know that's what he's asking."

I stare at her, then glance at the stall door.

"Bitch, if you walk out of here, I'm calling the police! Or worse, I'm calling your mother. Don't make me tell her everything else I know."

I swallow, texting him quick, shoving my phone back in my purse.

"There! Happy now?"

"Look, don't use me for one of your lies again."

"I won't need to. Korey is taking me on tour with him!"

"What?"

"We're gonna sing duets onstage! We're gonna work on my album."

Gab chuckles. "Girl, you really are crazy if you think your mom is ever gonna let that happen."

# *Chapter 29*
## THE PROPOSAL

My mother's body runs mid-July-hot all year long, despite her tongue being a cool breeze after a rainstorm.

But once you get her mad, there's no telling what category hurricane will brew.

"How dare you plaster my daughter's face all around the internet without consulting us first?"

"Mom!" I gasp.

"Then you pop up at her school, without our permission!"

"Mom! Please!"

"I am talking to Mr. Fields, young lady," she seethes. "Not you!"

Korey smiles from the other end of our kitchen table, with

Jessica sitting beside him. Sweat forms on the back of my knees. I'm embarrassed by the homely look of our . . . home. We're broke compared to his lavish lifestyle. But Korey insisted on driving all the way here to make his proposal.

"You're right, Mrs. Jones. My apologies. I never intended to be disrespectful."

I glance at the living room. On the sofa, the Littles stare wide-eyed at the back of Korey's head. Through the front window, his bodyguards lean against their black trucks.

"Enchanted asked me, on behalf of her school, if I would stop by," he continues. "I thought it would be cool."

Daddy taps his fingers on the table, side-eyeing me. I bite my lip. I never asked Korey to come to my school.

"I said it before," Korey continues. "I think Enchanted has some amazing potential. I mean, no lie, my phone's been blowing up with producers and record labels wanting to know who this mystery girl is. I think it's time we take the show on the road."

"What does that mean?" Daddy says.

"With your permission, I'd like Enchanted to be a special guest on my acoustic tour."

Mom gapes at him. "Not a damn chance in hell."

"Mom!"

"I know it sounds crazy, right? But—"

"BUT the answer is still no," Daddy fumes, voice taking up every corner of the house.

Korey cocks his head to the side with an amused smirk.

"If I may, Mr. and Mrs. Jones," Jessica jumps in. "I have

been working with Korey for quite some time, and what we see in Enchanted, we've . . . never seen in any of his other protégés. The label is really invested in grooming her, and then we can work on setting her up with her own record deal."

Mom's eyes widen with a jerk.

"I'm happy to act as a legal guardian," Jessica adds. "This has been done for dozens of underage stars in the past."

"And I'm sure Enchanted could use the money," Korey chuckles, glancing back at the Littles, sitting next to Daddy's freshly printed protest posters. "With school . . . and all."

Daddy swallows back some rage. "The answer is still no."

Mom chews her bottom lip.

Daddy's nos are firm, walls built of concrete.

But Mom's nos are made of drywall. Can be penetrated with the right force and tools.

# *Chapter 30*
## A MOTHER'S GRIP

"Never Knew Love Like This Before," by Stephanie Mills. That's the song he sent me.

Once again, I'm wondering what he means between the song lyrics. Is he saying he loves me?

Because I think . . . I mean, I know I love him.

Never knew love could feel like this. That spent-all-day-swimming-in-the-ocean breathless feeling. I can hear the sea in my ears. Taste the salt water in the back of my throat. Korey makes me feel like home. My *real* home. Only mermaids can swim in emotions this deep.

I'd do anything to feel this type of love forever.

• • •

*I'm sixteen years old. I'm not a child!*

That's the line from *The Little Mermaid* that keeps popping into my head. The way Ariel snapped at her father, even when I was little, made my muscles clench. Couldn't imagine talking to Mom or Daddy that way and living to tell about it.

But now they've pushed me.

The brisk fall air squeezes through the cracks of my jacket as I stand outside school, waiting for Mom.

Late, again.

Shea shivers next to me. "You're being selfish. You know that, right?"

I roll my eyes. "Mind your business, Shea. This has nothing to do with you!"

"Daddy and Mom barely have enough for next semester," she huffs. "You know how embarrassing that's gonna be? And you're worried about singing."

I pull a hat over my baldy, ignoring the gnawing in my gut. Korey hasn't returned any of my text messages today. What if he's done with me? What if he doesn't want to be bothered with my drama? What if he's already moved on? The desperation chills my backbone.

Mom whips her car around the corner, and I hop in the front seat.

"Wipe that look off your face, Chant," she snaps. "You're not going. End of discussion!"

"Mom, you have to let me do this."

Shea rolls her eyes and pops in her earbuds. "Here we go again."

"There's no way one of us can take off work for weeks to follow you around the country."

"But you won't have to. Jessica will watch me!"

"Jessica is a stranger!"

"She works for the label. She'll watch me. And what about the money? The label's gonna pay me fifteen thousand dollars! We're just gonna turn that down?"

"What? How do you know all that?"

I gulp, gripping the phone in my pocket.

"I . . . that's what I heard background singers make on tours."

Mom shakes her head. "Your father said no."

"But this is my chance! People would kill for this opportunity."

"There will be others, Chant. You're seventeen! You just have to be patient. Besides, what about school and swim?"

"I can homeschool!"

"What about the Littles?"

"Is that what this is about? You won't let me go 'cause I won't be home to watch the Littles?"

Mom's face flatlines.

"So I'm grown enough to watch your kids but not grown enough to live my life? That's not fair! I'm missing out on being a kid watching YOURS! Damn, how much do I have to give up?"

The car grows painfully silent. In the back seat, Shea sits with tears in her eyes, not waiting for the car to stop before jumping out into the driveway. Mom turns off the ignition, leans her head against the steering wheel. She's been working extra hours since Daddy's strike started.

"Chant, I can't keep fighting with you. I'm . . . tired."

"You have to let me go," I plead. "I know the money for tuition is due soon. You can use what I make for Shea."

Mom lowers her head farther to hide her shame.

"But if you don't let me go . . . I won't be the same. I promise you, I'll never ever be the same. Please, Mom!"

Mom looks at me, understanding flooding her eyes.

One thing I know about fish: you keep them on land too long, they'll die.

# Part Two

Part Two

# *Chapter 31*

## BEET JUICE 2

*NOW*

"Police. Open up!"

My toes are covered in beet juice and piss. They clash with my pedicure.

I should clean up, before anyone comes in here. Korey will be so mad if people see the place a mess.

Wait.

Wait.

No.

I look back inside the room. At his slumped-over body. His eyes are closed. Maybe for good. I hope for good.

No! Don't think like that.

He loves you, remember?
Another three hard knocks again.
I'm frozen. A statue.
What have I done?

# Chapter 32

## ON GOD

*THEN*

Korey presses record on his camera. Now when I go to the studio, I make a point to wear my cleanest shirt and gloss my lips, never knowing what's in store.

He sits behind the piano, playing the familiar keys, and smiles.

"Ready? Practice makes perfect, Bright Eyes."

I pat my new mini fro, unaccustomed to the tight dark brown coils slipping through my fingers. Daddy hasn't given me a shape-up in a while since he isn't exactly talking to me.

"You look beautiful," Korey says with a wink. "Relax."

Korey's words are always so sweet, thoughtful. Not like boys. Boys fumble, word vomiting wants, attacking my lips and hips like feral dogs. But men, men like Korey? Men are patient.

Why would any girl want a boy after she's had a man love them?

*"Like sweet morning dew,
I took one look at you . . .
you were my destiny . . ."*

His words caress my cheeks and I almost forget my lines. I squeeze up to the mic, my new soul mate.

*". . . I sacrifice for you,
dedicate my life to you . . ."*

Of course the perfect song for us would be "You're All I Need to Get By" by Marvin Gaye and Tammi Terrell, crafted in the stars just for us.

Every time I sing, I turn into a new kind of animal. The kind that loses all its dense bones and just floats. I'm flying above myself, because I can't imagine any girl in the world being as lucky as I am. To have the hottest singer in the world in love with her. To be going on tour. To have all her dreams come true.

Korey plays back the track while writing notes on a loose sheet of paper. He can be so focused, it's no wonder they call him a musical genius.

"Aight, I'm thinking we open with that number, yeah? Then, maybe do 'The Closer I Get to You.' Followed by your solo."

Blood drains from my head and I wobble.

"You . . . want me to do a solo?"

"Of course. Like I said, baby, you're talented. And beautiful."

Korey's eyes darken, gliding down my body before shooting a glance at the door, hopping up to lock it. Turning the music high, he drowns out the world, wrapping me in his arms.

"You *are* my destiny, Enchanted," he whispers, nuzzling my neck. "It was no accident that you walked into my life. It was fate."

Korey goes into a tangent about God, Jesus, the devil, and church. He preaches, his voice shrilling, full of twists and turns, and I'm nauseous from the ride.

"And your daddy out here talking about y'all come from fish," he says, rolling his eyes. "Pfff! God brought you to me. Without me, no one would know who you are. Fish didn't do that. God did."

I never know what to say in these one-sided conversations. Saying nothing seems like the best idea. Because otherwise, he might let go, and there's no place I'd rather be than wrapped up in his arms. So I bite my lip, something I read that girl did in *Fifty Shades of Grey*. Hoping maybe, just maybe, he'll kiss me again.

There's a bang on the door. Mom stands behind it, next

to Jessica, holding her purse, face tight.

"You didn't hear us knocking all that time?" she snaps at me.

I wiggle under her stony gaze. "It's kinda loud in here. We were rehearsing."

"For her solo," Korey adds, leaning against the door.

Mom regards him, and there's a slight flicker in her eyes. Like she *knows*. My lungs squeeze shut.

"Then why was the door locked?" she says in that familiar accusatory tone she gives my siblings when something is broken or missing.

I shoot her a pleading look. Please don't embarrass me. Please don't embarrass me. Please don't embarrass me.

"My bad, Mrs. Jones," Korey chuckles with a shrug. "Habit. But glad you're here! Mary J. Blige's Christmas show is next week. Gonna hook you and your husband up. She'd love to meet you."

Mom's shoulders relax, her face smoothing.

# Chapter 33
## ONCE UPON A DREAM

"You ready?" Korey says behind me, breath on the nape of my neck.

"No."

He chuckles. "Stop lying. You were born ready!"

Korey always knows the right things to say, even when my pulse is hammering.

Is this really happening?

One minute, I'm on my first plane ride, to Chicago, head dizzy with the altitude, next I'm here . . . standing shoulder to shoulder with Korey Fields, lacing our fingers together in a way no one can see.

"Let's do it," he whispers, with a quick kiss to the temple.

Korey walks out onstage, waving, and the crowd screams. A drum set sitting in the middle of the stage is moved up.

"What's up, Chi-Town! Ladies and gentlemen, thank you for being with us tonight. I'd like to bring out . . . a very special guest."

Eyes closed, I press my lips together, breathing through my nose.

"A girl you've probably seen before, but here for the very first time onstage . . ."

There's water in my ears, the sounds of lazy, calm waves licking the shore. As much as I miss living in my seashell, there's nothing like hearing your name through a million speakers.

"I introduce you to Miss . . . Enchanted!"

The cheers crash through the curtains. Jessica shoves my back and I stumble onto the stage, the lights blinding, gawking at the most people I've ever seen in my entire life.

Cheers. They are cheering for me.

I shuffle up to the mic on his left and it yells back at me. I shoot Korey an unsure glance. He plops on the stool behind the drum set, adjusting his mic. We catch eyes, something unsaid passing between us as the familiar rush of heat creeps up my neck. But then he smiles and an overwhelming sense of calm washes over me.

And then we perform "Fool for You" by CeeLo Green.

With only eyes for each other. We're in our own world in front of the entire world, but it feels like just the two of us.

●  ●  ●

"So! How's it going?" Mom asks on FaceTime, the Littles surrounding her. We talk twice a day, every single day, in my hotel room.

"It's . . . amazing, Mom. Did Jessica send you pictures?"

"Yeah," Shea says. "Chant, your makeup looks fire!"

"Thanks. Is Daddy there?"

Mom gives me a strained smile. "No. He's out right now."

Daddy hasn't really had time to call. With his union on strike, he's been on the picket line day and night. At least that's what I tell myself.

Gab hasn't answered any of my text messages since our fight in the bathroom. Not even when I called to wish her Happy New Year.

Few minutes after I hang up with the Littles, Korey walks through the connecting door of our hotel rooms.

"Finally," he says, plopping on my bed with a grin. "Alone at last! So what you wanna watch tonight, *Beauty and the Beast* or *Cinderella*?"

He turns on the TV, changing the channel, volume up to sixty.

"Did you iron my shirt?" he asks, popping some peanuts into his mouth. "Last time the sleeve was still a little wrinkled."

I dodge his reaching embrace, storming across the room.

"Yeah, it's in the closet," I say drily.

"Yo, what's wrong with you?"

I shrug. "Surprised you're here. Thought you were gonna hang out with the dancers. Like you did last night."

He smirks. "Aw, you jealous?"

"No," I mumble.

He wraps his arms around me, nuzzling my neck.

"Did I tell you how happy I am that you're here? Remember how I told you I felt mad lonely on tour, even when I was in a room full of people? But now I have you. It's like you're my little secret I don't have to share with no one." He kisses my temple. "You were wonderful tonight."

I take a deep breath, leaning into his love. There he is. MY Korey.

"Korey, when are we going to head into the studio and work on my album . . . like you promised?"

A knock on the door startles me. Korey rolls his eyes and answers.

Jessica. Her eyes widen, toggling between Korey and me.

"Yes?" Korey barks, and I jump in my skin.

Jessica gulps. "S-sorry. I'll come back later."

"Good," he says and slams the door in her face.

# Chapter 34

## MELISSA

Her name is Melissa.

She is dark brown, silky, twenty-six inches, and fits tight around the crown of my head.

I immediately hate her.

"How's that?" the hairstylist asks, glancing behind her.

Korey leans against the adjacent makeup counter, studying his phone. He looks up, beaming.

"Perfect! Enchanted? What do you think?"

"Um . . . it's OK."

He frowns, tucking his phone away. "Give us a moment."

The stylist nods and leaves the trailer.

"What's wrong, Bright Eyes?"

I bite the inside of my cheek. "Um, why do I need a wig?"

"It's for your look. We're trying to build your brand, remember? And you know what teen fans want? Girls with hair. They want that Beyoncé—you have to give it to them."

He touches the ends of Melissa, twirling her around his fingers.

"You know, it says in the Bible that women shouldn't shave their heads. It's a sin against the Lord."

My mouth opens, but no words come out. How do I argue with the Bible, something he knows so well and I . . . don't know at all?

"Besides, it'll make me happy. Cool?"

But . . . I thought I already made him happy. I thought he liked the way I looked.

I swallow back all the rising questions and wince a smile. "OK."

"Bet. Make sure you wear her tonight."

# Chapter 35
## TV NOTES

Tonight's concert afterparty in Los Angeles is being hosted by BET's *Music LIVE* at the Mandarin Oriental.

I stand off in the corner of the roped-off VIP area. Sweat is building under Melissa but one quick breeze could blow my too-short skirt off my ass.

Korey glances at me from across the room and winks. It's our special little message to each other. He doesn't like to be seen in public with me. Thinks it may give people the wrong impression; they won't understand. So I stand by, faithful to my man.

My man. Korey Fields is MY man. And I'm really in

California. I've touched palm trees and seen the Hollywood sign in the hills up close. Had to pinch myself several times to make sure I'm not dreaming.

Next to Korey, Richie pours himself another glass of champagne.

"So, what'd you think, fam? I think it'd be a hit! You know, your life story," he continues to explain. "Take all that home-video footage, spice it up with some exclusive interviews—it'll make a fire documentary for BET, HULU, or even Netflix."

"Man, you really trying to get that executive producer money, huh?" Korey laughs. "You want the Emmy bad! I mean, I'm down. If you say it's gonna bang, I trust you."

Richie smirks. "We could even make it a series! *Life and Times of Korey Fields*. Has a nice ring to it, right?"

"So, what you need from me?"

"All your home videos. Old and new."

Korey chuckles. "Well, not ALL my home videos. Some of them gotta be for the private viewing, feel me?"

The men cackle. Richie shakes his head. "Hey, man, leave the X-rated stuff at home. But we should highlight some of your wild-boy days. Then come back to how you found God."

Korey turns real serious. "Yo! I've always knew God. Don't get it twisted!"

Richie holds up his hands. "My bad, bruh. No disrespect."

My ankles crack as I struggle to walk in sky-high heels in search of a bathroom. So many people, yet I don't see Jessica anywhere. Not that she's much of a chaperone, and I've caught her rolling her eyes a couple of times at the most basic questions.

"Hey, Enchanted, right?"

A boy in a light blue blazer and white sneakers leaning against the bar waves a hand.

"Yeah. But how did you—"

"I remember you from your audition, back in New York. Derrick Price, Richie's son." He eyes Melissa with a squint. "I . . . uh, almost didn't recognize you."

I shift on my heel. "Um, yeah. New look."

He has dark brown skin with a mop of curly brown hair and kind hazel eyes. "Well, Pops and I don't share the same taste, but I thought you were dope!"

"Thanks," I say, pushing a strand of Melissa hair behind my ear. "So you work for your dad?"

He laughs. "Yeah, intern. Or my official title is executive assistant. How old are you again?"

"I'm eighteen."

Derrick frowns. "Huh, that's weird. I thought your application said you were seventeen."

I breathe in, practicing the line Korey fed me.

"Ha! I know, I look young for my age."

Derrick's eyebrow cocks up. "Uh, right. My bad, I thought you were still in high school like me, that's all. I'm a senior."

"Um, so . . . dope party," I say, changing the subject.

"Yeah," he says then his eyes grow big. "Yo! Over there! You see that? That's Jasmine Keith, from *Love and Hip Hop*."

I glance around the room until I spot her by the bar.

"OMG! That is her!" I can't help but grin. "Aight, so I know I shouldn't be about black folks fighting on TV, but I was cheering when she whooped Megan B.'s ass during the season finale."

"So you watch *Love and Hip-Hop* too? Dope, right?"

"Well, my sister does. And most of the time, I'm nearby . . . pretending not to be."

We laugh, walking closer to the bar. "I feel you. I know I shouldn't be all into it, but it's like crack TV."

"Wait, hold up. If you're in school, what you doing in LA? On a school night."

He smirks. "My pops writes me a note whenever I want to shadow him. Getting ready to take over the family business. Yo, that reminds me! When we're back in New York, we should link up. A couple of my homies from school produce they own beats and we record all the time."

"Really?"

"Yeah. They got over five hundred thousand followers on SoundCloud. They sick with it! Add that voice of yours and you'd be killing it with us!"

Whoa. Never met anyone in high school producing music like that. Unheard of at my dry school.

"Hey, over there," I whisper. "Check out Monica with Cardi B." For a split second, I think of Shea and how she would be losing her mind seeing some of her favorite celebrities in here.

"You know," Derrick says, trying to wave down a bartender. "I heard Jasmine used to be in Will and Willow and got kicked out for trying to sneak in a boys' room during Teen Conference."

"Wait! You're in Will and Willow? I'm in Will and Willow too! I mean . . . was."

"Oh, word? Didn't think they let us into these parties! Thought we were too bougie for this crowd."

Derrick and I spend the next fifteen minutes exchanging W&W stories and playing I Spy the Reality Show Star. It was fun, just kicking it, and I can't help but notice he's the first person my age I've seen in weeks. Mom is always talking about how small the world is. Maybe I would've met Derrick at a W&W conference or a dance. But then . . . I would've never met Korey. I'm all he has here; I bring him peace.

"Anyway, I better get back. Korey's probably looking for me."

Derrick cocks his head to the side, a question on his lips.

"You . . . with him?"

"Nah, no. We just, uh, sing together . . . like Marvin Gaye and Tammi. They weren't together in real life either."

He shrugs. "Well, looks like your boy has his hands full anyways."

Across the room, Korey is whispering in a girl's ear. Not just any girl. Amber. The one with the gold curly hair from the *Music LIVE* audition. She's in a tight sequined green dress, shimmering like a mermaid's tail. Her giggle is unnerving.

"Um, yeah," I say, my voice fading. "Well, it was nice meeting you, Derrick."

"Word. I'm sure I'll be seeing you around."

On the way back to the VIP area, I text Gab, hoping she'll be up. I need advice on how to handle girls creeping up on my man. Jay was popular in his neighborhood, and Gab had to put several girls in their place.

"Hey, Enchanted, hold up!" Derrick chases after me. "You left your purse."

"Oh! Thanks."

"No prob," he says, touching my arm before jogging back to the bar.

When I look up, Korey is staring, his eyes stone-cold. I give him a smile.

He doesn't smile back.

# Chapter 36

## ICE BUCKET

On the way back to the hotel, I'm invisible. Well, at least to Korey.

"Is something wrong?" I ask.

He ignores me, glaring out the window of the Suburban. My stomach in knots, I bite the inside of my cheek until I draw blood, trying to figure out what went wrong as we take the elevator up to the penthouse.

Inside, I trail behind him, keeping a distance, then kick off my shoes, toes throbbing.

"Korey, what's wrong? Can you talk to me? Please?"

A shadow crosses his face, eyes ten shades darker.

"What the fuck were you doing talking to some other man right in front of me?"

I blink twice. "What are you talking about?"

"Don't act stupid!" he screams. "You know what I'm talking about."

An unfamiliar panic rises in my throat as I replay the evening.

"Do you mean Derrick?"

He stares at me, face contorting, almost unrecognizable in anger.

"That's Richie's son! Your friend. I was making conversation. There was no one else to talk to. Plus, you were busy."

"Don't give me your bullshit excuses!"

"But I didn't do anything. I was just—"

"Shut up!" he roars. "All I asked is for you to be faithful to me, and you do me like this!"

His voice pounds against the walls and I back away, my head spinning. I don't know what to say except, "I'm sorry."

"I said stop with the excuses," he screams in my face, nostrils flaring.

I yelp, falling back onto the carpet, and burst into tears.

Korey shakes his head. "You need to stay in your room. Don't come out until I tell you."

Is he grounding me, like a child? "What you mean? I—"

"You leave this room . . . I'm going to make you regret it!"

The depth of his voice stuns me to silence. He storms out, slamming the door shut.

• • •

By noon, I'm pacing, the door calling my name.

I have to go to the bathroom.

Korey told me not to leave the room.

But still . . . I have to go to the bathroom.

I've been in here for over twelve hours. My mouth is dry. The hot sun and giant windows have turned this room into a sauna.

My cell is dead, and the charger is in the living room. Mom is probably wondering where I'm at. What if she calls Jessica? What will she say?

But still . . . bathroom.

I pace around in a circle, wondering how long. How long he'll keep me in here, how long he'll be mad at me, how long I can hold my piss.

Jessica opens the door, takes one look at me, and smirks.

"Your mom called. Want to talk to her?"

I pace in place, staring past her, feeling the cool breeze from the air-conditioning sweep in.

"Is . . . is that OK?" I say, my voice scratchy from sobbing.

"I don't know. Did you ask him?"

"How do I ask him?"

"How did he say to ask him?"

I pace again. "Jessica, I really need to use the bathroom. But Korey said I can't leave."

Jessica rolls her eyes and walks off. She returns with an empty ice bucket, placing it on the floor.

"Here you go. Have fun."

. . .

Sixteen hours.

That's how long I've been in this room. In this outfit. With no food or water. I'm sweating. Hungry. Thirsty. Dizzy. And the half-filled ice bucket in the corner makes me want to vomit.

I met another Korey last night. That's the only explanation for it. He must turn into a different person when he drinks, like Dr. Jekyll and Mr. Hyde. I've heard of people blacking out while drunk. He's going to wake up and not remember a thing that happened. He'll be so apologetic, begging for my forgiveness . . .

Or maybe he had a point. Maybe I shouldn't have been talking to Derrick. Girlfriends aren't supposed to make their boyfriends jealous.

But boyfriends shouldn't lock their girlfriends up like prisoners.

I grip my dead phone. I don't want to call Mom. Don't want to hear the I-told-you-so speech. Plus, I can't keep calling her whenever I have a problem. She'll keep treating me like a baby, and if I want freedom, I have to work this out on my own.

The door clicks open. Korey stands at the threshold and gives me a once-over. I jump to my feet, heart pounding. Who am I meeting today?

"Get dressed. We're going for a ride."

The moment I leave the room, I rush into the bathroom to drain my bladder then drink three bottles of water. Jessica is sitting on the sofa, watching *Keeping Up with the Kardashians*.

She doesn't turn in my direction. I refuse to acknowledge her either as I carry the ice bucket into the bathroom.

After a shower, feeling brand-new, I glare at Melissa, ready to flush her down the toilet. But maybe it'll make him happy.

"Ready?" Korey says as I emerge from the bathroom. He stands by the door, smiling. The familiar smile I know. My back muscles loosen.

"Where are we going?"

"I've got a surprise for you."

# *Chapter 37*

## WHERE FAIRY TALES END

The LA sunset creates a beautiful pink-and-baby-blue sky, dotted with palm trees. I sit passenger side as Korey zooms down the highway.

"Where are we going?" I ask again.

Korey glances in the rearview and sighs.

"You know . . . you ask a lot of questions. It makes me feel like you don't trust me." He glances at me, his voice deadpan. "So? Do you trust me?"

I nod my head like a faithful puppy. "Yes! Yes, you know I do!"

"Then quit all that talking. Enjoy the ride."

I lean back in my seat as that strange gnawing in my stomach returns, a mixture of fear, hope, and love.

Ten minutes later we pass a sign that makes me shoot up and gasp.

"OMG! Disneyland!"

He smirks. "Told you I'd bring you here one day."

Korey wears his sunglasses and hoodie to the most magical place on earth. On a Monday evening, with the park near empty, it's the perfect time to be incognito on Splash Mountain.

Even though I'm at the most magical place on earth, with my dream man, living my dream job, an ache inside me longs for the Littles. I thought my first time at Disney would be with them.

But still, being two kids in a massive playground had its perks. Korey was himself again, and I forced the images of last night out of my mind. Couples fight, then they make up. Mom and Daddy fight. Gab and Jay used to fight all the time.

We walk to a bench, with the perfect angle of the castle, holding a large cotton candy tube, bushes concealing us.

"I haven't been here in . . . years," Korey says, a dizzy smile on his face, and wraps an arm around my waist. "Thank you. For reminding me what it's like to be a kid again."

There's a sadness in his eyes that quickly flutters away. A shot of red then blue burst in the sky. Disney is famous for its evening fireworks show.

Korey grabs my hand and pulls me near the water's edge. He cups my face with both hands, staring down at me, but I can only see myself in the reflection of his glasses.

Or a version of myself, with Melissa on my head.

Slowly, he bends, lays one long kiss on my lips. Even as it happens, I can't believe it's real.

Rockets scream around us, but nothing could match the burst of my heart.

As the park closes, we walk into a gift shop. Still on a high, I float over to the Little Mermaid section, picking toy action figures of Ariel and her father. I think of Daddy and smile.

Korey picks up a large stuffed Flounder.

"Yeah, this is perfect," he mumbles, and takes it to the register.

"Did you have fun today?"

"Mmhmm," I nod with a yawn, hugging Flounder tight to my chest. "It was the best. Thank you!"

Korey follows me into my room, and I set Flounder on the desk. A reminder of this perfect day.

"Well, good night," I sigh. "See you—"

Korey is taking off his hoodie, chain, watch, and rings. He looks at me like I'm something to eat. The air changes and I back away.

"Korey?"

He kisses me hard, hands everywhere. I can't catch up. I push away but he grabs my chin, nails digging, and pulls my lips to his.

My body freezes as he lays me on the bed.

"You're so beautiful, you know that?" he whispers. "I'm sorry I yelled at you, baby. I just can't stand the thought of someone stealing what's mine. You're all I have."

His words thaw me a little.

"You have me," I say. "I'm not going anywhere."

He kisses my neck, more and more, his body heavy on top of mine. My shirt is gone. So is his. I'm being dragged underwater and can't breathe. The sound of his zipper rips the room apart. That's when he grabs my wrist, leading it down his stomach.

"Wait," I mutter, yanking my hand away. He sits up, hurt in his eyes.

"What? What is it?"

"I . . . um? I just . . ."

He sighs, shaking his head.

"I thought you cared about me."

I shoot up. "I do care about you! I really do!"

"Then I need you to make me feel good," he says, pushing my hand toward his crotch again. "Don't you want me to be happy? After the way you hurt me last night?"

That panic returns. I'm back in the hotel room with Creighton. Trapped. Alone. Scared. But . . . Korey saved me then. So why don't I feel safe now? His words replay on a loop, he said he'd wait. He said, *When you're ready, I'll be ready.*

"Korey, do you love me?"

Korey smiles. "Of course I do, Bright Eyes. Why else would I do all this? Only for you."

I nod, the answer not as satisfying as I'd hoped. Thought my heart would burst and flood the earth with our love; instead it races loud in my ears. My muscles tense, bracing themselves.

"Shhhh . . . relax," he whispers.

Then, I give in, and let him lead my hand down his pants, into his boxers. Something slimy flops in my palm.

He doesn't kiss my lips. He just grabs my breast, hard, panting, twisting, and it hurts.

It. Hurts.

Holding back tears, I stare at Flounder, sitting on the dresser, watching us. I don't want him to see me this way. So I squeeze my eyes shut and float away, back to the sea, the waves, the seagulls, Grandma . . .

Korey lets out a moan clipped by a slight scream then an "Ah! . . . That's my good girl."

# Chapter 38

## WITNESS STATEMENT

*NOW*

*Witness Statement: Tim Houlihan, doorman at The Cour-lander*

*On May 20, I started my shift around 6 p.m. Ms. Enchanted Jones came in around 10:30 p.m. Almost didn't recognize her since her hair is usually short, cut like a boy's, and she was always with her mother or father. But that night, she came alone. I called Mr. Fields to alert him of a visitor. Told me to send her right up. Seemed a little surprised but happy.*

*Around 11:30 p.m., Mr. Jones came in, demanding to see his daughter. I called upstairs twice, but no one* answered. He called the police, but it's private property and she's eighteen. He stayed until around 1:30 a.m., when Ms. Jessica Owens stopped by. They talked outside.

My shift ended around 4 a.m. Ms. Jones never came back downstairs.

# Chapter 39

## JUICE BOX

### THEN

Caesars Palace in Las Vegas has a giant pool. The fake water calls, begging me to dive in from the penthouse floor.

I want to swim. I need to swim. I need to submerge myself, wash my thoughts clean. Erase the memories.

But Korey doesn't want me walking around in a bathing suit.

I should be happy. Korey is like Edward from *Twilight*, doting over Bella with his overprotectiveness. Except, I don't feel happiness. I feel . . . tired. Exhausted from being woken up in the middle of the night over and over.

I feel . . . used.

"Again!" Korey bellows, standing next to his stylist, Leigh. Step, step, step. I practice strutting in four-inch heels, each step wobbly, worried that at any moment my ankles will snap like twigs.

The room is crowded with Korey, Leigh, Jessica, and Tony. Korey says I need to wear more designer brands. Gucci, Balmain, Chanel, and Versace. Makes sense since I'm in his world now—I should look the part.

Except . . . all these clothes are super tight. They cling like a second skin, pinching my sides.

"She's coming along," Leigh says, giving me a sympathetic smile.

"She has terrible posture," Jessica comments from the corner.

He nods. "Yeah, and she need to lose some of this belly fat. And tone up these arms."

I glance in the mirror as he grabs a piece of skin, mistaking it for fat. I try to be on my best behavior. Because the last thing I want to do is piss in an ice bucket again. Maybe my arms aren't as toned they used to be, after weeks of not swimming.

"Well, we won't have to worry about buying her some new tits," he says. "She got them Ds, but we gotta work on that ass."

"I'll call Dr. Adams when we get to Miami," Jessica says. "She'll need recovery time."

"Add some teeth whitening, too."

I bite my lip, wondering what Mom would say. Shouldn't I ask her first, before going to doctors? Gab told me those surgeries are dangerous—girls walk around with cement in their butts.

"And get her some new panties. Sick of seeing those grandma

drawers," Korey says, lifting the elastic around my waist, giving me an instant wedgie. "I want nothing but thongs!"

Leigh blinks at him, gaping. She studies me and I give her my best fake smile, holding back tears.

Still no studio time. No talk of an album. No singing lessons. My songbook, stuffed deep inside my suitcase, cries for air.

All we practice is how to look like anyone but me.

**Gab, don't know if you're going to be free or not but we're performing in Connecticut on Saturday. Maybe you and Jay can drive up? I'll have tickets at the box office for you. Miss you. Wish you'd just talk to me.**

"Drink."

Korey's outstretched hand holds a cup of clear liquid. Just like the night he saved me in Jersey. Except the conditions have changed.

"I don't really want any."

"Think I care what you want? I said drink," he slurs. "Standing around here looking stupid. Embarrassing me."

The greenroom is tight, smoky, and clogged full of unfamiliar faces, mostly groupies who don't pay me any attention. The more tour stops we make, the more groupies he collects like souvenirs.

"I said drink," he barks. Korey is drunk again, and I think of making a run for my room, where I can at least hide for the night. Tony stands by the door like a wall. Even if I try to leave, he'll probably stop me.

He's stopped me before.

I check my phone several times, hoping Gab will call. Text. Even to say she's not coming. Mom couldn't take off work, leaving Daddy at home to watch the Littles. Don't think he wanted to come anyway.

I sip and sip until the room is a dizzy haze.

Food arrives. Food he requires on his talent rider. Enough food to feed my entire family twice over that he never touches. Just nibbles on a few crackers or peanuts.

"You need a steak."

"I don't eat meat."

"You eat fish," he counters.

"That's . . . different."

"Well, that's what you need to do. I'm not going to put all this work into an ungrateful ass," he barks. "Now I'm telling you what to do, so do it or I'm sending your ass back home. Eat the fucking steak!"

He shoves the plate in my direction. The room grows quiet. My neck tightens as I pick a slice of bloody meat with my hand and pop a chunk in my mouth, feeling the cow screaming for its life.

The party continues. I keep drinking, the alcohol taking the edge off my misery. Mr. Hyde, that's all I'm dealing with. He'll be Dr. Jekyll soon enough.

"Nah, Enchanted got that Juice Box vibe."

"What does that even mean?" Someone laughs.

"Yo, let me show you. Ma, come here!"

A girl from across the room struts over and I almost didn't

recognize her. It's Amber. Her hair is bone straight, dyed black, long and silky . . .

Like Pocahontas.

"See?" Korey says, showing her off like a model car. "Look at Amber, now look at Enchanted. See the difference? One is shaped like a coke bottle . . . the other like a juice box."

Korey bursts into laughter. The room nervously laughs with him.

"Damn, man, that's cold," his friend laughs.

Amber twirls around, smirking at me. Vomit builds in my throat.

I stumble, catching a glimpse of myself in the vanity mirror. Not myself, but someone who used to be me. Tears brimming, I pour myself another glass of vodka.

"That better not be your only cup!" Korey says to me from . . . somewhere. I can't tell. Everything is a blur.

I check my phone one last time. Still nothing. Anger rises with bile. Some damn best friend I got. We have one fight and she cuts me off like some dead ends she needed to trim. She wouldn't even try to be happy for me. This is all I've ever wanted. Does she even know what she wants besides Jay?

I drift toward the door.

"Tony, has anyone come . . . looking for me?"

"Nah."

My knees clash together.

"You need to sit on down," he says.

I do, flopping back on the sofa, letting my eyes close on one last thought—Gab and I are done.

# *Chapter 40*
## FRICTION

My throat is lined with sandpaper. Hangovers and a moving tour bus don't mix. But the show must go on. Except tonight, my performance was stagnant. Fake. Forced. Voice cracking at the end of my solo.

Korey noticed. And he's not happy about it.

"What the fuck was that?" he screams. "This isn't karaoke."

"I know. I'm sorry," I cry.

"You made me look like an idiot out there! Damn, can't you do anything right?"

"I'm just t-tired," I stutter. "I need some sleep . . . alone."

There's a knock on the door. Before Korey can respond,

Jessica enters the greenroom, eyes toggling between us.

"We have a problem," she states.

"Yeah I know," he snarls. "Someone ain't got her shit together!"

"Not that. Well, not that exactly. It's her parents. They've been calling. They want to arrange a visit."

"Well, tell them she's busy," he says, arm motioning to the stage. "It's not like we're just kicking it on the beach. We working!"

"I know, but I can't hold them off forever."

Korey shoots me an angry look. "When do you turn eighteen again?"

I gulp. "Two months."

He exhales. "Good! Then we can finally be fucking rid of them." He plops down on the sofa, pouring himself a drink. "You know they've been breathing down my neck ever since you came into my life."

I blink. "But . . . they've been nothing but nice to you."

Korey snickers, shaking his head.

"Damn, I keep forgetting, you don't know nothing about nothing. Ma, they practically *begged* me to take you. One less mouth to feed."

That's not true, I want to shout. But fear and shock sew my lips shut.

"Been trying to control you 'cause they know you their big money ticket out of being some broke-ass niggas."

Hands trembling, my eyes narrow, and for a moment, the old me crawls her way out of the dark.

"Don't talk about my mom and daddy like that," I hiss.

He raises an eyebrow, as if impressed. "Oh, you don't believe me? Ask Jessica—she'll tell you. I can show you the texts they've sent. Asking for money, asking for what I owe. Man, thirsty as hell. That's how parents be. They be using their kids just to fill they own pockets. Right, Jessica?"

Jessica's eyes widen for a split second, and for the first time, through her cold demeanor, I see someone real, not just a block of ice. A real woman with emotions. Actually, no, not a woman.

A girl.

Maybe it's the way she carries herself, bone straight like a number-two pencil, but now I can't unsee the fact that Jessica is young.

"Plus, I've been paying their bills," Korey carries on. "How else you think your little sis still going to that expensive-ass school?"

My face feels numb. "What are you talking about?"

He groans, rubbing his face.

"Just . . . just get her out of here," he says with a flick of his wrist. "Tired of explaining myself."

In the car, I dare to ask the question. "Jessica, how old are you?"

Tony, behind the wheel, glances in the rearview mirror, and she shoots me a soul-piercing glare.

"That is none of your business."

# Chapter 41
## DECLINE

Hey, how's school?

> Kool. Everyone's been talking about you. You're like a celebrity. Which makes me a celebrity!

And the Littles?

> They kool too. You talk to Mom? You're not calling like you're supposed to. Heard her trying to reach you through Korey.

I reread Shea's message several times, willing it to change. Korey wasn't lying. Mom really was texting him.

Outside my window, on the top floor of our Washington, DC, hotel, I can see the Washington Monument, standing tall, snow covering the grass of the National Mall. I sit with the cold, hard facts Korey laid at my feet.

Shea is still in school because Korey is paying for it.

The Littles still have a roof over their head . . . because Korey is paying for it.

First, I was used as a resident babysitter, so I didn't have a life of my own, now I'm being used again. This time for money. I don't know what's worse.

Korey enters, carrying Flounder.

"You . . . left this in Connecticut," he says, setting the doll on the dresser.

"Sorry," I mumble, continuing to gaze out the window.

"Nah, I'm sorry," he says, falling to his knees in front of me. "I'm sorry I went off on you like that. I just . . . get so mad at the thought of anyone taking advantage of you. You so sweet and beautiful and I gotta protect the people I love."

Korey holds my hand, looking up expectantly at me, and my throat closes. How could someone be so angry one minute, then love me so hard the next?

"It's OK," I relent. "I know it's because you love me."

"I do," he says, cupping the side of my face. "I'd do anything for my Bright Eyes. I want to look into these eyes for the rest of my life."

He stares at me, and there he is. My Korey. Sweet, caring, protective as ever.

"When you turn eighteen, I'm going to marry you."

My heart surges. The smile growing across my face reaches my earlobes.

"Really?"

He grins, bashful and shy. "Yeah. I know I'm supposed to surprise you with a ring and all. But we already know what it is. Plus, no secrets. Right?"

I nod eagerly. "Right! No secrets."

"We gotta have a big wedding, though. No Las Vegas joint with Elvis or nothing like that."

"OK," I laugh, wrapping my arms around his neck.

He flicks out his wrist, holding up his gold watch. "You see this? It's a Richard Mille custom, there's only one like it. See those diamonds in the middle? Those were from my grandma's ring. I'ma get them to bust this open and put it in your ring when they make it."

"Really? You'd do that . . . for me?"

"I'd do anything for you! My most prized possession on my most prized possession."

The watch is different from his other jewelry. Crisp and understated. I've never seen him without it.

"But before all that, we gonna go to my spot in Atlanta and record that album. You gonna love it. Gonna be living like a real princess. Nah, a queen! Have whatever you want. Even have your own room for a change. No sharing everything with all your brothers and sisters. Maybe even get you that car you wanted."

My phone rings and I glance at it.

Mom.

I hit decline and continue listening to the life Korey plans to make for us.

# *Chapter 42*

## GROUP CHAT: SETTLEMENT

*W&W Squad (w/o the Jones sisters)*

Sean: **Y'all see that shit on the news?**

Malika: **Yup! And I told y'all. Korey Fields is a creep.**

Aisha: **Girl, calm down. OK? All it said was that he settled out of court with some lady. They didn't find him guilty.**

Malika: **The lady said she was fourteen and Korey was twenty-three.**

Sean: **It's his word against hers, tho.**

Malika: **Her word ain't enough?**

Sean: **Does she have proof? You know girls be lying and trying to trap a bruh.**

Creighton: And it ain't like she didn't know what she was doing. Back then, he went triple platinum and was on a world tour. My dad said she probably didn't even look fourteen.

Malika: So EVERY chick that comes forward is vengeful? That's stupid as hell. Even if she did, HE knew better. Not looking their age don't change their age. Your dad is being messy.

Sean: She took that settlement money tho.

Malika: That was nothing but hush money. Bet you that's happening to Enchanted right now.

Sean: Ew, dude. Don't put that image in my head. She's like our sister!

Malika: You've seen the videos of them? They singing in each other mouths onstage. Korey was dancing on her too.

Creighton: They were just performing. Chill.

Malika: Nah, that's like your auntie twerking on you.

Creighton: CHILL! I don't need the visual!

Aisha: Has anyone heard from her?

Sean: No.

Creighton: Nah.

Malika: Nope.

Aisha: Her sister hasn't either. And she ain't returning any of her parents calls.

# Chapter 43

## CANDY

Candy Cole. That's her name. Sometimes goes by CC.

I've only caught mere snippets of information from the news, but not much since Jessica keeps the TV off and I don't dare google it since Korey checks my phone. He's even changed my password.

But from what I've gathered, CC, the twenty-year-old aspiring singer, is a big liar. She has to be. Because what she's saying about Korey, what he did to her, isn't possible.

Korey would never hit a woman, ever. He'd never lock her in her room or force her to have sex in his studio. Korey is a complete gentleman. He opens doors, buys me flowers before our shows, sends me the sweetest notes and songs . . .

Then I think of Mr. Hyde, the ice bucket, Flounder . . . and the hairs on my neck spike up.

"The promoter isn't budging," Jessica whispers to Korey after finishing her call, her voice soft yet direct. "They've decided to cancel the show. They think it'd be too . . . risky for their brand."

Korey stares off into the sea from our suite inside the Fontainebleau in Miami. I lick my lips, inhaling the familiar salty air. I'd never been to Florida, but I've heard of their white-sand beaches and crisp ocean. Korey glances at me, his eyes softening. For a moment, I think I see the same yearning, to run and dive into the blue waters, and a spark of hope ignites in me. But then he rips his eyes away from me, typing on his phone.

"As long as I get my check, I don't give a shit," he says unconvincingly.

Across the room, Richie and his camera crew are standing by. They've been following us this last leg of the tour. Stealing interviews when they can. But today, they are quiet, making themselves small, pretending to be deaf.

Richie clears his throat and joins us in the sitting area.

"Aye, my man, don't sweat it, playboy," Richie offers with a laugh. "You know how these chicks be. Spreading gossip for attention."

"Yeah," another one of Korey's friends says. "It's mad convenient she talking now, right after they announce that endorsement deal. All she sees is dollar signs!"

Jessica holds a blank face. I guess the rest of his team

doesn't know that Nike canceled the endorsement deal as of this morning.

Korey slouches in his seat, hands folded across his stomach. The most defeated I've ever seen him. This is the third show canceled this week. After the news dropped about the case, fans are demanding refunds.

Richie tries to inject optimism into the room. "Don't let this get you down, bruh. You know all this me-too shit is just a phase. You'll bounce back, baby. You always do! Yo, you know what we should do? We should get you on *Love and Hip Hop*! My homeboy is an executive producer on the show. It would tie in well with the release of the doc."

Korey twists up his mouth with a snarl.

"Man, that show is for has-beens! D-shit celebrities. What you take me for?"

Stunned, Richie tries to smooth the waters. "Calm down, playboy. I'm just messing with you. Lighten up."

The door to the suite opens, and in walks Derrick with two trays of Starbucks.

"What's good, everybody! Order up! Here you go, Pops," Derrick says, passing Richie an iced coffee. He notices me at the table and waves. "Hey, Enchanted!"

"Hi," I say in a quiet voice, keeping my eyes down.

Korey raises an eyebrow, toggling from me to Derrick. "You two know each other?"

"Yeah! We met at your afterparty in LA," he says, and you can almost hear the *duh* following it.

Richie rubs his knees, cracking a stiff smile.

"Aight, son, let's get out of their hair. Help the team load up the gear."

"Cool. See you later, Enchanted!"

As everyone leaves, Korey glares at me.

"Get in your room," he growls under his breath.

I shuffle across the suite to the connecting door. Jessica's voice eases through the thin wood on the opposite side.

"Maybe we should send Enchanted home."

"Why?"

"Well, 'cause she's . . . just think how it'll look to people. Having . . . another young singer around while you are going through all this might not be the best idea."

"Yo, why are you always trying to get rid of her? You jealous?"

"No! But consider what the lawyer said. Think of the optics. Also, I'm worried about you. Enchanted . . . she has trouble following the rules."

"She's not going anywhere. She's staying here. With me."


The thick Miami humidity creates a muzzle of sweat around my neck, holding me back from what I want most. To jump, to fly, to glide . . . right into the ocean. The yearning is physically painful, like holding in a sneeze.

I sit outside on the balcony, and can't remember the last time I sat so close to the ocean.

Or maybe I can. Maybe it was that time on the boardwalk, right before climbing into the back seat of Dad's truck as we drove away from Grandma's house. I clung to the memory like a lifeline, the last ounce of hope that Mom would change her mind about moving to the suburbs. That maybe they would see we weren't meant to live in the shadow of some damp woods. We were made to live by the sea, in the sun.

"You ain't leaving," Grandma said from her recliner, shaking her head even as the last boxes were carried out.

"I am, Ma," Mom barked.

"You take them, you're gonna be sorry! You can count on that!"

Their voices clapped like seashells, and Mom vowed to never come back. You can try all you want to control the wild sea, but in the end, it'll always do what it wants. And Mom was done with Grandma's stubborn irrationality for good.

So here I am again, sitting by the beach hoping that someone's claim is a lie.

The sliding glass door opens behind me and I catch a whiff of his cologne. He plops next to me, bottle in hand, and I can't hold the question in any longer.

"Did you really work with that girl?"

He rolls his eyes. "Yes."

"Why didn't you tell me? Why all these secrets? Thought you said we didn't have secrets?"

He sighs. "I didn't want to tell you this 'cause I didn't want you blaming yourself or nothing."

"Huh? Why would I blame myself?"

"She's . . . jealous. She's seen us perform, knows we're gearing up to do an album . . . but she wasn't as talented as you. I could only help her so much. That's why she's jealous. Of you, of what we have. So she's hurting me, to hurt you."

This is all because of me? It doesn't make sense.

"Were you two . . . together? Like us?"

"No! No, of course not. We . . . we're different."

He must read the skepticism on my face.

"You don't believe me, do you?"

I want to believe him. My heart longs to believe him . . . but then I think of the ice bucket and my emotions lock down. Wish I could just wish the thoughts away.

"I know I've . . . made some mistakes. But love ain't no fairy tale, ain't no Disney movie. Love . . . REAL love . . . is complicated. It's hard. It's gonna hurt some days. Then some days it's not."

His face cracks, and he breaks down crying, falling to his knees as he sobs.

"I don't know why they coming for me like this! After all I've done! I'm a good man! Take care of my fans, give to the poor . . . what more do they want from me?"

I've never seen a man cry. Never seen someone so broken. It's a strange, unbalanced puzzle. I hold my chair arms, glancing at the ocean just to anchor myself.

"If they ever arrest me . . . I can't go to prison. It'd kill me. Just kill me. I'll kill myself!"

He clambers around me, wiping his wet face on my stomach.

"You're all I have, Bright Eyes. It'll just be me and you. I swear, we'll record your album and then maybe . . . maybe we can go somewhere. Live by the beach. Watch Disney movies, eat popcorn, and make music. That's all I want. OK? Is that OK?"

I nod. "Yes."

"But you gotta promise you won't ever leave me, Enchanted. Promise it'll just be me and you. You'll protect me and I'll protect you. Together, forever."

He gathers me up in his arms, clutching my back, his body shaking. A fresh wave of love washes over my heart. No one has ever needed me like this before. Maybe the Littles, but this feels so much more . . . desperate.

I look over at the ocean, at what was once my home, so close yet so far, then back at Korey. My new home.

"I promise."

# Chapter 44

## GROWN

**Voice mail #1:** Enchanted? It's Mommy, give me a call.

**Voice mail #2:** Enchanted? It's Mom. Again. I've been calling you for the past three days and the only way I know you alive is because of your Instagram. Call me back.

**Voice mail #3:** Enchanted? It's Mommy. What's going on?

**Voice mail #8:** Enchanted, this is your mother.

This is my eighth message and you haven't called me back once! Call me. I mean it.

**Voice mail #10:** Enchanted, what is going on with you? I see you on the news performing but that's the only way I know you're alive. Look, you better call me! Your father and I have had just about enough of this, and we can't seem to get any answer from Jessica. Call me back TO-DAY!

**Voice mail #13:** Oh, so you think you GROWN now? Think I don't see you hopping around stage in that cheap getup and wig. Enchanted, I'm sick and tired of these games y'all playing. You better call me back!

**Voice mail #17:** Enchanted, baby . . . I don't know what's going on with you. I don't care. I just want you to come home. We're real worried now. It's been three weeks since I've heard your voice. You just need to come on home now, OK?

**Voice mail #21:** Enchanted, it's Daddy. Call me.

**Voice mail #28:** Enchanted, it's Daddy. Just come on downstairs, baby. It's OK. It's OK. No one's gonna hurt you, I swear.

***Voice mail #29:*** Enchanted! Your father is
  downstairs. PLEASE, Enchanted. Please, go down,
  go talk to him. Please.

***Voice mail #30:*** Enchanted, what's going on?
  Please, they're hurting him. Just answer the
  phone. Stop this!

***Voice mail #42:*** Enchanted, it's Mommy. Please,
  baby. Please, just talk to me. Why won't you
  talk to me?

Voice mail almost full.

# Chapter 45
## CONNECTION

On the Parkwood Instagram page, I see my friends. A picture of Hannah and Mackenzie at the last swim meet, grinning in soaking-wet suits. Pictures of the basketball game against our rival. There's a picture of Shea, with her group of friends, handing out roses for the annual Valentine's Day fest. The junior student council posts a message, reminding people to purchase their junior prom tickets and pay student dues.

I wish there was a picture of Gab, somewhere. Anywhere. I'm starting to forget what she looks like.

On Will and Willow's page, Creighton posts pictures from the recent Presidents' Day trip to the Smithsonian African American museum in Washington, DC, a video of their sing-along on the bus ride down, and pictures of them eating red-velvet cupcakes, my favorite.

Everyone is going out, living their lives. Two months, and it feels like the whole world has moved on . . . without me.

"Why you all up in his page?"

The airport terminal lights cast a shadow across Korey's face. His voice is hard, cutting. I look down at my phone, realizing I clicked on Creighton's profile, on a post about the upcoming Group Five spring-break trip, a drive down the East Coast to visit historically black colleges, even staying on campus.

It all sounds like fun. Real fun. I barely remember what that is.

"I'm not. It's . . . um, Will and Willow's page."

Korey's face is unreadable. He snatches my phone, shoving it in his pocket.

"You don't need this anymore anyways. We're going home."

# Chapter 46

## GLASS JAR

The house is a glass jar of French vanilla pudding in an Atlanta suburb. Everything is cream, white, and stone. Cream curtains, cream sofa, cream carpet, and dining table. The only spot of color is the black wrought-iron railing snaking up the double staircase.

"Welcome home," Korey says, his arms spread wide under the giant crystal chandelier that hangs from an impossibly high foyer ceiling.

Nothing about this place screams home. It screams museum or mausoleum, smelling as if it was dipped in bleach. It burns my nose the moment I step inside.

"Shoes off," he orders, holding a gold champagne bottle.

I set my bag down, unlacing my sneakers and take in the surroundings.

No pictures. No memorabilia. Nothing that says this place belongs to anyone specific. It could almost double as a model home I've seen on those real estate commercials.

I suddenly miss the smells and tight quarters of my house. Burning sage, roasting rosemary, and Daddy's aftershave. I even miss sharing a room with Shea. But I can't go back home. Parents probably wouldn't let me through the front door. The only place left for me is with Korey. Plus, he loves me. He needs me.

Love is complicated.

"How long will we be here?" I ask, noticing a tiny security camera on the ceiling.

"We're recording the album here," he says, picking up something that looks like a baby monitor. "So as long as it takes."

Wow. It's really happening. We're going to record my album. The words in my songbook are about to come alive. All I ever wanted.

I wrap my full self around him in a tight hug. Surprised and alarmed by the warmth, he leans away.

"Thank you," I whisper, kissing his cheek.

Slowly, he thaws, rubbing my back. "Anything for my Bright Eyes."

Over his shoulder, I have a clear view of a monitor in his hand, a grid of black-and-white video images. He has a camera in almost every corner of the house.

He releases me, a confused look in his eyes, then smiles

before clicking a button. Music blasts at deafening levels.

"JESSICA!" he screams.

Jessica? She's here?

On the first landing, Jessica appears, wearing a loose-fitting black sweat suit, face devoid of emotion.

Korey waves at me. "Show her around."

I meet Jessica with my bag. She sizes me up, then starts down the hall.

"Korey expects this place to be spotless. No tracking in dirt or dust, and absolutely no shoes in the house. Don't eat until he tells you. Don't drink until he tells you. Don't talk to the other guests, especially the men . . . but I'm sure you've learned that lesson by now."

"What other guests?"

"That's none of your business," she says, clipped and cold as ever.

We walk up another flight of stairs to a long hallway. To the left are gold double doors.

"That's Korey's room."

Jessica walks the opposite direction, opening the last door on the right.

"Don't leave this room until he tells you."

My room is what you'd call a perfect square. Dull hardwood floors, a tiny desk, a queen-size bed with white sheets, and a closet with a few baggy track suits on hangers, just like Jessica's. The flat-screen TV on the wall seems dwarfed by the vast plainness. It doesn't match the opulence of the rest of the home. No cameras . . . or at least not that I can see.

"No skirts or dresses around here, in case any of Korey's friends stop by. And they will, so stay in your room."

The window faces a pristine backyard with manicured hedges that look like part of a large maze surrounding a giant swimming pool. A small dose of relief pours into my heart. I live here. I live in a home with a pool. I have my own pool.

As I back away, my leg brushes against something metal. Something I didn't see, halfway hidden by the cream curtain kissing the floor. It almost seems out of place with the rest of the decor. I push the curtain aside and gasp.

A metal bucket.

My heart stops and starts up again in time for me to turn around and watch Jessica close the door, locking it from the outside.

There's this scene in *Cinderella* that always pops in my head.

It's at the very end of the movie, when she hears the prince is looking for the mystery girl who lost a glass slipper. Cinderella floats upstairs, never noticing her evil stepmother's realization. She follows Cinderella to her room and locks her in so she's unable to try on the glass slipper.

Maybe that's what Jessica is, the stepmother, trying to keep me from Korey. No way all those rules are his idea.

Korey enters with two Styrofoam cups and Flounder under his arm.

"Here, drink this."

It tastes familiar. Sweet, like a Jolly Rancher. Bubbly, like Sprite. But something else. A slightly bitter medicine taste.

"What is it?"

"Something to help you relax. See, I'm having some too."

He sets Flounder on the desk, angling him toward the bed. I haven't touched Flounder much; he reminds me too much of going to Disneyland, and I'd rather forget that day. But in some strange way, seeing him brings me comfort of softer times, when I was a mermaid who sang and played with little fishes. I wonder how the Littles are doing without me.

"Enchanted . . . such a pretty-ass name," Korey says with a smirk, his words slurring. He flops onto the bed next to me. "What's the story behind that beautiful name?"

My heart softens, and I feel my defenses loosen. It's been so long since it was just the two of us and him smiling that I almost forgot how just being near him feels like flying.

"Mom said I was born with the type of eyes that takes your breath away," I say, taking a sip.

"That's it?" He chuckles. "All Moms say shit like that."

Without thinking, I shoot back, "Is that what yours said?"

"No, she . . ." His voice fades, eyes staring off into the void. "She . . . I, um, doubt she saw anything good in me."

He sits up, grabbing the remote from the nightstand, clicking on Netflix. In an instant, I feel guilty for bringing up his mom, but I also feel loose and wobbly. Korey rubs my knee, his arms like an octopus, the room spinning.

I look inside the cup after one long blink. The drink is purple.

How sweet, I thought before flopping back. He knows purple is my favorite color.

# *Chapter 47*
## JELLYFISH

I was stung by a jellyfish once.

Back in Far Rockaway, while snorkeling close to the rock bank, I noticed a plastic bag floating nearby. Or . . . at least I thought it was a plastic bag. People are always throwing their trash in the ocean. But when I moved closer, the bag came to life, its tentacles darting, and a three-alarm fire broke out on my arm. I popped up to the surface with a scream. Daddy rushed in and carried me to shore. Mom doused the fire with salt water. Lifeguards brought the first-aid kit. Shooting stars covered the clear blue sky as the intense burning raged on.

At Grandma's, while she soaked my wound in vinegar wraps, I looked up facts about jellyfish:

Jellyfish have no brains.

"Nah, I never said anything about recording an album. You imagining things. Oh, so what, you don't trust me now? Get in your room!"

Jellyfish have no hearts.

"What you mean? Of course I love you. Why you keep asking me that shit?"

Jellyfish have no eyes.

"You don't see that? That dirt right there! You better clean that shit up. I mean it, clean all that shit up."

Jellyfish are spineless.

"Swimming? What the fuck I look like swimming? Nah, ma. That pool is just for show. We're not going in there."

Jellyfish don't purposely sting humans, only when provoked or touched.

"Why do you make me so mad? Why can't you do what I tell you? Do you want to go home? Is that what you want? I'll send you home, I swear."

At night, I drink my purple drink, wondering if Daddy will come and save me again.

# Chapter 48

## READY PLAYER ONE

Korey is addicted to video games.

"Ha, ha! Got 'em!"

Mainly, he loves playing Grand Theft Auto: San Andreas.

He likes for me to watch while he plays. So that's what I do. I sit next to him on the white sofa for hours, tapping a pen against my songbook, hoping he'll catch the hint. That we should be working, not playing games.

"How many songs do you need on an EP?" I ask.

He shrugs, still focused on the screen. "Like, four, maybe five. You shouldn't be worried about all . . . oh, hold up! Hold UP!"

It's been weeks and we've only recorded one. It'll take months at this rate.

Just need three more. I breathe in the thought, flipping through the warped pages of my book. And once I have them, he won't be able to take them away from me.

"Yuuupp! Got that bitch!"

Guess he beat some level or something. The scene changes, a man with a fro in the dank, messy bedroom with a half-dressed girl. She gives him head. Then they're on the bed, having sex, all controlled by Korey, while fro guy narrates: "I ain't never understood the phrase meaningless sex . . ."

Creighton used to play this game too. Now I see why. Don't understand why the girl is naked, while the guy is fully dressed. It's kinda weird. It's kinda gross. But Korey takes his time, pressing the button, following instructions:

*Push UP and DOWN in rhythm.*
*Joy 3 Change view.*
*Joy 1 Change position.*
*Joy 4 Quit.*


"You know, first time I had sex," he says, without sparing a glance, "I was fourteen."

My eyes shoot over to him.

"This . . . fine-ass woman. She taught me a few thangs. Ha, Richie was there!"

The girl on the video game moans.

"Like, in the room with you?"

"Nah. But he was around. Somewhere. Happened right after I signed to RCA. At a Grammys afterparty. Shorty took me to the coat closet or something. I ain't gonna front, I was SHOOK. Never been with a woman before."

The sex scene is awfully long.

". . . Come on, girl. I ain't insecure, just tell me I'm great."

"That's . . . really young."

He shrugs. "Nah, I was a man by then. Grandma died, all on my own so had to grow up fast, you know?"

". . . Come on, girl. I ain't insecure, just tell me I'm great."

*Fourteen years old—that's Shea's age*, a voice inside shouts. Poor Korey, he doesn't even realize he was taken advantage of or how much he's been hurt. Maybe that's why he has such a dark side.

Judging my silence, Korey quickly adds, "But, I mean, I ain't grow up like you, Bright Eyes. We all got . . . something."

I shift closer, pay more attention to his game, loving him a little harder.

And if I love him hard enough, maybe, just maybe, I can keep the dark side away.

# Chapter 49

## CASE FILE

*NOW*

SUMMARY REPORT OF AUTOPSY

**Time of Death:** Body temperature, rigor
and livor mortis, and stomach contents
approximate the time of death between 10:30
and 11:45 p.m.

**Immediate Cause of Death:** Multiple stab
wounds to the chest and abdomen

**Manner of Death:** Homicide

**Remarks:** At the death scene, there was a
large pool of blood in the bedroom, with
secondary pools and stains trailing from the
living room to the bedroom, blood splatter

on the walls and door. Defensive wounds to
hands, wrist, and arms.

EXCERPT FROM INITIAL DETECTIVE NOTES
Partial footprint found in bedroom near
death scene. Impression lifted from blood
splatter. Similar impression in living room
carpet. Initial findings estimate the print
belongs to a male, size 11–11½, left foot.
Does not match any of the victim's shoes
or foot size. Sent for further analysis of
specific footwear.

Possible third unidentified individual was in
the apartment at time of death.

# Chapter 50

## WELFARE CHECK

### THEN

"Enchanted, would you come here, please?"

The word "please" is a stranger in this house. So when I hear Korey say it, I bolt out of my room and freeze on the first staircase landing.

At the front door is Tony, another bodyguard, Richie, Korey, and two police officers. I scurry down to join them.

The officers, a white man and a black woman, never cross the threshold, but their presence is loud, fills up the entire house.

"Yes?" I say, twisting a strand of Melissa around my pinkie.

"Are you Enchanted Jones?" the woman asks.

"Um, yes."

"We need to talk to you in private."

I look at Korey, unsure if I'm allowed to speak. He gives a small nod.

"About what?" I ask, my voice shaky.

Korey steps in, his voice light and pleasant. "As you can see, she's not chained up in the basement. She has free range to walk around the house as she pleases."

Something about his demeanor makes me think he's done this before.

"Pssh! You think a brother like Korey Fields need to lock a bitch up to keep 'em?" the bodyguard quips. "Bitches be lining down the block just to get a taste!"

The woman gives him a once-over. "May we use your living room?"

Korey slaps on a sweet smile.

"Yes, ma'am, of course. By the way, she's seventeen. Age of consent in Atlanta, I believe."

She raises an eyebrow. "Yes, thank you for pointing out you know the laws in Georgia so well."

A tense silence falls, bugs fluttering through the open door. Korey shoves his hands into his sweats pockets.

The white officer reads the room, then proceeds. "We'll be right in there."

"Fine. Do what you gotta do!"

Richie pulls Korey aside, whispering in his ear, keeping him calm. Korey's jaw stiffens, never taking his eyes off me as the officers lead me into the living room. Even as the woman closes the double doors in his face.

"Hello, Enchanted," the white officer says. "We received a call to check on your well-being."

My teeth chatter loud enough to hear down the block. I rub my arms. "By who?"

"We're not at liberty to say but per protocol, we need to ask you a few questions."

"Enchanted, are you being held against your will?" the woman asks bluntly.

A shiver zips down my back. We had practiced every scenario we could ever think of, but this is new and frightening. Lying to fans and strangers is one thing but lying to the police is another. My mind races, thinking of the settlement with Candy, the way he broke down on the balcony in Miami . . . and the promise I made.

"No."

"Are you in need of assistance?"

The double door cracks open, just slightly. Someone else would confuse it for a gust of wind, but I know better.

"No, I'm fine," I say with a stiff smile.

Out in the hall, I hear Korey clear his throat.

"Everything's fine here," I say, stronger, louder. "We're recording my album."

Something slams against the wall. The officers exchange a glance but carry on.

The woman officer says, "So you WANT to be here."

"Yes. Yes, I want to be here." I almost believe the words coming out of my mouth.

The woman gives me another once-over, eyeballing my oversize sweat suit.

They ask me a few more questions but quickly realize my answers are going to remain the same.

Back in the foyer, Korey and Richie are waiting.

"All done?" Korey asks.

"Yes," the woman says.

Korey smirks. "Well, thanks for stopping by."

The woman nods at me, just me, and walks back to the patrol car. The man waits until she's a few feet away before turning with a grin.

"Sorry about all this. But, uh, hey, can I get your autograph? My wife, she's a *huge* fan and she'd kill me if she knew I met you and didn't at least try."

Korey thickens his charm.

"Sure, man! Sorry y'all came all this way for nothing. You know, trolls stay trolling."

As he signs the officer's flip book, offering to pose for a selfie, I creep away slow, willing myself invisible.

Maybe this will all blow over. Maybe it won't be that bad.

But no more than two feet into my room, the front door slams. My lungs shrink as his feet stomp up the stairs. He charges in, face emotionless.

"You know it was them nosy-ass parents of yours who sent them cops, right?"

"You . . . talked to them?"

"Yeah, they said they were going to do this shit," he snaps, shaking his head. "They texted me."

"Can I see?"

He cocks his head to the side, stepping toward me.

"Why you need to see? What, you don't trust me?"

Panic surges and my arms go limp.

"N-n-no, of course I trust you. I . . . just wanted to see what they said. That's all."

He cuts his eyes before flopping onto the bed.

"They said they wanted more money. Said I ain't paid them enough for you. I think I've given them plenty. Shit, I'm over-paying, after all the shit you've put me through!"

"Can . . . can I have my phone back. Please?"

"That's all you got to say to me?" he roars.

"No! I mean I can call them and try to—"

"After everything I've done for you, all you want is your phone back? You should be on your knees, begging me to keep you. Get on your knees, now! Now!"

I hesitate before kneeling. Korey approaches and I have to crane my neck back to look up at him. He steps closer, crotch in my face, and my stomach drops.

"Please, Korey," I whimper. "I don't want to fight. I love you."

Korey blinks, as if the word *love* broke him out of a trance. He mumbles a curse and brushes by, storming out the room. When the studio door slams below, I exhale the breath I'd been holding, hands trembling.

If only he'd give me back my phone. Then maybe I could convince my parents to back off, just for a little while. They're making things harder for us. For me, really. But if they give us some space, maybe he'll return to normal.

## Chapter 51
### FOLLOW THE RULES

Korey's label organized a small six-city Southern tour to show love to all his loyal fans. Could've been nicknamed the Apology Tour or the Love Me Again Tour, after the rounds of terrible press from Candy's lawsuit.

Still, it's a blessing. We're out of the house and back on the road, on a tour bus this time. Korey doesn't want to do duets but lets me sing background, even though my voice is raspy, and I have trouble staying on beat. Sometimes, during sets, I catch him stealing glances, and I can tell he's singing just to me.

Korey says love is hard. Love is complicated and a lot of work. The rules are different when you love a celebrity. They're under so much pressure. And as his girlfriend, I need to support him. Be understanding, rather than be a headache. So that's what I do. Sing my heart out from the shadows, stage left. Make sure he has plenty food, water, and space when he needs it. He's given me, and my family, so much. It's the least I can do for him.

Just follow the rules.

Backstage after our Charlotte show, I pass Richie's team shooting what's called B-roll footage for the documentary. Richie's in the shadows, talking to Jessica. More like consoling her. She seems real upset. Maybe I should . . . no. No!

Mind your business. Follow the rules.

No eye contact, I head straight for the tour bus when I spot her strutting down the hall.

Amber.

She's wearing a tight pink strapless dress, her hair tight and curly.

What is she doing in North Carolina?

"Hey! Enchanted, right?" a voice says behind me.

A tall Latino man with a thick New York accent stands by the exit. His curly hair shines like silky black snakes.

"Um, yes. I . . ."

"What's up! Louis Santiago. My friends call my Louie. I've been waiting to meet you!"

"I . . . I, um . . . who are you?"

"Don't worry. Korey and I go way back. He said it was cool if we talk."

My spidey senses tingle, and I spin around to see if Korey is nearby.

Just follow the rules.

"Um, I think I better . . ."

"Aight, well I won't hold you," Louie says, talking fast. "Just gotta say that . . . I think you are an incredible singer. I've worked with a lot of artists, but you, young lady, have a VOICE. Even on background, you outshine everyone onstage. Was wondering if you're looking for representation?"

"You're . . . a manager?"

"Yup. Manage a couple of artists. But like I was saying, I think we can really make something happen. I know you have allegiance to Korey, but here. This is my card. When you done with your tour, call me. You hear what I gotta say, and see if I'm a good fit."

Follow the rules.

The card is a beacon of light in his hand. Maybe this is a good thing! I'm only two songs away from my EP goal, and I'll eventually need a manager once I'm done. I glance over my shoulder until I spot Korey, standing outside his dressing room, talking to someone, but watching me. He's smiling but his eyes aren't. Did Korey send Louie my way as a trap? Or did he really want me to meet this guy? Maybe this is a different type of test, one to see if I can handle myself businesswise.

"Um, sure. OK," I mumble.

"Bet! Looking forward to talking soon."

The moment I grasp the card and look back at Korey, I know I've chosen wrong.

# Chapter 52

## TWO MINUTES

Beach lifeguards can hold their breath for two whole minutes. It's a part of their aptitude test. So that's what I do. I hold my breath, right before he strikes me.

"Why'd you do it, huh? Why do you keep on disrespecting me? After everything I've done for you? I gave you your career and you do me like this?"

The first time he hits me, the sky goes bright white, like I shot up into the clouds.

The second time he hits me, my ears ring like cowbells.

Lightning can't strike the same place twice. But thunder? Thunder is omnidirectional. You can hear it from every side of you.

"I told you not to talk to men, didn't I! You look that man in his face!"

The room spins and I'm dizzy from holding my breath while bracing for his blows. Curling into a ball on the bed, I sob. I thought Mr. Hyde was the worst of Korey, but now I see he can be so much worse.

"So that's it? You want to leave me? You gonna go be with Louie? That piece of shit. Where are any of his artists, huh? You so stupid, just listening to anything anyone tell you."

Korey paces around the hotel room, huffing. I lift myself upright, licking my lip, tasting blood on the corner of my mouth.

"Korey . . . Korey, this is too much."

My words confuse him. "What do you mean?"

"I can't . . . I can't . . . do this anymore," I sob. "I . . . I think I need to go home."

Tears pooling in his eyes, he nods incessantly.

"First my grandma, now you. Everyone always leaving me, man!" He grabs both of his ears, pinning them to the sides of his head. "I can't take this no more. I swear, if you leave me . . . I'm just gonna kill myself!"

The words are another blow, another lightning strike and thunderous roar all at once.

"What?" I gasp.

He nods, as if convincing himself. "Yeah! That's what I'm going to do. I promise that's what I'll do if you leave me."

"No! You, you can't! What about your family?"

He scoffs. "What family?"

"Your friends?"

"Psh! Those leeches! They just here for the money."

"Your fans? They need your music! You . . . you're their hero! They love you!"

He shrugs. "Well, then, guess that's what you'll have to live with. All that heartbreak will be your fault 'cause you pushed me to do it."

# Chapter 53
## THIN WALLS

*W&W Squad Chat (w/o the Jones sisters)*

Sean: **Aight. I'ma tell y'all something but damn.**

Creighton: **Yo, what's up?**

Malika: **Spill it.**

Sean: **My dad talked to Mr. Jones. He said, once he heard about the rape case, he drove down to get Enchanted.**

Creighton: **Yoooooo.**

Aisha: **OMG! What happened?**

Last show. Just have to get through the last show, I promise myself. Then, you'll go back home. Not home home, but back to Korey's house in Atlanta. You'll work on the last song for your EP. Then, when you fly back to New York for his big concert in April, you'll make your escape.

Two a.m. and I can't sleep, going over all my options, solidifying a plan. But I needed someone to bounce the idea off of. Any other time, it would be Gab. She was always the other voice in my head.

If I had my phone, I would have called her for the millionth time or at least sent an email.

Email . . . there's a business center in this hotel. With computers.

I flip through the hotel menus to a map on the back page. The business center is on the second floor, close to the elevators.

What if someone sees me? What if Korey comes and finds I'm not here?

But this is my only chance. Once I'm back in that house, there won't be another.

I grab my keycard and the ice bucket, glancing over at Flounder.

"I'll be gone ten minutes, tops," I say, shrugging on a robe.

Flounder looks worried as I slip out the door, sprinting to the elevators barefoot.

The business center's computers are old, the internet slow, the wide glass door easy for someone to spot me.

"Come on, come on," I whimper to the booting monitor. It takes over six minutes to log in to Gmail. But once it's up, I hit the compose button and type quick:

Hey Gab,

Korey has a big show at MSG next month and I really need you. But don't tell anyone you're coming. Just wait on the corner of 33rd and 7th. I know you're still mad at me because I lied and I'm sorry. But I really need you. Please. You're still my best friend.

Love,

Chanty

Send.

It's been more than ten minutes. Can't wait for a reply; I'll just have to trust she's coming. But before I log off, a message pops up—

The message that you sent could not be delivered. Permanent error.

Did I send it to the right address? Shit, there's no time.

I log off, clear the cache, deleting any evidence of my existence, and race back to the elevator as a voice creeps inside my head. One that says, *What about Korey? He says he needs you. How can you leave? How can you live with yourself after everything he's done for you? How can you use him for songs? He loves you.*

Love is complicated . . .

Back on my floor, I step off the elevator and find the police at my door.

BOOM BOOM BOOM! "POLICE!"

Shit.

"I . . . I was just getting ice," I croak as I approach, showing the ice bucket.

"Ma'am, is anyone in there with you?" the officer standing at the threshold asks.

"No. Just me."

"Is Korey Fields here?" the other one asks. "We had a call for a 10-56A. Some type of suicide pact."

The floor is ripped from underneath me as I bring a trembling hand to my mouth.

Korey.

"Oh God," I mumble, dropping the bucket.

A door swings open behind me.

"Hey, what's going on?" Tony says.

"Miss! Where are you going?" the officer shouts.

I fly into my room, rushing to the connecting suite door, wild thoughts chasing me.

It's my fault, it's all my fault! He's killed himself because I wouldn't listen. He said he would and I didn't listen.

"Oh no, oh no, oh no. Please, please, please."

I burst in, running straight to his bed, slipping on something wet and rubbery, like a jellyfish.

"Korey!" I scream, diving toward his pillows, and turn on the light.

"What the fuck?" Korey roars . . . as Amber's head pops up from under the covers.

All the air charges out of my body.

The police are behind me now. Korey is enraged. Words are exchanged. Amber wraps a sheet around herself; it trails behind her as she shuffles into the bathroom.

"What the fuck are you doing? You let them in here?"

I can't feel my feet. And I don't know what to do with the icicles that used to be my hands.

Voices swim around me.

"Suicide pact? Hell no, there's no fucking suicide pact. What are you even talking about?"

I back away, noticing a used condom on the floor by the bed.

The very one my bare foot slipped on.

The smell of fried fish, mac and cheese, and baked ziti roasting in the kitchen downstairs makes me want to climb the walls.

I'm so hungry.

Jessica brings me two meals, usually fast-food takeout, burgers with cold fries and flat Sprite, which only makes me crave my purple drink. Jessica doesn't talk despite being the only human contact I've had in over a week since we've returned to Atlanta. My room is the tiniest fish tank I've ever lived in.

But I can hear Korey. I hear his music leaking through the vents from the basement. Hear the parties he throws downstairs with at least a hundred people, including strippers. Hear him having sex with Amber . . . right next door.

The walls of my room are thin. Thin enough to feel like I'm with them.

So, I sit beside them, watching what he does to her body. Watching him call her sweetheart and her call him daddy.

I vomit in my bucket, yearning for the same attention he used to give me yet sickened by it.

Korey serves me a second cup of purple drink. I guzzle it, fast and desperate.

"If I can't have sex with you, I have to have sex with someone else," Korey says, stroking my cheek. "It's your decision to wait, and I respect that. But I'm a man, baby. And a man has needs."

That was his explanation for Amber. He tells me we will be our own kind of family now and that we are following God's will.

"Men in the Bible had many wives. It was written by Jesus."

I listen, his words slowly soaking in as I slurp more drink.

"I know you upset about Amber. But you need me and I need you. Your folks, they not gonna want you, not after all this. They were never gonna let you go. They would've had you up in that house, taking care of all those kids forever, when you were meant to sing. I saved you. You don't need them no more. You got me. You, me, and Amber, we're our own family. Just us. No one else. Family over everything."

I nod and hold out my cup, my voice slurring. "Can I have some more?"

# Chapter 54
## SISTERS

There's a party downstairs and I'm not invited. Neither is Amber. That's why I know she's in her room, listening to the music and laughter.

They don't lock the door anymore. They know I'm not leaving. So I have no problem slipping into the hall to use the bathroom while they're distracted.

Which is exactly where I find her.

"Amber," I whisper, my voice groggy. "Amber?"

She drops her head, speeding toward her room.

"Wait," I shout under my breath, peering down the stairs again, checking if the coast is clear.

"We're not supposed to talk to each other," she whispers.

"I know but . . . are you OK?"

She stops short, then turns to face me, her right eye dark purple.

"I'm fine," she hisses.

"I know the rules . . . but Korey says we're like sisters. And if any of my sisters got hurt, I'd be the first to check on them."

Amber's lip trembles, the tears pooling in her eyes fall. We both glance at the stairs. Safe. For now.

"How many sisters you got?" she sniffs.

"Three. And one brother."

"Dang, that's a lot of kids."

I chuckle. "Yeah. I know."

Amber is quiet for some time. "I have a little brother. Gets on my nerves. Can't understand why I miss him so much."

"Yeah, Ain't that annoying?"

Amber and I sit in the doorways of our respective rooms, chatting. Unlike me, Amber was a professionally and classically trained singer. Been in competitions since she was four. She met Korey the same night I did, but through Richie.

"Dang, feels like forever since I've talked normal to . . . anyone," I say.

"Yeah. Me too. My school back home is real big so we have like a gazillion kids in it I talked to every day."

School? The word rings a bell and reminds me of something.

"Hey, how old are you?"

She pauses, her face straightening.

"I'm eighteen."

My tongue sticks to the top of my mouth. She's lying.

"Yeah, so am I," I mumble.

"Well, yeah, duh," she giggles. Even her voice sounds young.

I make more small talk. About books, hair, clothes, comparing the songs we love to sing.

"Oh, I know that one," I say and slip in the question. "Think it came out the year we were born, right?"

She tells me the year and I do the math in my head quick.

"You're fifteen," I gasp.

Amber's face falls, eyes darkening. We stare at each other for a brief moment before she jumps to her feet, closing the door behind her.


Today, Korey's allowed us to come to a listening session in his studio, swimming in baggy sweats. Plenty to drink, so I drink until I'm no longer myself, only longing for the pieces of myself that are left.

"That lean got Enchanted leaning," someone jokes.

The room ripples with laughter. I spot Richie in the bunch. Amber sits in the opposite room, far from me, far from the memory of who she used to be too.

My mouth waters for more purple drink but Korey slips the cup out of my hand and whispers in my ear.

"Think you had enough. Go to your room."

No sense in arguing. It'll only end in pain for me.

Ignoring the laugher at my back, I drift out of the studio, up to the first floor, craving my bed but craving food just as much. With everyone downstairs, maybe I can sneak some leftover pasta.

I tiptoe into the kitchen, spotting the camera, aimed right at the fridge.

Damn.

Abandoning hope, I spin around and run right into his chest. Derrick.

"Shit," I shudder.

"Hey. You OK?" he says, and I don't remember him being so tall . . . or handsome.

Out of practice more than instinct, I divert my eyes to the floor. "Yeah. But . . . um, I have to go."

The room tilts to the left and I stumble. Derrick catches me. "Whoa, hold up."

"Stop it. Don't touch me!"

I backpedal, grabbing hold of the counter. Or at least I thought I grabbed the counter. Someone moved it, and I flop onto the kitchen tile.

Within seconds, Derrick is by my side.

"I'm fine," I slur, swatting away hands that seem to be coming from every direction.

"No. You're not," he says, then whispers, "Enchanted. I know you're not eighteen."

The room stops spinning long enough for me to look at him. "What?"

"You're seventeen. Your birthday is not for a few weeks. April eighteenth, right?"

My mouth goes dry. "How did you . . ."

"A friend of mine from Brooklyn Will and Willow knows your chapter brother Creighton."

Creighton. The name makes me want to vomit.

"Him, of course," I snap, shoving his chest.

"Wait, Enchanted. I hollered at peeps from your chapter. They all worried about you. They've been trying to get in touch with you, ever since that shit went down with your dad."

"My dad?"

"Yeah. He came down to try and get you, but Korey's boys roughed him up." He pauses. "You didn't know about that?"

My heart is a drum in my ear, drowning out Korey's music thumping around us.

"No," I moan, running a tongue across my dry lips. "Just leave me alone."

Derrick looks over his shoulder, then pulls me to my feet.

"Listen, you have to get out of here. Korey, he's . . . a sick dude."

"I don't know what you're talking about. I don't—"

"There were others, Enchanted."

"Other what?"

"Other suits and settlements. Candy isn't the first one. There were other girls. All fifteen and sixteen and so on. One girl even tried to kill herself after dealing with Korey."

I sway with the spinning room.

"Other girls are coming forward. And everything they saying . . . look, you have to get out of here. Pack a bag or don't, but just go. Dude is dangerous."

My knees give in again and I lean against the counter. "No. No . . . I can't . . ."

"Here, take my phone number. Call me and I'll . . ."

Without shoes, his steps are soundless. That's why I didn't hear him coming. But the moment I see him, my stomach sinks, breath catching.

Derrick turns, remaining stoic, positioning himself in front of me.

"What's up, Korey. My bad. Got lost and started talking with my FRIEND, Enchanted."

Korey looks straight at me, as if Derrick didn't exist, eyes speaking of my near future. A grim and painful one.

"Go to your room. I'll deal with you later."

# *Chapter 55*

## RUN

Watching the sun peek over the trees, tears pool in my eyes. Five a.m. Dawn. My purple drink is empty. I haven't slept. Haven't even sat down. I just stood in the middle of my room . . . waiting. Waiting for Korey to come "deal" with me like he said. Dread ties several knots around my throat. I suck in air, wheezing, trying not to imagine the pain.

Run.

The voice is so loud, so familiar and crystal clear that I spin around to see who's in the room with me.

"Grandma?"

Silence. I'm alone. And when Korey walks in here . . . he may kill me.

Run.

The bedroom door glows golden. I test the knob. It's unlocked.

Run.

My bare feet touch the carpeted steps. Gently, one by one, down I go, my balance off. No one is around. Music blares; the speakers vibrate with the bass. I slip on my sneakers, glancing up at the camera. Is he awake? Does he see me?

Run.

My hand touches the cold front-door lock. I inhale, press my lips together, and slowly click it right. I burst through the doors, the corner of the gate clipping my shoulder.

Run.

The bright sun in the sky disarms me. Where am I?

Run.

I smell pine trees, wet grass, and car exhaust. A driveway. A street. A stop sign. What do I do? What do I do?

Run.

Can't call Mom. She's so mad at me. She may hang up. She may leave me here.

Can't call Daddy. He'll do the same.

Run.

What if he wakes up? What if he finds I'm not there? Cameras? He knows! He's coming, he's coming.

Run.

Slip, swoop, down. I'm up and running again. Converse hitting the pavement. Laces undone. Run, faster, harder. Nothing looks familiar. What do I do? What do I do? What do I do?

Run.

Into the woods. I'm safe in the woods. He can't find me here.

Run.

Telephone wires make music sheets in the sky.

Thicker wires lead to a highway. The highway. A yellow sign, yellow Scrabble letters. A Waffle House. Police car in the parking lot.

Run.

The door is heavy. My arms are weak.

Two cops sit at the counter. Coffee, black. Plates, empty.

Ask me if I'm OK. Ask me. Ask me. Ask me . . .

"Sit anywhere, bae," a waitress says, walking by with plates of sizzling eggs and bacon. "Be right with ya."

I limp and stumble to the counter, opposite the cops, lips quivering. It's so cold. I left my jacket, my songbook, my everything.

The cops laugh, joking about something they see on their phones. I had a phone. But it's gone. Along with everything else.

Dirty bleeding wound on my legs from a fall. Customer notices and stops eating.

Open your mouth and sing. Sing! Sing!

But my throat is full of sand and hunks of coral. I can't sing. I can't talk. How do I explain I'm a caught fish who needs to be thrown back into the sea?

"There you are! You got lost?"

Tony. I can't see his eyes behind his sunglasses, but his

forehead is damp with sweat. Hand gripping my forearm, breathing hard, he leans down to whisper.

"One word, you'll never talk to Gab again."

Everything in the sky comes crashing down and the earth shakes.

Sing!

"I can't," I tell the voice. He knows about Gab.

"Come on. Let's get you home," he says, an arm around my shoulders.

I gape across the counter at the cops peeping our interaction.

"Hey. Everything OK?" one of the officers asks.

"Oh yeah! We fine," Tony says with a smile and nods. "Y'all have a good day."

They nod back as I'm led to the car.

# Chapter 56
## GET HELP

I don't recognize myself in the bathroom of Terminal T.

Melissa is on top of my head, glued secure, yet loosening after wear. My makeup is thick, lipstick bright. But I don't know the girl staring back at me on her eighteenth birthday.

She has weak arms, potholes under her eyes, a sagging belly, and she can fall asleep standing up. At the same time, she's malnourished, surviving off McDonald's and the purple drink she chugged before leaving for the airport.

My wounds are invisible, weeping invisible blood. Can anyone see the black-and-blue marks painted on my heart?

What if that's it? What if I'm invisible? That's why no one

has tried to save me. Why no one can hear my screams, inside and out.

I wash my hands in the basin, the faucet automatic. And right on the lower righthand corner of the mirror, there's a sticker:

If you are a victim of human trafficking, call this number.

The word "victim" glows red. Or . . . at least I think so. I pat through my bag, forgetting I no longer have a phone.

Just my songbook.


Korey hates flying. He especially hates flying commercial.

After some crazy storm, flights are canceled, private planes are grounded, and the only way he'll make soundcheck is if we fly on Delta.

But as the plane rattles up twenty thousand feet, Korey wants nothing more than to skip the entire tour.

"Shit," he mumbles, taking a shot of vodka.

We hover above the angry clouds in first class—me by the window, Korey by the aisle. Amber, Tony, Richie, and crew are scattered in coach, the only seats available.

Korey grips the armrest, shaking his head. He reaches out, squeezing my thigh. Once, his touch used to be thrilling, now I only flinch in terror.

I peer out the tiny window, at the giant, dark gray, mountain-shaped clouds full of lightning, the plane maneuvering around them.

"Hello. This is your captain speaking. Sorry about that takeoff there! We've just reached our cruising altitude. We are expecting some rough air closer to landing, so I'm going to leave the seat-belt sign on for the time being and anticipate an on-time arrival. So, sit back, relax, and enjoy your flight."

The plane levels off, finding some smooth air, but Korey doesn't let go of my leg.

A black flight attendant stops by, beaming.

"Sir, care for another beverage?" she asks with a taut smile.

Korey opens one eye. "Yeah. And one for her too."

The flight attendant glances at me, frowning at the hand on my thigh. I read her gold nameplate: Nicole.

"Um, sure, can I see some ID, ma'am?"

Korey rolls his eyes, flicking his wrist.

"Just get me my drink."

There's a brief pause as the plane tightens. You can almost hear the metal contract.

Nicole's eyes narrow before she walks away and mumbles something to another attendant. They peer over their shoulders, glaring at us. The cabin grows sticky and humid.

Korey continues to drink, listening to music on his iPhone. I stare out the window, the sky an oil painting, the sea below calling me home.

"So yo, I've been thinking," Korey whispers, vodka on his breath. "We ain't gonna start you with a solo career."

The plane shakes. Or at least I think it does.

I blink. "What?"

"You need to be in a girl group first. We already got Amber. We need two more."

"Two more girls?"

"Yeah. So when we get to New York, you should invite your friend Gabriela to come by the studio."

Something thumps and claws against the side of the plane. "Gab?"

"Yeah," he says, gripping his armrest with a gulp, waiting for the plane to fall apart midair. "You said she can sing, right?"

I don't remember telling him that. "Um. Yeah."

He slips a phone out of his hoodie. "Here. Text her. Tell her to roll through tomorrow."

I palm the phone, thoughts churning. "I . . . I don't think she would be . . . she's hard to work with. You'd get mad, and I wouldn't want you to be upset."

Annoyed, he relents. "Aight. What about your sister?"

In an instant, I'm a deboned filet of fish, sliding down my seat.

"Shea," I croak out.

"Yeah. Can she sing?"

"No," I answer quick, heart racing.

"Well, let me text her and see."

"Y-y-you have her number?"

He smirks. "I got all the numbers in your phone."

My mouth dries. The thought of him in Shea's phone, the way he was in mine . . . I'm out the window, on the wing, ready to jump. But I can't. Because if I jump, there will be no one to protect Gab, Shea, Mom, Daddy, or the Littles from this monster.

He's a monster—the thought sharpens, drenched in resolve.

"Leave her alone," I mutter.

The plane rumbles. Harder now. Korey's drink almost slides off his tray.

"Huh?" he says, glancing upward as if expecting the oxygen masks to drop.

I turn to him. "I said leave her alone."

Korey's face transforms slow, from Dr. Jekyll to Mr. Hyde. My stomach drops, the feeling of a falling roller coaster as the plane tilts. He lunges and I reel back, hitting my head on the window with a yelp.

"Miss, are you OK?"

Nicole appears at our side. Korey straightens, remembering we're in public.

"Hm? Oh, nah, she's fine," he says with a light chuckle. "All this turbulence got her shook."

Nicole stares at him then at me, unconvinced.

"Miss, do you need to use the ladies' room?"

Korey cocks his head to the side, and I fear for Nicole.

"I said she's fine."

"Sir, I'm asking *her* a question."

The plane tips upward, pressure building against my eardrum. Nicole steadies herself, surfing the ride.

Korey realizes his intimidation tactics are no longer working and goes straight for charm.

"Oh, I see what it is. You've been reading them blogs about me, right?" He chuckles, standing. "Don't trip, sweetheart. I'm not the monster they paint me to be. I'm a gentleman. I got her, aight? She's cool."

Nicole raises a vicious eyebrow. "Sir, if you don't take your hand off my shoulder and sit down, I'll have the captain make an emergency landing and the police waiting for you at the gate."

Commotion stirs in the cabin behind us. "Hey, Boss, what's going on up here?" Tony shouts. "Do you know who he is?"

Soon, everyone talks over one another. The flight attendants yell about federal regulations. Tony barks about his boss's needs. Korey vents about how the world is trying to attack him.

The wings seesaw. Korey falls into his seat and I press into the window, widening the distance between us. He leans into me, his mouth on my neck.

"If you embarrass me on this fucking plane, you gonna wish you were fucking dead," he whispers.

Outside, the brewing storm is a beautiful chaotic show.

"Miss!" Nicole, now shouting. "Do you need help?"

"I'm . . . I'm . . ."

"See? She says she's fine! Why you harassing her?"

"Miss, are you fine? Do you need help?"

"What are you doing?" The white flight attendant scolds Nicole before whipping around to Tony. "Hey! Sir, I said back off. You need to return to your seat!"

The plane rocks. Small yelps escape the other passengers. A bell dings.

"Flight attendants, please return to your seats!"

Nicole doesn't move. "Miss, do you need help?"

Holding my breath, I look at Korey, at the panic in his eyes, the eyes I once loved, then exhale from my diaphragm before letting go of my dream.

"Yes. Yes . . . I do."

# Part Three

# Chapter 57

## BEET JUICE 3

*NOW*

*BOOM BOOM BOOM!*

"Open up!"

I rush into the bathroom and wash the beet juice off my face and hands.

It turns the soap into pink bubbles, water coloring the sink. I use a towel and wipe down my face, arms, and hands. Use the same towel to wipe the basin.

"OK, OK, OK," I mumble to myself. "Deep breaths. Breathe from your diaphragm."

I hold my stomach, noticing the beet juice on my shirt, mixed with purple drink, and press a nail into my palm.

Think.

Think.

Think.

They don't have a warrant. They can't enter without a warrant. That's what Korey would say. He knew all the loopholes to keep us safe.

Just stay inside. Wait for them to come correct.

I'm walking across the living room, hoping he's really dead, when a voice stops me cold in my tracks.

"Enchanted? It's Daddy. Please, baby. Open the door. Let us know you're OK."

# Chapter 58
## SLEEPING BEAUTY

*THEN*

Coming off a high feels exactly like dying.

First, your body thinks it's freezing, even though you live inside an oven. So you sweat through all your pajamas and bedsheets.

Next, your stomach twists, turns, and quakes.

Then, you're puking. Anything and everything that remains. Most of the time, you're gagging on your own thick white saliva.

You cling to the toilet, leaning against your baby sister's bath toys, while your mom props you up to keep you from choking on your own vomit and pumps you full of fluids she stole from the hospital.

Then, you sleep like you're dead, wishing you were.

But also secretly wishing a prince would kiss you and wake you from this terrible nightmare.

Only to do it all over again, for the next four days.

"Well, there she is! Sleeping beauty! Was wondering when you were gonna wake up."

Mom is in the kitchen, which I'm sure the whole neighborhood knows since the juicer has been going off for the last hour.

"Hi," I croak and sit at the table. My throat is sore and achy. The wreckage of puking for days. After this week, I wonder what will be left of my voice.

"Here you go," she says, setting a glass of something thick and red on the table.

"What's this?"

"Beet juice!"

"Ew. Gross."

"I saw it on Dr. Oz. Supposed to balance oxygen and increase stamina. And you need all the energy to fight off this . . . flu you got."

Mom turns quick so I can't see her face crumble, but I've never been happier to see our beat-up sofa, the weeping pine trees, and empty streets. Never want to see another hotel as long as I live.

On the sofa, the bedsheets are still laid out.

"Shea slept out here again?"

"Yes," Mom says. "You've been, um, having nightmares. Screaming in your sleep and such."

The psychiatrist warned of nightmares. Warned of flashbacks, difficulty sleeping, jumpiness, and distrust. All I can say is, I can't take closed doors. Not even to use the bathroom.

Mom sets a tray in front of me: soup, water crackers, fresh orange juice, and two Zoloft pills.

"Where is everyone?"

"The Littles are at school. Well, they'll be out soon. And Daddy is on the picket line. He'll grab them on the way home."

Mom nods at the tray and I take the pills obediently.

"What day is it?

"Tuesday."

"I . . . don't know why I asked that." I sigh. "Not that it matters."

"It matters. It all matters." Mom winces a sympathetic smile. "You think you're up to talking today?"

She means with the therapist. I shake my head so violently the house trembles.

"OK OK! It's all good! No rush but you know it's a must. So, how about some fresh air?"

Mom speaks to me as if I'm alien. Wide-eyed, hesitant, and timid of her footing. I imagine this is what it's like for parents of a recently kidnapped child who has been returned. After just a few short months, I'm a stranger in my own house.

"Mom, aren't you missing a lot of work taking care of me?"

With a crooked smile, she wipes a counter she's already wiped twice. "Stop worrying about me. I have plenty of days saved up."

I'm not sure how true that is, but I'm too exhausted to press her further.

"So? How about that walk?" she asks again, another fake smile.

I look over to the sofa and sigh. "Maybe later."

Destiny is the first to bust through the door, flying right to the table, followed by Pearl and Phoenix, then Shea, closing the door behind her. Daddy doesn't come inside.

"Chanty! Chanty! You're up."

"Hey, little bits," I say weakly. "How was school today?"

Destiny nods her head. "Good. You feel better? You still got a tummy ache?"

Shea rolls her eyes and walks to our room.

I gulp down the beet juice, wishing it was purple.

Mom buys me a refurbished phone. We take it to Verizon and find we can't salvage my pictures, contacts, or messages from my old phone.

In my room, I power it up, and the wave of text messages floods my screen, phone seizing in my hand. The newest one from Korey, sent this morning. A link to a song. Usher's "Throwback."

*You never miss a good thing till it leaves ya*
*Finally I realized that I need ya*
*I want ya back.*

There are almost fifty messages from him. All songs.

The smell of his cologne makes the room dip into a haze. The phone tumbles to the floor like a brick and I shoot up. Pulse racing, chills descend.

Alone. I'm alone. But I could have sworn he was right behind me.

"Mom! I need a new number."


I text Gab a few times from my new number, telling her it's me and that I'll be starting school next week, but she doesn't answer. She must have seen the stories by now. Page Six of the *New York Post* called it "Nightmare at 20,000 Feet."

It's kinda clever.

Korey is all over the news, but not for what you'd think. It's about his forthcoming gospel album, featuring some of the hottest names in the music industry. They're all over Instagram, tagging him in every photo. His new music video premiers tomorrow. Documentary produced by Richie announced . . .

He's everywhere, like water, spreading fast, and flooding.


My muscles . . . aren't what they used to be. Mostly from the lack of exercise and nutritious food. Surprised the doctor in the emergency room didn't find any bruises, breaks, or sprains. Just dehydration and an addiction to codeine.

I fight to fit my new curls under a swim cap. Mom and Coach sit on the sideline, murmuring to each other.

As I slip into the cool water, I roll to my back and stare up at the ceiling, inhaling deep, waiting for relief.

*Water can heal anything*, Grandma once said. But does it heal hearts?

It's not the same as floating in the ocean. Nothing seems to be the same anymore. I let myself sink, the world finally quiet.

"What I tell you about showing all that skin!"

Korey!

Bubbles full of my screams reach the surface before I can.

I yelp, thrashing and splashing, whipping my head around.

Is he here? Is he?

No one but Mom and Coach, now up on their feet.

"Chanty?" Mom asks. "You OK?"

I doggy-paddle to the edge of the pool, resting my head against the cement.

Trying to reclaim your life is a lot like drowning. You attempt to stay above water as waves of new information hit you sideways, carrying you further into the unknown. People throw life preservers, but the ropes can only reach so far, and once a riptide catches you by the ankle, all you can do is wonder why you ever thought you'd be OK jumping into the deep end, when you could barely manage the shallows.

# Chapter 59
## BARBERSHOP TALK

Daddy has been avoiding me.

Thought it was just my imagination. Everyone has been giving me space. But Daddy . . . his absence is blatant. When I walk into a room, he walks out. When I say hello, he mumbles back. Eyes always down, never meeting mine, and even when they do, they seem sad and distant.

Mommy and Shea cut veggies for soup as the Littles gather around Daddy in the living room, watching *Bambi*.

"Um, Daddy?"

The entire house jumps at the sound of my voice.

"Yes?"

I hold up the clippers. "Can you hook me up?"

Daddy glances at Mom, something unsaid passing between them. She gives him a sharper glare and he hoists himself up quick.

"Sure."

I straddle the toilet seat like I always have, the smock buttoned around my neck while Daddy sets up his tools. Mom pretends not to be watching from the kitchen, peeling yams. Shea entertains the Littles.

The bathroom is . . . tighter than I remember. I claw at my inner palm, breathing through my nose, out through the mouth. It's just Daddy, I tell myself over and over again. I'm safe with him. I'm home and I'm safe.

Safe. Safe. Safe . . .

Daddy uses scissors on the top to cut down my curls as close as he can. The ringlets fall, bouncing off my shoulders.

"Been a while since I done this," Daddy says, uncertainty in his voice. "Nice having the floor clean for a change."

His voice is so flat I'm not sure if he's kidding.

"You still charge the same?"

He shrugs. "We've gotten pretty popular since you've been . . . gone. Charging seventy-five now."

I sigh with relief. "You can add it to my tab."

The bathroom seems to open, just slightly.

"So. School on Monday? You, um, feeling up to it?"

"Yeah. Just want to get back to normal, you know?"

We glance at each other in the mirror, knowing we'll never be normal again. He sets down the scissors and lifts the clippers. The buzzing makes me flinch.

"You OK? You want me to stop?"

"No," I whimper, clutching his shirt. "No please, stay."

Daddy takes a long breath. "Hold still, baby. Don't want to, you know, nick you."

Daddy has aged since I've been away. The creases on his face are deep; he breathes harder, like his lungs are defeated. I tell myself it's the strike, it's the bills piling up, and the picket lines in the cold. But I know what it's really from.

Me. I did this to him. I stressed him out. All the trauma I've been through . . . my parents probably have been through way worse, worried about a kid who wouldn't even pick up the phone.

The tears I've been holding for God knows how long bubble up and let out the cry hidden deep in my belly. I cry and cry until my body is convulsing.

Daddy turns off the clippers and holds me close. I bury myself in his shoulder.

"It's all right, sweetheart."

"I'm so sorry, Daddy."

"None of this is your fault. Not one drop of it. No child should ever take the blame for a man's actions."

I sniffle into his shirt, crumbling.

"It's gonna be all right. I promise."

# Chapter 60
## SCHOOL DAZE

The halls of Parkwood High School are not much different from being onstage. All eyes follow me. Waiting for me to open my mouth and sing.

But I stay quiet, keep my head down, walk quickly to home-room, hoping to see Gab beforehand. It's hard to reconnect with anyone over text. But maybe if we see each other, it would make a difference. I wonder if she's been eating lunch in the cafeteria or if she still eats at our spot.

Mackenzie and Hannah give me a quick wave but don't meet my eye. Coach won't let me back on the team yet but says I can practice, good for my therapy.

People part the hallways like the Red Sea and clash back

together the moment I pass. Voices hit my back like pebbles.

I walk into biology, our only class together. Except Gab's seat is empty. And stays empty.

When class ends, I call Gab again.

And again.

And again.

She's not in the cafeteria when I pick up my fries and salad. She's not at our spot near the award case.

I pull out my songbook, the only thing I managed to salvage from my time with Korey, trying to soothe the aching loneliness. Because the biggest loss I've experienced in all of this is the loss of a best friend.


I wait for Mom outside, pretending not to notice everyone staring as I shuffle through the notes from my teachers, all saying the same thing: I'm failing. Couldn't keep up with my schoolwork while I was gone and I couldn't explain why. All they saw, or really assumed, was that I was living the celebrity high life and couldn't be bothered with math quizzes or English essays. I want to tell everyone what happened . . . but where do I even start? How do I explain what I hate facing about myself, and how stupid I've been through all of it?

Shea stomps down the steps, a deep frown on her face, but in her eyes is a touch of sadness. Dried white tears stain her cheeks.

"How's school?" I ask as she plops down next to me.

Shea scoffs. "A mess. But not as messy as your life."

First day back and the knives are sharp.

"What the hell is your problem? Do you really think I wanted all this to happen?"

Shea examines her manicure with a sniff. "I think you got exactly what you wanted, no matter who it hurt. It just didn't turn out the way you expected."

Mouth dry, my stomach churns. "But . . . I risked everything for you."

"Me?" Shea laughs. "Oh, please."

"Yeah. I made sure that you could stay in school. Korey paid for it!"

She flashes me a hard stare.

"I would've rather dropped out," she hisses. "Like, do you think I wanted this? It's hard enough being the only black girl in ninth grade, but having an older sister be some grown-ass man's . . . I don't know what. All I know is I'm not allowed over my friends' houses because of you. When people talk about you, they're talking about me, wondering if I like old men too. When they talk about you, they're talking about Mom and Daddy, wondering what kind of fucked-up parents would send their daughter off with some man. You wanted to be with him, no matter what it made *us* look like."

Shea turns her back to me. I can't find the words to accurately describe what I feel. Shock. Guilt. Shame. I thought if I told her all I did, how I gave up my dream to protect her, she'd have to forgive me.

But it doesn't seem right to shove that in her face. That's something Korey would do.

• • •

"How did you find us?"

Mom's voice is sharp, but Louie doesn't seem to notice. He's busy sipping Mom's limeade, appreciating the family photos on the wall. He's a strange artifact of my recent past sitting on our sofa in my present.

"I got friends in high places," Louie says. "Looking good, Enchanted! I'm digging the buzz cut."

Daddy jumps to his feet, bellowing, "Aye, it's time for you to go!"

"Hey, hey! Easy! I'm messing with y'all! Chanty, your friend Derrick? He hooked me up with your info."

Daddy's and Mom's heads snap at me and I give an approving nod.

"It's all right. Derrick . . . is a friend."

Louie takes a relieved sigh, clutching his chest with a sheepish smile.

"Sorry. Figured a little humor would lighten the mood. Especially after everything you've been through."

I squirm in my seat. "You know?"

He shrugs. "The music industry is small. We hear things."

"So everyone knows?"

He sets down his glass. "I mean, I don't know exactly what happened with Korey. I've heard about his . . . taste in the past. Everyone has."

"And y'all just allow it?" Mom says, hands on her hips.

"He makes RCA millions. It's easy for them to ignore and bury whatever stories may come up. Christ sakes, the guy is a *rock star*! Known all over the world!"

Mom shakes her head in disgust. "Just a bunch of grown men letting another grown man chase after children! Cowards!"

"I couldn't agree more," Louie says.

"Well, we're waiting until she's up to it to go to the police," Mom says. "We don't want to put her through any unnecessary stress yet. But maybe we should go now."

"I'd hold off on that. Just for the time being."

"Why?" Daddy snaps. "I want that fool behind bars, so I'm not tempted to kill him."

"I'ma keep it real with you. Your daughter's dream is to be a star. If you go to the police, labels will blackball her. She won't stand a chance. It'll be some little girl's word against Korey Fields. But if we build up her name, it'll be *Enchanted*'s word against his. That holds more weight."

I sit back as it hits me. "You still want to be my manager?"

He smirks. "Well, I didn't come all this way for the limeade, which is delicious, by the way."

"Even after everything?"

Louie shrugs. "Call me crazy, but all I know is I have a daughter your age. And I would kill a man for . . . well . . . if my kid had the amount of talent you had, I'd just about bleed dry trying to make sure everyone in the world knew it."

I chew on my inner cheek, tossing the idea back and forth. The thought of singing again both scary and invigorating.

Louie leans forward, his expression serious. "Enchanted. Don't let that asshole snuff out your dreams. Success is the best revenge." He looks at Mom and Daddy. "We'll get the son of a bitch. It won't be easy, but you have my word."

# Chapter 61

## SHINE BRIGHT

"OK, you're up next." Louie holds my shoulders. "Ready?"

I nod in the dressing room mirror, admiring my own makeup job. I look like . . . myself. Fresh baldy, lip gloss, a little mascara, and some hoop earrings. Mom lent me one of her smaller-fitting dresses, short boots, and a leather jacket.

Music thumps from the stage outside. The narrow greenroom of the Apollo Theater smells of perfume and all-purpose cleaner.

But I'm happier being here than anywhere.

"I . . . don't think this is a good idea," Mom sputters behind me, almost hysterical. "Maybe we should wait. We shouldn't be doing this!"

Louie's mouth drops.

I jump from the makeup chair, taking both of her hands. "Mom, you promised! You promised we weren't going to let what happened stop me."

"Yes, but I meant you can still go to college."

"That was your dream, not mine."

Mom shifts on her heels, eyes wide and glassy. "This all . . . seems too rushed," she says, bottom lip trembling. "We just got you back, now we're throwing you back into the spotlight."

"But this is where I want to be," I beg.

"This is a small showcase," Louie insists. "Just to get her feet wet. Get her back in the water. Only a few artists. Nothing major."

"She's not ready!"

"I'm fine. Really!"

Mom gathers me in her arms, her tears trickling down my jacket. I can sense her spiraling and try to hold her close.

"I failed you, baby. If I was more of one of those stage moms . . . if I had paid attention to what you really wanted, if I was there, with you . . . none of this would've happened. If I didn't work so much or if I was a better mother. Then maybe . . . maybe . . ."

I hug her and whisper, "You were exactly what I needed you to be. I'm fine, Mom. I swear."

She searches my face then nods, kissing my forehead.

"OK. I'll be right here, waiting."

• • •

The lights are blinding. I haven't been onstage in weeks, but the moment my hand touches the mic, it brings me to life, the two-ton truck on my chest lifted.

I snap my fingers along to the rhythm and give a dazzling smile.

"*Ba ba bada. Ba ba bada . . .*"

At first, when Louie suggested Beyoncé, I immediately cut him off. But he made a great point. We needed to show audiences that I'm versatile, youthful, and have range. So I picked a song that has an old-school vibe but kicks it hard—"Love on Top."

I spin around, dancing across the stage, the audience clapping along. Despite everything, I feel free. Like flying again. I missed the stage. Missed the rush of adrenaline that comes with it. A different type of high . . . until I see him.

Korey.

I blink, my vision blurring, and pray I'm seeing things. I spin again, glancing at the band behind me, and there he is. Playing drums. Even with the sunglasses and hoodie, I couldn't mistake that smile.

He's here. Onstage with me. Again.

I turn back to the crowd, and somehow, I keep up with the song, while my insides scream.

He's here he's here he's here he's here he's here.

My eye twitches, the lights too bright and I'm too terrified to blink. I almost forget the modulation at the end of the song and go up an octave.

*"Baby, 'cause you're the one that I love*
*Baby, you're the one that I need"*

Fear keeps me moving. I spin again to sneak another look. Korey is grinning, having the time of his life. He looks . . . proud.

Don't look at him. Don't. Run!

I go up the next octave. And the next one. And the next one. My voice nearly cracks at the end.

How did he get in here? Did Louie invite him? Was this all a trap from the start? What if he takes me? What if he . . . he . . .

"Love on TOP!"

A roaring applause caps off the song and I sprint stage left, into the darkness, toward the back door. A pair of hands grabs me, and I scream.

"Enchanted! Holy shit! That was amazing!" Louie cheers, lifting me off the floor. "Do you hear that crowd! Look at them!"

Teeth chattering, I shake my head. I can't go back out there. He's here, he's here, he's here . . . *run!* Need to tell someone, but the words are stuck. My mouth moves but no sound comes out.

"Look, Enchanted! Look! They're all on their feet."

I peer over my shoulder, only to look onstage. The band set is empty. Korey's gone. But the crowd . . . they're cheering.

A bubble of hope inflates. Maybe I really could be something without him.

"Hey? Everything OK?" Louie says, suddenly serious. "Look like you've seen a ghost. Want me to get your mom?"

My blood turns to ice, veins throbbing. Should I tell them? No. Mom can't know. She'll never let me out of her sight for as long as I live.

And then . . . I'll never sing again.

# *Chapter 62*

## LEGALESE

"Korey Fields sent a copy of your contract."

At Sylvia's restaurant in Harlem, Mom and I meet Louie for our weekly strategy meeting. Mom wants to be more involved in my career moves. But this news took us both by surprise.

"Contract? What contract?" Mom asks.

Louie sighs, digging in his messenger bag.

"That's what I thought. I let my lawyer take a look. Apparently, you signed to Korey's label."

Mom and I share an equally confused look.

"What label? What are you talking about?"

"You don't remember signing any documents?"

Mom shrugs. "Only the proxy paperwork that girl Jessica gave me."

"Did it look something like this?"

Louie passes her a stack of papers. The instant I see its thickness I know we're in trouble. Mom flips through the pages, nodding slow.

"Well, yes. She told me it's all standard. Like a big long permission slip to go on a class trip."

Louie rubs his face, eyebrows creased.

"Korey had you sign to his label, Field of Dreams Records."

"He has his own label?" I ask. "Since when?"

"It's an imprint under RCA, relatively new. He was going to announce this fall, with a roster of new up-and-coming artists."

"So RCA sent this to you?" Mom asks. "Then, they gotta know what he'd done to her by now!"

"They do. And this is their first way of silencing you." He pokes the papers in Mom's hands hard. "According to this contract, he pretty much owns any music you produce for the next three years."

It feels like the final gutting. The last chop to my mermaid tail. He knew how to slice into me where it would hurt the worst.

"But my songs . . . I've worked on them for years. They're mine."

Louie shakes his head.

"I'm sorry, Enchanted. Unless we can get out of this contract, there's not much we can do."

# Chapter 63
## ROAD TRIP

"Look who's home just in time for Teen Conference," Malika grumbles, rolling her eyes. "Ain't that convenient."

Malika Evens has a mansion, one in a gated community around the corner from our house. It always amazes me how we can be so close and yet so far in every way imaginable.

Our W&W group gathers in the driveway, loading up the van for our weekend trip to the National Teen Conference. Malika's and Aisha's moms offered to be our chaperones. They give Shea and me dubious glances with strained smiles.

"Hi, ladies. Right on time," Mrs. Evens says.

"What's up, superstar," Sean says, winking. "Glad you can

kick it with us common folk! Guess you got the guap to buy us some bottles this time around, right?"

Veins tighten around my neck and I fake a smile. Malika rolls her eyes. Shea grabs my arm before I can lift our suitcase into the trunk.

"You sure this is a good idea?" she whispers.

"We already paid for it," I shoot back. "Mom's been making payments for months. We're going."

"Yeah, but maybe Daddy needs . . ."

"Daddy needs to watch the Littles while Mom works. And with the way things are looking with the strike we might not even be in Will and Willow next year."

Shea freezes, realization gut-punching her. "But . . . are you going to be OK?"

"I'm fine," I insist. "Really. Besides, I'm safe . . . with you."

Her mouth cracks a little, eyes softening. As if she's sorry for me. Which I can't stand, but it's better than her being mad at me.

"OK," she concedes.

"Nice to have you back with us," Aisha says, smiling as we climb into the van. "We gonna be the lit-est with a celebrity in our chapter."

Creighton gives me a meek smile and a hey before jumping in the front seat.

"Hi, Creighton," I say. "How's stock club going?"

Creighton turns to me with a shy smile. "Um, it's cool. We made five thousand last quarter."

I decided to forgive Creighton. What he did was stupid. But

not nearly as horrendous as Korey. Plus, he saved me, sending Derrick my way. I might have still been in that house.

"Bruh, she paid her dues. Who cares if she hasn't been to a meeting in the last few months?" Sean snaps. Everyone in the van turns around to see him and Malika arguing in the driveway. "Get over yourself. She's coming!"

The Will and Willow National Teen Conference is like a giant Teen Cluster. Once a year, chapters from across the country gather in a select city. A grand finale before summer break. Our chapter is staying at the Renaissance Hotel near Boston Harbor, about three blocks from the convention center, where the breakout sessions, panels, and speeches are being held. We're expected to dress business casual, like professionals to be. Skirt suits, blazers, ties, heels, and hard-bottoms.

But . . . I don't exactly look ladylike, crawling around our hotel room on all fours in my charcoal-gray suit.

"What are you doing?" Shea snaps.

"Lost the back of my earring. I dropped it somewhere."

I use my phone flashlight to check under the bed.

"We were supposed to be downstairs ten minutes ago!"

"Yeah, but I can't go without earrings. They'll say I look like a boy!"

The room phone rings.

"Ugh, it's probably Ms. Evens wondering where we are," She whines, crossing the room.

"Don't answer it," I shout, grabbing her wrist before she can reach the handle. "She'll know we're still in here. Just . . .

head to the elevators, tell her I'm in the bathroom or something. I'll meet you down there!"

She groans, throwing her hands up and exits.

Back on the floor, I search high and low. The phone rings again as I pat down the tight space between the nightstand and bed. A twinkle of gold catches my eye.

"Got ya!" I cheer.

The phone rings again, right in my ear. With a groan, I grab the receiver.

"Yeah, yeah. I'm on my way!"

"Come outside."

My throat clenches shut at the sound of his voice.

Korey.

I jolt upright, muscles tensing, and turn to the door, miles away.

"I know you're there, Bright Eyes. Come outside."


Stiff as a board, I inch across the near-empty hotel lobby, biting the inside of my cheek, tasting blood. Everyone is already on their way to the convention center for the evening's keynote.

Even if I call, no one would make it here fast enough to save me.

I'm spit outside by the revolving doors and can smell the salty water drifting from the bay, the convention center a few blocks away. Maybe I can make a run for it. Jump into the water and swim home.

"Enchanted."

Another familiar voice. Tony.

I think of calling Shea, but I don't want either of them near my sister. I'd give up my life first.

"This way," he says, leading me down the block to a black truck. He drives around the corner to the underground parking, then down three levels.

There, a car I don't recognize sits parked in the far back, engine running.

Tony opens the back door and shoves me inside. In an instant, I'm wrapped in Korey's arms and my body turns to stone.

"Bright Eyes," he coos. "Damn, I've missed you so much."

I pull away from him, sliding on the red leather seats, squeezing myself to the door.

Korey's black hoodie is pulled up. But even in the darkness of the back seat, I can see he's hurt by the move.

"What . . . are you doing here?"

"I—I thought you'd be happy to see me. Here I am, come to save you again."

I'm stunned to silence. Korey looks broken, shattered . . . older. And the part of my heart that loved him beats a little harder, despite how I willed it not to.

He hangs his head low.

"You left me," he murmurs. "You promised you'd never leave me."

"Korey, please," I beg, trembling. "You have to let me go."

"We belong together, remember? Like Tammi and Marvin."

"Tammi died."

"So did Marvin. Is that what you want me to do? Die?"

For a bristling moment, I almost say yes.

"Just . . . please, you can't be here."

"Aight, one more question, then . . . I'll leave you alone."

I swallow. "OK."

"Did you ever love me?"

It's the same question I've been asking myself for weeks. Did *he* ever really love me? Because I loved him. Our love felt deeper than the ocean, endless and beautiful.

"Yes. But . . . I can't be with you anymore."

He pulls me into his arms again. "I'm sorry, baby. We'll . . . we'll try again. It'll be better this time. I've changed. I saw you sing the other day. You were so beautiful."

He was there. I knew it!

"I . . . I have to go."

"Bright Eyes, you're eighteen now. We can be together like we talked about."

"Please, Korey," I sob, grabbing the door handle. "I can't."

His face darkens. "You leave me again, you're going to regret it. You need to come back where you belong."

A small flame flickers in my belly. Something I'm not used to. Water and fire don't mix. But now, I'm made of both. Thinking quick, I grab my phone, opening up the maps.

"What are you—"

I hold the phone up to his face. "There's a locator on my phone that shows my exact location. I was supposed to be at dinner ten minutes ago. If you don't let me out, they are going to come looking for me. Right here."

Korey glances at the screen then back at me.

Shea is standing in the lobby of the convention center when I arrive, arms crossed.

"Where the hell have you been? I've been calling!"

"Sorry," I mumble, still stunned my bluff worked.

She frowns. "You OK?"

"Yeah," I squeak. "Ready for dinner?"

Three exits, no windows. Bathrooms on the left.

The evening's welcome party is held in the convention center's ballroom. Another dance with a trash DJ and strobe lights. Except there are over a thousand affluent black kids here, smashed together in the shadows. Shea is kicking it with Aisha, taking Snapchat selfies. Sean is dancing with some girl from the Miami chapter in the corner. Creighton doesn't leave his seat at the far end of the ballroom.

Three exits, no windows. Bathrooms on the left.

How can I be so numb but can feel every atom floating through my body?

Worse, I'm craving my purple drink. Bad.

A few other Will and Willow members recognize me, or heard of me, but with the bald head, I no longer look like the girl I was with Korey. I'm back to my old self but somehow new.

Three exits, no windows. Bathrooms on the left.

Can't stand facing one direction too long; need eyes on

every door. What if he shows up, another surprise performance? What if he's already here? What if he finds Shea first?

"Shea," I gasp, spinning around to search the crowd. Across the room, my eyes refocus on a familiar face, chest tightening.

Derrick gives me a slight wave, and I let out a relieved laugh, maneuvering through the crowd. We make our way toward each other, meeting in the middle.

"There you are! Like, the REAL you. Not that chick I met on the road."

"Hey, that chick you met still has horrible taste in TV," I shoot back with a smirk.

Derrick nods. "It's good to see you."

"Surprised I'm here?"

"No. I'm glad, though! How are . . . things?"

"'Things' are OK. For now."

"For what it's worth, I'm mad proud of you. I know that . . . took a lot."

I press my lips together to keep them from trembling. "Thanks," I say, voice cracking.

"Yo, that Creighton guy," he says, nodding in his direction. "He ever come clean about what happened between you two?"

"What? How'd you know about that!"

Derrick rolls his eyes. "Man, dummy confessed to one of my boys, saying how guilty he felt but afraid of getting kicked out of W&W. It's why he wanted to help you."

"Oh. Well, it's whatever. And he did help me get away from Korey, by sending me you."

Derrick's face turns up into a snarl, his voice stern.

"Yo, you can't keep burying what happens to you, thinking it'll solve itself. Your voice ain't just for singing, you know? You gotta speak up. If not for you, then for the next you, 'cause there's gonna be one if you let people think they can get away with hurting you."

Guilt pulses up my spine. I nod my head. "You're right."

Derrick takes a relieving breath before his eyes light up. "Yoooo! Did you watch last week's episode?"

Within minutes, the mood shifts, and we're back to shit-talking, debating which we like more, *Love and Hip Hop* NY or ATL. I'm always a fan of NY but ATL has some characters. I laugh, like really laugh with my whole chest, for the first time in months. Feels good. Almost normal.

From the corner of my eye, I see Malika—hard to miss being the only person in the middle of the room not dancing, a bright phone screen reflecting off her face. Hand to her mouth, she gapes in horror before her head pops up, looking dead at me.

A sickly feeling takes over.

Malika rushes across the room to Sean, jamming her phone in his face.

Derrick is still talking as I watch them. His phone buzzes. He takes one look and flinches.

"Oh shit," he mutters, eyes wide.

"What is it?"

Phones chirp and buzz around us, like that day the world saw our YouTube video. Except I know it's not as innocent as us singing. From everyone's shocked expressions, I know it's something . . . more.

"I . . . I . . . fuck," Derrick says, grabbing my hand. "Come on, we have to go."

For a split second, I wonder if Korey killed himself like he said he would. Maybe out in the parking lot. And it would be all my fault.

Once in the lobby, I can't take the suspense and yank away from him.

"Would you just tell me what's going on?" I snap.

Derrick bites his fist, seeming torn. "Aight, there's a video . . . a sex tape. With Korey."

My stomach lurches. I blink slow. "A . . . a what?"

He stands next to me, pressing play on his phone. It's a blurry video of Korey naked . . . with a girl in his house . . . his house in Atlanta . . . in my old room . . . naked.

Derrick studies me, sorrow covering his face when it finally hits me. And I let out a delirious deep belly laugh.

"Oh, you think that's me? Nah, that's not me."

Derrick's jaw clenches, holding a grave stare.

I shake my head. "It's not, Derrick. That's not me!"

# *Chapter 64*

## GROUP CHAT

*W&W Squad (w/o the Jones sisters)*

Malika: **Well, that was a memorable Teen Conference.**

Sean: **Y'all. Bruh! Son! WTF!**

Aisha: **Some girl in the Danbury chapter said that our chapter is now known as the Porn Hub Squad.**

Malika: **That's disgusting.**

Sean: **OK, but the real question . . . is that Enchanted or nah?**

Malika: **Seriously?**

Aisha: **Really?**

Creighton: **LOL!**

Aisha: It ain't funny!

Sean: I mean, I watched the video. Well, the clips I could find. And I ain't gonna front, the girl has a striking resemblance.

Aisha: Really?

Malika: Of course it's her! Is everyone blind? Even with that shit quality and their backs to us, I could tell it's her.

Creighton: The girl had hair tho.

Aisha: It was a wig.

Sean: Surprised it stayed on the way he was flipping her.

Creighton: LMAO! Damn bruh, you wildin right now!

Sean: Kid, don't act like you didn't watch it either.

Malika: Did you?

Creighton: Dude on my soccer team was playing it in the locker room.

Malika: And you let him?

Sean: You want to see? I got a link.

Creighton: Nah, don't do her like that. She been through enough.

Aisha: Yo, y'all parents got that email from Nationals?

Malika: Yeah. They're wondering what kind of hood ass shit we got ourselves into, letting the Jones sisters join our chapter.

# Chapter 65

## SEX TAPE

On the news, Korey's publicist gives a statement in front of his condo building. "My client is extremely upset that someone would steal his personal and private property. However, we are confident that the individuals, whoever they may be, will be found and face severe consequences."

Shea stays home from school to avoid the onslaught. Don't know why, because it's not me.

Louie tells us to stay quiet and keep our heads down. Let the media circus blow over. He thinks it's me. But it's not me.

Mom is on the phone, talking with a lawyer. Don't know why, because it's not me.

Daddy's seen clips . . . and now he can't even look at me. He thinks it's me too. But it's not me.

It's not me.

It's not me.

I say it over and over to myself until it becomes a hum in my ear.

I feel like fall.

I am a heap of dead leaves, blackened, moist, reeking of mold. Rotting apples, dying grass, early darkness chasing away the sun.

Someone printed a screenshot of the video and taped it to my locker. Even the janitors give me questioning glares.

Mr. Walker turned red when I walked into AP English. He's seen the video. English used to be my favorite. Wrote some of my best lyrics in here. Now, I can't think of a single word to write.

Except, *it's not me*. I scribble it over and over in my songbook.

It's not me.

It's not me.

It's not me.

Chasing this dream has turned into a nightmare.

Out the window, pass the grassy knoll, wind hits the flags flying high on white poles. Mr. Walker's classroom is on the north side of campus, near the student parking lot. I strain to search for Gab's car among the BMWs and Audis. Rich-kid cars, Gab joked. She was proud of her Toyota Corolla. I cringe at the idea of Gab watching the video, maybe with Jay, in his campus dorm room, with the rest of school.

I asked a few people in class about Gab, but no one seemed to know who I was talking about. She was the only senior in our biology class—how could they not notice her?

At the very back of the lot, sunlight glints off the tinted window of a familiar black Mercedes parked near the exit. It's close enough for me to notice but far enough that no one would take a second glance. The jet-black opulence is unmistakable.

Korey.

I can't see through his tints, but I know it's him. Sitting there with his engine purring, watching and waiting. Waiting to take me, waiting to trap me.

Waiting to kill me.

Run!

A shudder shoots through me and I'm on my feet. Mr. Walker says something to my back as I sprint out into the hall. I keep running, though my legs ache and my body is full of dead things. I run. Straight down into the gym locker room.

What am I going to do? Am I ever going to be rid of him?

And . . . what if this is really my fault, like Shea said. I . . . sent him that Aretha Franklin song. I followed him on social media. I called him in Jersey. I wore that sexy top to the studio. I kissed him . . .

"Chant?"

A scream escapes, and I cover my mouth with both hands, voice echoing in the empty locker room.

Shea stands by the sinks, taking an unsteady step back.

"What are you doing down here? I saw you running past my class."

Was she followed? Did she shut the door?

"He's here," I whisper. "Korey. Outside, in his car."

Shea frowns. "You saw him? Are you sure?"

I nod, trembling. I have to tell someone, just in case I don't make it out alive.

"He's coming for me."

Her eyes grow big. "Enchanted. You're scaring me." She says it really harsh, like she doesn't believe me.

"He was at Teen Conference too. I saw him before the dance."

"What? Why didn't you tell Mom?"

"I . . . I thought I could handle him. Thought I could keep him in check . . ."

"How'd you think you were going to handle someone like him? He's Korey Fields! A superstar! You're just . . . you. We need to tell Mom."

Shea's right. Korey has all the money. All the power. I'm . . . just me.

# Chapter 66
## BEET JUICE 4

*NOW*

"Chanty? Baby? Are you OK?"

"Daddy?" I whisper. What's he doing here?

More voices. I look to my right, down the hall, something sticking out of the wall. A hidden door cracked open like a book. I peer inside at the short metal staircase leading to a glass door. That must be the studio, one floor below. I've never seen this door before.

Did we work on music last night? Maybe.

Think.

Think.

Beside my feet is a steak knife. The kind you find in a set, sitting in a block of wood on the kitchen counter. Except now it's on the floor, covered in beet juice.

Don't even know where the kitchen is, but I should clean up, before anyone comes in here. He'll be so mad.

As I bend, the front door lock clicks and swings open.

"FREEZE!"

# Chapter 67

## INTERROGATION #1

### *THEN*

*Transcript—May 13*

**Detective Fletcher:** Hello, Mrs. Jones, Enchanted. I'm Detective Fletcher. You've already met with my associate Detective Silverman. Nice to meet you both!

**Enchanted Jones:** Hi.

**LaToya Jones:** Yes, hello.

**Fletcher:** Detective Silverman asked me to join, but before we start, I just wanted to say, I was actually at that showcase you recently did. At the Apollo.

**E. Jones:** Really?

**Fletcher:** Yeah, my daughter is an aspiring singer too. You have an amazing voice!

**E. Jones:** Thank you.

**Detective Silverman:** So to confirm, you want to report Korey Fields for assault, battery, rape, and . . . stalking? Am I right?

**E. Jones:** Um, yeah.

**LaToya Jones:** We wanted to report this sooner, but we thought best to wait until Enchanted was strong enough. But now, Korey has been stalking my daughter and he needs to be stopped.

**Silverman:** And this happened around the time the sex tape surfaced?

**E. Jones:** That's not me in that video. We never had sex.

**Silverman:** Are you sure? You mentioned before that he often drugged you?

**E. Jones:** We . . . fooled around, I guess you can call it that. But not sex.

**Fletcher:** Oral sex is still considered sex, under the law.

**Silverman:** So you admit you were intimate?

**E. Jones:** Um, yeah.

**Silverman:** Did you perform oral on Mr. Fields?

**E. Jones:** Um, yes.

**Silverman:** And you did so willingly?

**L. Jones:** Look, she already went over this. She
said it's not her. I don't understand what this
has to do with him stalking her!

**Fletcher:** We need the full scope for the
investigation. Mrs. Jones, you said you gave
permission for Enchanted to go on tour with
Korey Fields.

**L. Jones:** Yes. We signed proxy documents. Well,
that's what they called them, that guaranteed
she would have a supervising adult guardian,
hired by the label, to watch her at all times
and make sure she kept up with her schoolwork.
That's the only way we would allow her to go.
But Jessica was just as bad as Korey, never
returning phone calls or messages. We tried
to contact the label, but it was like a maze.
Kept getting transferred from one person to the
other!

**Silverman:** But you're now saying a relationship
happened prior to you leaving on tour?

**E. Jones:** Yes.

**Silverman:** What did your relationship consist of?
Did you go on dates?

**E. Jones:** Um, no. We were at his studio,
recording. And he texted me. A lot.

**Silverman:** Do you have those text messages?

**E. Jones:** No. He took my phone. I got a new one
but . . . they should be on his phone. We

texted songs to each other.

**Silverman:** Did you know Enchanted was communicating with him?

**L. Jones:** No. I did not.

**Fletcher:** Talk to me about him following you. Can you give us more details?

**E. Jones:** Uh, yeah. First, he followed me to the annual Will and Willow conference in Boston. Took me to a parking lot nearby. He was also outside my school. I saw his car.

**Silverman:** And he was aware you no longer wanted to be in a relationship. This was made clear to him?

**L. Jones:** You keep saying relationship. She was seventeen. There's no relationship between a grown man and a *child*.

**Silverman:** Of course. Of course. But we find in these circumstances it's better to . . .

**L. Jones:** And I don't care! That *man* kidnapped my daughter.

**Silverman:** Well, we can't say kidnap. You did allow your daughter to go with him willingly.

**L. Jones:** Yes. And he kept her against her will!

**Silverman:** Those welfare checks, at his home in Atlanta, Enchanted, why didn't you leave then?

**E. Jones:** I . . . I was scared! I didn't know what would happen if I did.

**Fletcher:** Enchanted, could any of those incidents

that you mentioned, of him following you, could they have been considered . . . coincidental in nature? Example, he just happened to be in Boston the same time you were?

**E. Jones:** Nah. No way. He was even at the showcase! Onstage with me.

**Fletcher:** Onstage with you?

**E. Jones:** Yes. Playing in the band.

**Fletcher:** The band?

**E. Jones:** Yes.

**Fletcher:** There wasn't a band at the showcase.

**E. Jones:** Huh? Yes, there was.

**Fletcher:** Um. OK. We'll check that out.

**Silverman:** Can anyone else confirm your relationship prior to the tour?

**E. Jones:** Yes, my friend Gab.

**L. Jones:** Baby, who?

**E. Jones:** Gabriela Garcia. From school. She knew. She covered for me when I skipped to see him. You can talk to her.

# *Chapter 68*
## COLLEGE BOUND

Gab mentioned Jay worked on campus at the computer lab. Easy enough to find once I make it to Fordham's campus, near the Metro-North train stop.

I remembered his face, saved as a screensaver on her phone.

He walks around the lab, checking computers, straightening chairs, smiling, and is just as cute as Gab swore he was.

"Are you Jay?"

"Yep. What's up, how can I help you?

"I'm . . . a friend of Gabriela's?"

He pauses, not abruptly, more like a slow, questioning glare.

"Who?"

"Gabriela. Or Gab? Your girlfriend."

He scoffs, then laughs. "Girlfriend? Pshhh. Boo boo, you got the wrong guy."

I peep his curly brown hair, his soft features, his height. It's uncanny. No way—this has to be him.

"Gabriela. You're sure you don't know her? I'm her friend, Enchanted."

I describe her as best I could, wishing I'd printed at least one photo.

"Sorry, I don't know who you're talking about."

My eyes narrow. "You're lying."

He stares through me. "What? Yo, do you even go here? Security check your ID?"

I back away, rushing out the door, straight to the Metro-North.

As soon as I'm on the next train home, a text from an unknown number buzzes:

**Give me one night of you and this will all go away.**

A stack of bricks piles onto my chest. He'll never leave me alone. Ever.

# Chapter 69
## W&W MEETING MINUTES

*Minutes from Emergency W&W Mothers' Meeting*

**Dr. Marcia Patrick (Sean's mother):** I think we all
   know what this is about.

**LaToya Jones:** I don't, so why don't you fill me
   in?

**Dr. Patrick:** There has been a lot of activity
   surrounding our chapter given this controversy
   with Korey Fields. The national board has
   concerns and thinks it's best to . . . suspend
   your family's membership for the time being.

**Ms. Jones:** Wow. Just like that?

**Karen Evens (Malika's mother):** To be associated

with this right now. It's just not good for the
children.

**Ms. Jones:** Hold up! Now when we first moved here,
you all convinced us that we were family. And
in times of crisis, family supposed to come
together.

**Ms. Evens:** This . . . is different.

**Nicole Woods (Aisha's mother):** I agree with
LaToya. This is foolish, y'all! Come on! We're
supposed to be a group that cares and watches
over our children. It takes a village to raise
a child—that's the motto.

**Ms. Jones:** Our daughter was stalked, preyed upon,
and assaulted by a grown man. This is when we
need our village the most.

**Ms. Evens:** Well . . . not so sure about all that.

**Ms. Jones:** Excuse me?

**Ms. Woods:** Oooo, Lawd.

**Ms. Evens:** She wasn't exactly stalked, now was
she? She walked right into his house.

**Ms. Jones:** She was brainwashed.

**Ms. Evens:** Girls are smart. They know what they
doing.

**Ms. Jones:** Girls may THINK they know what they're
doing, but he's an adult. He knew better than
her.

**Dr. Patrick:** I agree. Adultlike decisions don't
make them adults.

**Tonia Stevens (Creighton's mother):** Then, might I ask, why did you let her go?

**Ms. Jones:** We were made promises. None of those he came through with. But she's not an adult. She's just a child. My daughter.

**Ms. Evens:** She's eighteen now.

**Ms. Jones:** And she was seventeen when he first started. And honestly, do you consider your eighteen-year-old smart enough to make her own decisions without all your hovering?

**Ms. Evens:** What are you implying?

**Ms. Woods:** Oooo, Lawd.

**Ms. Jones:** Just asking, would you be OK with your daughter seeing a twenty-nine-year-old?

**Ms. Evens:** No, no. My daughter would never do something like that. I know my child.

**Ms. Jones:** So do I. But they're still their own individual. They're all going to test the limits, and we're not with them twenty-four-seven.

**Ms. Evens:** Sorry, but my child wouldn't do something like that. I can't speak to how anyone else raises their child, but I know mine.

**Ms. Jones:** You mean to tell me your mother knew everything you ever did when you were a girl?

**Ms. Evens:** That's . . . different.

**Ms. Stevens:** Are you sure she didn't tell him she was eighteen?

**Ms. Jones:** So you calling us liars now?

**Ms. Stevens:** No! I'm . . . well, we've all been there. Hell, I had an older boyfriend in high school. And I didn't exactly have the body of a sixteen-year-old. So, I could understand if, you know, she told a little fib.

**Ms. Woods:** Oooo, Ms. Stevens, scandalous! Well, I guess if we're sharing, I, too, had a little thing-thing back in the day. It was . . . exciting! Remember it like yesterday.

**Ms. Stevens:** Yeah . . . I was scared to tell him the truth but really lived in fear of the day my mama would find out about us.

**Dr. Patrick:** Is this really the conversation we're having right now?

**Ms. Jones:** But see, there's a difference. You had boyfriends and, yes, they were older than you. And yes, you might have even lied about your age. But let me ask you . . . did any of them lay a hand on you? Kidnap you? Trap you? Starve you? Keep you from your mother? Make you pee in a got damn bucket?!

**Dr. Patrick:** Latoya, I think . . .

**Ms. Jones:** This isn't some little scandalous fling! He used his money and power to hide our daughter! He abused his power 'cause he had it. If he wasn't a celebrity, he'd be under the jail right now!

**Ms. Evens:** Innocent until proven guilty.

**Ms. Woods:** Yeah, and how many times has that little rule worked in favor of black women?

**Ms. Jones:** The point is, *he's* the adult. *We* are adults. Don't care how smart our babies are or how we broke the rules before—we *know* better now.

**Dr. Patrick:** OK. I hear you. So what do you need?

# Chapter 70

## INTERROGATION #2

*Transcript—May 18*

**Fletcher:** Thanks for stopping by on such short notice. So, we talked to Korey Fields.

**L. Jones:** OK. And? Are you going to arrest him yet? Did you talk to his label?

**Fletcher:** First, we have some follow-up questions for you . . . crossing our t's, dotting our i's, the usual. Korey has been very forthcoming. He takes these allegations seriously. As do we.

**Silverman:** Korey suggested that you may have been the one who leaked the sex video.

**E. Jones:** What?

**L. Jones:** Why would she do that?

**Silverman:** Fame. Ruin his reputation. Extortion of money.

**E. Jones:** I wouldn't do that. How would I even do that?

**Silverman:** He mentioned you had full access to his home. That you knew where he kept his cameras.

**E. Jones:** No! I . . . never left my room. Not even to go to the bathroom! I peed in a bucket.

**L. Jones:** Unbelievable. She's saying she had to pee in a bucket while being locked in her room, and you're worried about his nasty sex tapes?

**E. Jones:** He's been following me! Stalking me!

**Fletcher:** So, let's talk about that. You mentioned, he was outside your high school, right?

**E. Jones:** Yes!

**Silverman:** We followed up with your high school, and per security footage, Korey has only been on campus once, during last October's homecoming dance. The one Korey says you invited him to.

**E. Jones:** No! I didn't! I swear I didn't!

**L. Jones:** What about Boston?

**Silverman:** We're waiting for footage, but there is no record of Korey being in the state at that time. No train or plane tickets. No toll roads or hotel records. Not even a parking violation.

**E. Jones:** [crying] But Tony was there too.

**Fletcher:** He also gave us full access to his cell phone. No phone calls or text messages. We did see many with you, Mrs. Jones.

**L. Jones:** You mean when I was looking for my daughter? Damn right I blew up his line.

**E. Jones:** He . . . he must have called from another number. Another phone.

**L. Jones:** So, you think she's making all this up? What kind of twisted—

**E. Jones:** The showcase! He was in the band!

**Fletcher:** Korey wasn't at the talent showcase. There was no drummer. Only a DJ.

**E. Jones:** What?

**Fletcher:** There's no way he was at the showcase. Korey was in Las Vegas with his wife.

**E. Jones:** His . . . wife? What are you talking about?

**Fletcher:** Yes. There is video of him and his wife at a nightclub, timestamped the same day as your performance.

**E. Jones:** [crying]

**Fletcher:** Mrs. Jones, do you remember seeing a band onstage?

**L. Jones:** Well, no . . . but I thought she meant offstage or something. I was in her

dressing room. I didn't . . . I mean, I don't
think . . .

**E. Jones:** I'm not lying! I swear! Gabriela saw my
phone! She saw him texting me!

**Silverman:** And finally, we checked with the
school. There's no student by the name of
Gabriela Garcia.

**E. Jones:** What?

**Silverman:** They have no record of a Gabriela
Garcia. And the phone number you gave us
belongs to a Martin Anderson of White Plains.
Age, thirty-five.

**E. Jones:** No. That's . . . that's impossible.

**Fletcher:** Mrs. Jones, have you ever met Gabriela?

**L. Jones:** [pause] No. No. I've . . . I've never
met her.

**Fletcher:** Mrs. Jones . . . your mother suffers
with mental illness, does she not?

**L. Jones:** H-how did you know that? And what does
that have to do with Enchanted?

**Fletcher:** Has your daughter ever had a mental
evaluation?

**E. Jones:** Mom?

**L. Jones:** Don't say another word, Chanted! We're
done here.

# Chapter 71
## WHO IS GABRIELA?

"Shea, I want you to be honest with me. Do you know someone named Gab or Gabriela?"

Mom and Daddy sit with Shea at the kitchen table while I pretend to be asleep in my room. But these walls are thin.

"For the last time, I don't know who you're talking about."

"Shea, this is serious," Daddy says, exasperated.

"I get that, but doesn't change what I don't know!"

"Gabriela," Mom repeats herself. "A Spanish girl? There can't be many of them."

"Yeah, a Spanish girl that looks white. And a senior? That's a needle in a haystack. I barely know the kids in my own class."

I text:

**GABRIELA! STOP IGNORING ME!
THIS IS SERIOUS!**

"Can you ask around?"

"None of my friends are talking to me, so sorry I can't ask them either," she says bitterly.

"Can we go up to the school, ask about her?" Dad asks.

"I don't think the school's allowed to give out information on other students," Mom replies. "Please, Shea. You must have seen your sister with somebody."

"No! I haven't, OK? She mostly hung out by herself. She didn't even eat in the cafeteria. I don't want to call her a loser, but . . ."

**Gabriela, please!**

"Your sister is in trouble, baby," Mom says gently. "We need to do everything we can to help her."

Shea sighs. "I'll ask around. Can I go to bed now? It's late."

"Sure, baby."

Shea enters our room and I keep my head to the wall, squeezing my eyes tight to hide the tears.

A text flashes. From Gabriela.

**Dude, for the last time. WRONG
NUMBER!!!**

"You never heard her mention . . . anybody?" Daddy whispers.

"I don't remember," Mom sighs. "Then again, I can barely remember what happened yesterday, let alone six months ago. We've just been so busy with work and I . . . all I remember her talking about is her teammates. Shit, I'm the world's worst goddamn mother! First I didn't want her to sing, then I couldn't go on tour with her, now I don't know her friends. I just . . . never thought I had to worry about her. She always seemed to be OK."

"Not your fault," Daddy says cautiously. "But do you think . . . ?"

"I don't know, but please. Let's . . . not talk about that right now."

# Chapter 72

## HOW TO BUY BACK YOUR LIFE

The number is still written on the kitchen whiteboard in big, bold red. Mom said she called it five to six times a day when she was looking for me. The evidence of her fight is all around the house. Receipts, tour schedules, articles, tickets, concert photos . . . now she's on the phone with another lawyer, one recommended by the W&W moms.

There's no escaping Korey. He's everywhere. I'm back in that house again, door locked, trapped. And this time, I've brought my family and friends with me.

I dial the number and slip into the bathroom, throwing the shower on to buffer the sound.

"Jessica. It's Enchanted."

There's a brief pause on the other end of the line.

"Oh. You," she says, voice seething. "What do YOU want?"

"I need to speak with Korey."

Another long pause. Mumbling. She's talking to someone.

"Well . . . I'm not with him. He's in New York."

The phone is on speaker now. Korey must be with her.

"I know that. He's been stalking me," I snap, hoping the words burn him.

"Ha! More delusions."

"What does that mean?"

"Nothing. So why are you calling me?"

"Because you know how to get in touch with him."

"So?"

"So, tell him . . . I'll give him what he wants."

Silence. Whatever car she's in sounds like it's driving down a highway.

"I'll . . . relay the message."

Click.


There are steps you need to take to buy back your life:

First, you need to run away from home.

Next, you need to spend the little money you have on a cab from Metro-North station to the Upper West Side.

Next, you have to meet the devil at his penthouse, right above his studio.

Then, you have to brace your body for what's to come.

• • •

The place is just like his home in Atlanta, the cream foam on top of black coffee. I'm dressed in his favorite: tank top, jeans, Melissa on my head. Maybe seeing me this way will soften him. I'll be on my knees begging for my life soon. The thought makes me gag.

"Made you your favorite," he says, dancing the Styrofoam cup in his hand toward me.

The sweet scent of purple drink makes my throat scorch, like I've never been so thirsty in my entire life. Without hesitating, I clasp my hands around the cup, needing the liquid courage.

One sip. Then another. It's . . . stronger than I remember. On the giant TV, a video game is set on pause.

"Baby, I'm so happy you're here. You look beautiful. Let me give you a tour."

The tour was short. A quick walk from his living room to his massive bedroom. Cream from head to toe. Dim mood lighting. Another TV set to Netflix. On the dresser is Flounder.

"You still have it," I say, surprised.

"Well . . . yeah. That was one of the best days of my life."

I look up at him, feeling my heart soften, willing it not to.

"So, what do you want to watch?" he asks, plopping onto the bed. "*Swiss Family Robinson? Mighty Ducks?* How about *Pocahontas?*"

I sip again. "Can I . . . ask you a question?"

"Anything."

"You've heard me talk about Gab, right?"

He smiles. "Yeah. You said she's the exact opposite of you."

See, everyone? I'm not crazy. I swallow the cry building in the back of my throat but with another sip and the sight of his bed . . . knowing what I have to do, the tears bubble up.

Korey swoops in, gathering me in his arms.

"If you would've just listened," he coos into Melissa, caressing her.

A fish hook pierces my back and I reel away from him. He sways on his feet. Don't think I've seen him this drunk this fast before. But I also can't see too good.

"Crazy how all that happened, right?" he chuckles. "You've seen the tape? Here, let's watch it together."

He presses play on the big flat-screen. The video is clearer than the ones I've seen on blogs. It's the original. I move closer, cocking my head to the side.

Without the distortion, it's clearly not me. But it's someone . . . familiar.

I stare at him, revolted by his sleazy grin.

"You're sick," I slur out sleepily, the room growing fuzzy.

Korey is on top of me, hands everywhere.

"Leave me alone."

"Shhhh . . . just relax."

"Nooo," I moan, my arms heavy.

"I'm still making them mortgage payments," he whispers . . . from somewhere. "I'm still paying for school. You want Shea to go to a good school, right?"

Her name in his mouth makes my stomach curl.

"Get away from me," I shout, pushing him. Or I thought I shouted. Because next thing I know, my cup drops. My shirt is wet. He strikes me, then again, and the carpet nuzzles to my face before the room goes dark.

# Part Four

# Chapter 73

## BEET JUICE 5

*NOW*

"We have to get her to a hospital. . . . That can wait. She's scared. Hang on, now! You don't have to be so rough!"

The cuffs are cold. That's what I notice first. Sharp shards of ice pinching around my wrist. Hands patting down my jean pockets. The taste of drywall I'm pressed into.

"You don't have to be so rough! She's just a baby! You don't have to do her like that!"

I'm vaguely aware of Daddy begging nearby. All I can focus on is my bare feet, now in flip-flops. Flip-flops that are not mine. Are they Korey's wife's? Forgot about her.

Someone shouts, "Multiple stab wounds."

I had a feeling. Only that much blood can paint a room red.

• • •

*Transcript with LaToya Jones—May 21*

**Detective Arnold:** Detective Arnold. Homicide. Please, sit.

**LaToya Jones:** When can I see my daughter?

**Arnold:** You realize your daughter was the only one found at the scene of the crime?

**L. Jones:** She said she didn't do it. You saw her eyes when they brought her in here? She was clearly drugged. Something happened.

**Arnold:** Where were you last night?

**L. Jones:** Are you serious? I was at work!

**Arnold:** Is there a record of your shift?

**L. Jones:** I didn't clock in. The moment I arrived, victims were coming in from a five-alarm fire.

**Arnold:** So did anyone see you?

**L. Jones:** Of course, the other nurses on duty.

**Arnold:** Your friends.

**L. Jones:** My colleagues.

**Arnold:** Are these your text messages?

**L. Jones:** [long pause] Yes.

**Arnold:** For the record, Mrs. Jones is looking at copies of text messages sent to Mr. Korey Fields. Quote: "If you don't give me back my daughter, I'm going to put a bullet in your ass." Unquote. These text messages are pretty extreme.

**L. Jones:** I was upset! He kidnapped my daughter.

**Arnold:** But according to interviews you had with Detective Fletcher, you gave permission for your daughter to go with him.

**L. Jones:** I gave permission for a tour and promises were made. He broke those promises and our trust!

**Arnold:** You made several welfare check requests with the DeKalb County Police, in Georgia, correct?

**L. Jones:** Yes. It was all that I could do.

**Arnold:** And when you didn't get your desired outcome . . .

**L. Jones:** I called again and again. You not hearing me. That's my CHILD. I would walk through fire to get my child back.

**Arnold:** But during each of those welfare checks, Enchanted indicated she was fine. That she wanted to stay with Korey.

**L. Jones:** She was brainwashed. You can speak to her psychiatrist. She didn't know what she was doing.

**Arnold:** Are you sure this isn't all about money you were expecting?

**L. Jones:** HA! Please! Let me see the receipts of the money he's given us. 'Cause that man hasn't given us a dime!

**Arnold:** This isn't funny at all. A man was murdered! You could show some respect.

**L. Jones:** When are y'all gonna start showing us some? We went to the police to file a report against him, and them detectives gave my daughter the third degree like she was the one who did something, not that monster!

**Arnold:** Mrs. Jones, according to E-ZPass records, your car clocked into the toll entering Henry Hudson Parkway, southbound around 11:14 p.m., approximately one hour before Korey Fields was murdered. Care to explain?

**L. Jones:** What? I . . . that wasn't me.

**Arnold:** No? So who was it?

**L. Jones:** [long pause] My . . . husband had my car that night. We switched since he was picking up the kids.

**Arnold:** Why would he need to go to the city?

**L. Jones:** I guess . . . he was looking for Enchanted.

# Chapter 74

## PETER PAN

The Will and Willow moms hook me up with a no-nonsense lawyer named Seth Pulley. He has jet-black wavy hair, crisp blue eyes, and a lisp. He organizes papers and files on the table as I gently yank at the cuffs chaining me to the chair. The fluorescent light burns my eyelids.

"What's happening now?" I ask. "Out there. No one will tell me."

Mr. Pulley sighs. "Out there, the world is taking it pretty hard. Their favorite superstar was killed. They're in mourning. But I wouldn't worry about all that for now."

I can imagine Korey's memorial news reports. The photo collages on Instagram, top trending topic on Twitter.

"So everyone hates me," I state, slumping in my chair. "They have no idea who he really is. Was."

Mr. Pulley takes out a ballpoint pen. "I'm not going to lie to you, Enchanted," he says, straight to business. "You are public enemy number one."

I close my eyes and try to float out the room. When I open them, I'm still in a cage, surrounded by metal bars. A cage, not much different from my room in Atlanta, in a uniform just as baggy as the track suits he made us wear. Panic eats through my bones. Trapped again.

This is really happening.

"The good news: it's been almost forty-eight hours," Mr. Pulley says as he reads through some paperwork. "Meaning, they don't have enough for a formal arrest warrant, and they'll release you sometime this evening. But the evidence they're gathering is more than circumstantial. Being at the scene of the crime, partial prints on the weapon, and for the number of stab wounds, you would have had to hold that knife pretty firmly. There are also footprints they are trying to identify. They don't think you worked alone. Could have enough for formal charges as early as next week."

My tongue is too dry to moisten my quivering chapped lips. "I didn't kill him. I swear I didn't kill him! I wouldn't."

Mr. Pulley pats my hand. "I know, hon. But let's not worry about that for now. How about you tell me everything that you remember?"

• • •

Tonight's movie: *Peter Pan*.

The Littles sit on the opposite side of the sofa, clutching Shea, sneaking peeks at me every few minutes. They've been locked in the house ever since the media caught wind of where we lived, taking over our once-quiet street, circling like sharks.

In the kitchen, Mom and Daddy pore over some paperwork on the table, their backs to us, Mom quietly sobbing.

"All you need is faith, trust, and a little pixie dust."

Peter Pan kind of reminds me of Korey. Flying high on blissful thoughts, he was fine never growing up, wanted to stay a kid forever. He was also forgetful, self-centered, and cocky enough to put himself in danger, skating by without consequence over and over again.

Meanwhile, all I wanted to do was grow up fast, love him hard, and sing around the world. But the adult world pushed me down a plank and fed me to the crocodiles.

Maybe Korey had the right idea all along.

My phone buzzes. An unknown number.

Gab?

"Hello?"

"You're fucking dead, bitch!"

"W-w-w-what?"

"You're fucking dead! If I see you, I'm slicing your fucking throat, you little slut."

The line drops and I look at Shea. The voice was loud enough for her to hear.

She stares back then sighs, returning to the movie.

# *Chapter 75*

## PICTURES WORTH A THOUSAND WORDS

There are so many pictures of Korey when he was younger. Every news outlet shows them on repeat.

"Did you know Korey Fields couldn't read a single sheet's worth of music? He could just about play any instrument you put in front of him using his ear, like a blind man."

I scroll through the various feeds. Mom said to stay away from the news, but I can't help it. Seeing young Korey makes me long for the Korey I thought I knew. The big kid trapped in a man's body.

I scroll to another picture of Korey, standing next to Richie. Back then, he barely reached Richie's chest, hair in slick corn-rows, dressed in baggy clothes. The caption reads, "Grammy After-party. Luv U 4eva KF!" This was the party he told me about, where he lost his virginity. I flip to the next photo and my jaw hits the floor, at the woman standing next to him, his skinny arm wrapped around her tiny waist, his head just at her breast. Her hair is different, blond finger waves. Her face is different too. But I recognize her.

Jessica.

To anyone else, the photo would seem innocent. But something about the way she leans into his arms, his childlike arms, makes my stomach clench. I click on another link and it brings me to a Facebook post with almost three hundred comments:

---

**If you mourning him, you're mourning a pedophile!**

Pedophile? She was a GROWN ass woman.

Bruh, GROWN ain't SEVENTEEN

She didn't look seventeen. *shrugs*

But once you find out she's 17, you still gonna smash?

---

**So we just gonna jump and believe this girl?**

He abused other women too!

That wasn't proven. Just a bunch of settlements.

Children lie when they get caught doing something they not
   supposed to! That's what they do!

A group of children who don't know each other can't ALL be
   lying. That's called a pattern. That should be enough proof!

---

**You know there are three sides to every story: her side,
his side, and the truth.**

---

There's also FACT. And FACT is no man should be sleeping
    with a seventeen-year-old GIRL! PERIOD!

You see her body? Walking around in them tight dresses. She
    was just tempting him. Another fast ass girl.

Why are we blaming/shaming little black girls/women for being
    "fast" when they're simply being themselves? For just BEING.

What a woman wears or doesn't wear doesn't give anyone the
    right to touch them.

**Well, you know he's had a rough childhood. Abandoned
by his mom, didn't know his father, raised by his grandma
who passed.**

We've all BEEN through a lot but that don't give you no excuse
    to abuse girls.

You know how these groupies do. They was lookin' for a come
    up and didn't get what they wanted now they coming for the
    brother's neck. They were about that dolla dolla bill!

Money doesn't give anyone permission to treat them like an
    animal.

**You know that girl's probably from a broken home. Ain't
got no real man in her life to set an example.**

Did you pull a muscle with that reach? She was in Will and
    Willow and her parents are married.

Just cause a girl from a broken home, don't mean you get to
    piss on her. What the fuck is wrong with y'all?

**So why are we not just as angry at the parents who gave permission and took his money is my only question. Isn't it they job first to protect they daughter? IJS, charge them too they the pimps.**

Why is everyone so busy trying to find ANYONE to blame instead of the person actually responsible for committing a crime?

Everyone that worked for him knew those girls were too young and yet they let them.

If that was my daughter, he'd be six feet under.

**Where was all this outrage when the priest story came out? Or Weinstein? Wake the fuck up people! We rather talk shit about our own people, while you got a white man in the White House that clearly fucked up in the mind.**

I can walk and chew bubble gum at the same time bruh.

Still, how many Black Men are in prison because of something some chick said?

Don't care. Black white blue orange-haired. LOCK THEM UP.

Yo, don't all-lives-matter this. We ain't saying the other shit ain't wrong either. But we talking about BLACK WOMEN right now. That's it. FOCUS!

If these were white girls, Korey would be cremated and thrown in the sewer.

**I met my husband at 16 and he was 20. I don't see the problem with dating an older man.**

Yeah but your husband didn't abuse you. Didn't lock you in your
   room with nothing but a bucket.
Y'all talking about some imaginary sex dungeon that no one
   has ever seen.
So the girls word are not enough? Why don't people EVER
   believe women?
Why didn't she just leave?
She was being brainwashed.
Brainwashed? That's bullshit.
You never heard of a cult? Were you born yesterday?
FAKE NEWS!

**Yo, Malcolm X said it best. "The most disrespected
person in America is the Black woman. The most
unprotected person in America is the Black woman.
The most neglected person in America is the Black
woman."**

# *Chapter 76*

## THE OTHER WOMAN

Korey's wife . . . isn't what you'd expect.

She's a short, bite-size, petite woman. So short, they have to adjust the mic at the podium during the televised press conference. She's fair skinned with bright hazel eyes, dressed in black pants and a modest knit sweater. None of this really surprises me. It's her auburn pixie cut that gives me pause.

I think of Melissa and the way she made my scalp itch. The way she stuck to my sticky lip gloss whenever I turned my head. The way I glued her to my forehead, used a toothbrush to lay down her edges with gel. One hair out of place would enrage Korey.

Korey liked women with long hair. This woman couldn't

possibly be his wife.

But, through tears, she steps to the mic with the help of Tony, reading off a printed piece of paper.

"I typically wouldn't address the press. I always let my husband take all the shine. But he's gone. Someone took him from us in a senseless, cruel act of violence."

She looks directly at me through the TV, speaking like a Broadway actress, voice projecting . . . just like Korey taught me. My spine stiffens, and I glance across the living room.

"Did you know he was married?"

Louie stares at the TV, frowning. "Nah. Apparently, no one knew. Just people in his close circle. I've never seen her before in my life. Yo, should you be watching this?"

I nod. I needed to see her. I needed to see the other woman.

Cameras click, sounding like a forest of bugs. There's a dramatic pause as she tilts her chin up, blinking back tears.

"Korey was a loving, devoted, faithful husband. A brilliant songwriter and singer. A living legend and philanthropist. These . . . disgusting allegations against him are inexcusable, especially when he is unable to defend himself. There are people trying to sully his good name when all he ever did was love his fans voraciously."

"What allegations?" I ask Louie. "What is she talking about?"

"Some women are coming forward, claiming they were abused by Korey." Louie looks at me. "I say that to say, you weren't alone."

This doesn't make me feel better. Only angrier.

"We look forward to when justice will finally be served, and the real monster will be behind bars for good."

She thinks I'm a monster yet knows Korey. Intimately. We lived in that house for months, touring for weeks. I never saw her, not even once. How could she not have known?

As Korey's wife wraps up the press conference, I peep Jessica in the shadows. Cheeks sunken, dark glasses, black suit, her mouth a crooked scribble of a line. Even after everything, I feel kind of bad for her. Korey was the earth she rotated around daily. Now, he's gone and she's lost in deep space.

It's what I've felt daily. Except I'm floating in the ocean, farther and farther away from the shore that is supposed to ground me.

That's when it sinks in—Korey's really gone. A rough lump the shape of coral lodges in my throat.

"Excuse me," I whimper and race to the bathroom, chest caving in.

How can he be dead? We were supposed to sing together forever. He loved me, with a heart too big for his body so it leaked into his lungs, giving him a voice dripping with honey. Who sang with passion and made everyone believe they could be anything. Now the world will never hear his voice again.

Shouldn't I be happy? Relieved instead of torn and crumbling at the idea that the only love I've ever known was also my greatest torturer?

Love is complicated, he would say. But love shouldn't hurt. And deep down, I know I went to his apartment that night hoping he'd change. I was always hoping he'd change. But you can't hope or wish someone to be anyone that they're not.

My phone buzzes. Another unknown number and I'm tempted to answer, listen to the same woman threatening to kill me. I deserve it.

A news anchor cuts through my thoughts.

"And we have exclusive footage obtained of the suspect's father, Terry Jones, seen outside Korey Fields's apartment the night of the murder."

I rip the door open. "Wait, what?"

Louie is on his feet, turning up the volume. The video is blurry, black and white, taken from a distance, outside Korey's building. But there's Daddy, storming inside the building, at eleven thirty p.m.

"Whoa," Louie mumbles. "Where the hell is he going?"

# Chapter 77

## THE REAL HERO

The more time goes on, the more I see what Daddy went through while I was gone and how his quiet suffering wasn't so silent after all.

There's video footage of Daddy outside our hotel in Charlotte.

Footage of Daddy kicking and screaming while Tony and his goons tossed him around like a rag doll in the hotel parking lot.

Footage of Daddy on the phone in the lobby of our Columbia hotel, calling about the suicide pact, hoping it would draw me outside.

Footage of Daddy outside Korey's mansion, waiting for the police to do another welfare check.

The media has twisted it. They see Daddy stalking Korey . . . I see Daddy trying to save me this whole time.

*Transcript with Terry Jones—May 26*

**Detective Arnold:** I understand you've been unemployed the last five months.

**Terry Jones:** Not unemployed. Our union is on strike.

**Detective Arnold:** So you've had plenty of time to make trips down South.

**T. Jones:** Yeah. And I'd do it again. The man had my daughter.

**Detective Arnold:** Did it make you feel like less of a man that you couldn't protect your daughter?

**T. Jones:** Really? That's all you got?

**Detective Arnold:** OK. Tell us about what happened the night of the murder.

**T. Jones:** Front-door security turned me away. I told them my daughter was up there, but they wouldn't let me in.

**Detective Arnold:** And that's when you called the police?

**T. Jones:** Yeah. But they said there was nothing they could do since she's eighteen. That's when that woman came. Jessica or whoever.

**Detective Arnold:** So you're saying you never went inside the apartment?

**T. Jones:** If only I was given the chance . . . I
  wouldn't have killed him, but he'd be walking
  with a limp for the rest of his life.

*Knocking*

**Fletcher:** Hey! Sorry to interrupt but you better
  get down to the Marriott. Now!

**Detective Arnold:** What's going on? We're in the
  middle of questioning!

**T. Jones:** What's wrong? Is Enchanted OK?

**Fletcher:** She was attacked.

# Chapter 78

## PRESS CONFERENCE

The entire ballroom of the Marriott Hotel in Times Square is full of reporters. Louie said there would be limited seating, but that rule has already been broken.

Louie and Mr. Pulley decided to set up a press conference to counter all the negative talk and stop rumors.

"Normally I wouldn't suggest this," Mr. Pulley says in our hotel room. "But I think it would help. Plus, we need other victims to corroborate your claim that he abused you. I typed up a statement. You're going to remind them that you're a student, active on the swim team, a Will and Willow sister, aspiring singer and songwriter. Remind them that you're a victim as well."

They think putting me in front of the camera, showing that I'm just a kid, will help produce some sympathy, garner understanding, and maybe even stop the death threats. The same woman keeps calling. I know I should tell Mom, but she may change my number again and . . . I'm still holding out hope that somehow, some way, Gab will call.

"It's ridiculous to think Mr. Jones would set up his own daughter, the one he's been trying to retrieve after months in captivity, for the murder of Mr. Fields," Mr. Pulley says from the small podium on the platform stage. We stand on the sidelines, watching him address reporters. Behind me, Mom gives my shoulders a gentle squeeze.

"I'm going to let Enchanted speak in her own words about her time with Mr. Fields."

I should be used to walking out onstage in front of a packed crowd, full of cameras and gawking eyes. But this time, there's no warm applause. No cheering. In fact, the room drops in temperature. A collective breath holds.

"Um. Hello," I mutter, gripping my printed speech.

No one responds. Utter silence, a room full of frozen statues. Except one person. A woman, moving closer to the stage. For a moment I'm confused, thinking she's staff.

"You fucking bitch!"

She launches something in her hand toward the stage, toward me.

"ENCHANTED!" Mom screams before I duck. A brick flies over my head and crashes behind me. I pop up just as the woman reaches me, a knife in hand.

All the blood rushes to my feet as I scramble to flee but trip over the brick, landing on my knees, and she gives me one swift kick to my side.

"Fucking slut," she barks.

My ribs flare. I'm going to die. Here, onstage, the only place I ever wanted to be. I close my eyes, bracing for the pain as feet scuffle around me, security rushing in.

"Enchanted!" Mom grabs me, leading me off the stage. "Baby, are you OK? Are you hurt?"

The room explodes into chaos, cameras clicking.

"I'ma kill you, you bitch! He never loved you, stupid Bright Eyes!"

Bright Eyes?

I whip around, her wild eyes locked on me as she's carried out of the ballroom, screaming. She's sickly thin, tall . . . with a wig similar to Melissa. Her voice is familiar, and it doesn't take long to realize it's the woman from the anonymous phone calls.

But . . . how did she know about Bright Eyes?

"Get her out of here now!" Louie screams from somewhere as we pour into the opposite hallway.

Bodies bump into me. Security. Panic. Mayhem. A blond woman in a uniform. She's looking me in the eye. Is she trying to kill me too?

"What—"

"Take this," she whispers, stuffing something in my pocket, then passes by quick. Too quick for Mom to notice before I'm whisked away to the elevator, and up to our room.

Mom is on the phone with Dad, hysterical, and I slip into the bathroom to retrieve the ripped notebook paper.

*Meet at 421 Broadway for a KA meeting. Friday,*
*10 a.m. There are others.*
*You're not alone.*

# Chapter 79
## FUNERAL

Rain roars hard against the roof, lightning sparking through the gray fog. A flash flood warning sounds off. Every phone in the diner wails of it.

Including Derrick's.

"Thanks for risking your life to come visit me."

He chuckles. "Anything is better than being home right now."

Derrick and I sit in a booth in the town's staple diner, sipping chocolate milkshakes. The place is classic with a bar counter, mini jukeboxes on the tables, and decor they haven't changed since the eighties. I don't come often, but their fish sticks and sweet potato fries are pretty on point. I've had them here with Gab after school. The very Gab they say is a figment of my imagination.

I glance outside at the rain pummeling the fresh spring flowers, puddles turning into lakes.

The perfect day for a funeral.

"Figured you'd want some company today," Derrick says, hinting at the box TV mounted above the pumpkin-haired woman at the register, set on CNN. No sense in asking to change it. Almost every news station is showing the same thing.

Korey Fields's funeral is a massive A-list event being held at Madison Square Garden, the largest convention center in the city. Lines started forming before five a.m.

"I heard he got a gold casket. Like Michael Jackson," Derrick quips.

"Kinda fitting, right?"

"Ouch. Too soon."

I chuckle, throwing a fry at him. "You didn't want to go to the funeral?"

"My dad wanted me to. But . . . I'd rather stick glass in my eyes. Ain't no way I'm going to celebrate the life of that asshole."

"We are of the minority."

He shrugs. "Fine with me."

"So you're cool hanging out with an alleged murderer?"

"Man, if you really did kill him . . . I wouldn't blame you. I saw you in that house. No one else did. But I saw."

We stare at each other.

"I'm glad he's dead," he admits.

"Why?"

"He hurt you. He hurt those other girls. He hurt . . . everybody."

Derrick bites into a juicy cheeseburger deluxe. Gab loved the burgers here too. The thought of her makes me lose my appetite, our memories playing on repeat. Who could make up a laugh like hers? Her smile? I want to walk around to every person we ever met to say *Don't you remember her?* But I don't have one picture to prove she's real.

"Everyone thinks I'm crazy."

"Well, are you?" he asks.

I stir my milkshake. "I keep having these moments . . . where I'll remember things so clearly and know exactly what I'm talking about, only for people to tell me I'm wrong."

Derrick gives me a faint smile. "Reminds me of this picture my mom has in her office. It's fire. Maybe I'll show you someday."

"Don't think your dad would like it if I came to your house."

Derrick's face goes dark. "Well. He ain't living with us right now."

"Why?"

"Can't keep his dick in his pants. Ever."

"Oh. I'm sorry."

"It's whatever. He still comes by to get his shit every now and then. Still gotta be nice to him, 'cause he's really my only shot at breaking into the business after college."

Reminds me of Korey. How I felt there was no way I could

make a name for myself without him. Now I have a name, but not the one I wanted.

"I bet you can find another way," I offer.

"He came over after he found out what happened, all broken up and shaking. He was just with Korey that day," he says, eyeing his burger before glancing at the TV. "Speak of the devil."

On the screen, Richie is onstage, dressed in a dark gray suit with black glasses, giving some kind of speech. I can't tell since it's on mute. I almost turn away when the light hits his wrist at a certain angle . . .

"Oh my God," I gasp.

"What?"

I jump to my feet, moving closer, and I'm right. It's his watch. It's Korey's watch.

"What's up?" Derrick asks. "What's wrong?"

My mind runs full throttle, remembering Korey's words.

*"There's only one like it . . ."*

Derrick is by my side, worry in his eyes. But I can't tell him. As mad as he is . . . I'm not sure where his loyalty lies.

"Um, it's nothing."

When Richie steps off stage, he sits next to Jessica. And something strange passes between them. They clasp hands for a few seconds too long before releasing.

I look to see if Derrick notices. "What do you know about Jessica?"

He shrugs, paying the bill. "Jessica has probably been around the longest. She used to sing. My dad found her at some talent contest in Texas and introduced her to Korey. Always says he would do anything for her."

Derrick doesn't know.

Outside, the rain lets up, but the clouds remain, dark and threatening.

# Chapter 80

## THERE'S ONLY ONE LIKE IT

"You have some fucking nerve calling me after what you've done!"

Jessica is scalding hot. I'm surprised she even answered. So I don't give her time to hang up on me before I ask the question.

"Did you see the picture I sent you? The watch? Do you recognize it?"

"I shouldn't be talking to a killer," she seethes.

I wipe the acid off my face. First time someone's called me a murderer.

"The watch. In the screenshot. It's Korey's, right? Korey was wearing it when I saw him that night. He never took it off—you know that. It has his grandma's diamonds in the center."

"He . . . told you that," she murmurs in utter disbelief.

"Yeah. So how did Richie get it?"

Silence.

"What?"

"Richie has Korey's watch. He was wearing it at the funeral."

More silence. More breathing.

"Jessica, please. Just tell me, how did Richie get Korey's watch?"

"Why should I tell you anything? Everything that's happened has been because of you. Korey went crazy after you left him. He couldn't eat, sleep, or record. He loved you. More than anyone. Did you know that? He moved heaven and earth for you."

"You think it's right for him to love a kid?"

"You weren't a child! You knew exactly what you were doing."

"I was doing what he told me to do," I snap back. "But that doesn't matter anymore, Jessica. He's dead. I didn't kill him. I don't remember much, but I know he had his watch on that night. So how did Richie get it?"

Jessica takes a deep breath, righting herself.

"I don't know what you're talking about," she says in an impossibly calm voice. "Don't fucking call me again."

The phone clicks.

# Chapter 81

## CHARGED

"They've found sufficient evidence for an arrest warrant," Mr. Pulley says from across his desk, face sagging, as if already defeated. "Now that you're eighteen, they can try you as an adult."

Mom's bottom lip trembles as tears fall. Daddy rubs her shoulders.

A sob climbs up my throat. "I didn't do it, Mr. Pulley. I swear I didn't."

"I know, sweetheart. I know. But we should think about strategy. I spoke to the DA's office and worked it out that you'll turn yourself in on Friday morning."

Mr. Pulley continues going over our options, suggesting expert witnesses and psych evaluations, my PTSD diagnosis key to our defense. The question floats around my head until it nearly drowns me, and I gasp for air.

"Do you have a report of what they found on Korey?" I blurt out.

Mr. Pulley raises an eyebrow. "What do you mean?"

"Like, one of those lists of all the items they found on his, um, body?"

"What you wanna know about that for?" Mom asks, Daddy still holding her hand.

Mr. Pulley gives me a curious glance but combs through his files.

"Yeah, uh, sure. Right here."

I scan down the itemized list. No watch. But I know I saw the watch. I remember the light hitting it before he hit me.

Or am I confusing that with Atlanta? It's all a blur . . .

"What are you looking for?"

All the grown-ups in the room stare at me. I grip the folder, weighing my options. If I tell them what I'm thinking, they may think I'm really crazy. Not even sure if the theory makes sense, and I hate upsetting Mom. If only there was a way to prove that watch was on Korey.

"Um, nothing."

Mr. Pulley raises an eyebrow. "Enchanted, is there anything you want to tell me?"

I shake my head.

"OK. Well . . . you'll have two days to turn yourself in. I suggest you . . . spend time with your family. Then be ready to fight like hell!"

# Chapter 82
## A VISIT

As birds chirp to the rising sun, I hear the unmistakable sounds of an old clanking engine puttering to a stop in the driveway. The squeaky storm door slams. Then Mom's snappy voice interrupts the peace of the morning.

"What are you doing here? And at this time of day!"

"I still get the news," a woman answers back, and my chest tightens.

Silence falls between them.

"All right, come on then," Mom yells. "Let's hear it!"

"Hear what?" the woman says, amused.

"The 'I told you so' speech. Go on. That's what you came here for, right?"

"Don't need to tell you something you already know."

Her words cut deep. They always have.

"Now, can I see my granddaughter or are you going to keep me out here all day?"

"We . . . have to bring her in tomorrow," Mom sniffles through tears.

"Then let me have today."

In the distance, green water spirals into waves, barreling toward me. I tread for a moment, then kick hard in their direction, before they're too treacherous, and split them sideways.

The waves foam white as they hit the sandy shore. Nearby, Grandma pops up from under the water.

"Ooo . . . water nippy today. Skin can't seem to get warm."

From some angles, Grandma looks like Ursula from *The Little Mermaid*. A shock of short snow-white hair, skin a tint of purple, a round tummy, and a boisterous laugh, her tentacles everywhere at once, enough to wrangle me and the Littles.

We're buoyed in silence as another wave forms in the distance. I swim toward it, Grandma on my tail. Even at her old age, Grandma is an excellent swimmer. Taught me everything I know about the unpredictable ocean, its propensity for violence. Those lessons were lost on land.

There are only a few dedicated swimmers and surfers out here. In early June, the water still has a bit of winter's chill, not the warm bath conditions we have in the summers. The water sinks its icy teeth into us but feels just fine to me.

"So. How long we gonna float out here? Getting late. Think

we should head in? Maybe pick up some Popeye's on the way home? Crispy shrimp?"

The salt water burns the back of my throat. Nearby, a plastic bag floats and I think of the jellyfish. I can almost feel the remnants of his sting, the force of his hit, the rage in his eyes, the ice bucket . . .

I turn, waiting for the next wave.

She chuckles. "I guess not."

"Just a little while longer," I finally say.

Don't know when I'll be able to do this again.

There's a rancid smell in Grandma's apartment that makes it impossible to eat.

As she fixes us hot cocoa in the kitchen, I search for the culprit, digging through boxes of old newspapers, bags of empty plastic bottles, and crates of records piled to the ceiling, blocking the sunset. Behind another set of boxes in the corner is an old empty fish tank. I peer at the horror inside.

"Um, Grandma . . . I think the turtle is dead."

She scoffs. "No, it's not, honey. He's being silly. Come on now, before your cocoa gets cold."

I draw in a breath, re-covering the tank and cracking a window to air out the suffocating stench. We sit in the dark living room, watching her old box TV with the funny clicker remote. Daddy set up her Amazon fire stick to watch, but she's committed to basic channels.

Her home has either shrunk or I've grown. I always considered this place a castle, but now I see it for what it really is. The clutter, the random articles from the beach she found with her metal detector. Forks, spoons, half-broken jewelry. She was fascinated by humans' trash. Just like Ariel. It was the perfect house for that hoarder show Shea likes to watch.

How did we all fit in here before?

"Grandma?"

"Yes, honey?"

"What happened when you found out you were sick?"

She laughs. "I'm not sick, baby. That's the problem. I see things clear as day. It's everyone else that don't see what's right in front of them. People see what they want to see all the time."

I nod, cooling my cup.

Grandma glances at the chair next to her. "Oh no, she wouldn't want to do that."

I look at the empty chair then back to her. "Do what?"

Grandma giggles, waving me off. "Oh nothing, you know they just love your voice, that's all. They want you to sing."

The empty chair says nothing.

"Um, sure, Grandma. Why not?"

Grandma nods at the chair. "Ain't my grandbaby something? Y'all say thank you. Not every day we get a real star in here."

The crates of old vinyls are covered in two years' worth of dust.

"OK, you want some Whitney or Aretha?"

"No, we need a classic! We just came from the sea! They want that!"

"Little Mermaid?"

"Yes! That's the one."

"OK, Grandma," I laugh.

I sing "Part of Your World," which is always fun, singing a cappella, something I haven't done in a while. My voice is raw, unhinged even. Something about being back here, performing in the place I found my voice feels . . . different.

Grandma sways as she listens, glancing over at the empty seat, nodding in agreement, then claps when I'm done.

"You know why I like that movie?"

"Because you like my singing and know I like to swim?"

"Ha! Well, that too. But no, I liked it 'cause the princess saved herself."

"No, she didn't. Eric saved her, the prince. And her dad, the king."

"No, no," she laughs, the light from the TV bouncing off her dark skin. "She saved herself from the sea long before that silly prince came flopping along. She took hold of her life, didn't care what anyone else had to think or say. Even if they thought she was crazy, she did what she wanted, and folks just had to deal. Like when you cut off all your hair. You didn't care—you just did it! Some brave guts you've always had. Get that from my side of the family."

Grandma sips her hot cocoa, allowing the chocolate milk mustache to sit on her top lip. I glance around the room again, refocusing my lens to what this place used to be. A treasure trove of the most wondrous things.

"Grandma . . . I'm in trouble."

She nods. "Yes, baby. You are."

"And I don't know what to do."

"Well, what would Ariel do?"

"Maybe run away from home?" I chuckle. "Trade her voice for some legs?"

Grandma shrugs and flips a few channels, humming, landing on E! News. There's Richie. Talking about the upcoming Korey documentary. No watch on his wrist. Jessica must have told him. I doubt she'd take it, knowing how it could implicate her. She's smarter than Richie. She must have told him to get rid of it. But he wouldn't throw it away, and he couldn't be dumb enough to pawn it. So he must still have it . . . somewhere.

"Grandma, I have to go."

"Where to?"

I smirk, zipping up my hoodie. "To save myself."

Grandma smiles. "OK, baby. Have fun."

# Chapter 83

## FAMILY OVER EVERYTHING

"Hey! Surprised you called," Derrick says, opening up the peach french doors to his Upper West Side condo.

"Was in the neighborhood," I lie. The hour-and-change commute from Queens into Manhattan gave me enough time to brainstorm all the lies I'm about to tell him.

"Well, I'm glad you're here. Heard about the charges. I'm . . . sorry, Enchanted."

He rubs my shoulders and I lean into his warm hands. It feels good to be held. Something I miss . . . with Korey.

Panic beats against my chest, and I step back, turning in a circle.

He's not here, Enchanted. Korey is not here. You're safe.

"Hey, you OK?" Derrick asks as I rub my temples, trying to regain control.

"Uh, yeah. So, is your dad stopping by any time soon?"

"Nah. And my mom is on some business trip. It's just us two."

There's a hunger in his eyes that makes me fidget.

"Um, you said you wanted to show me a photo?"

"Oh! Yeah! Come on, it's in here."

Derrick's home is lavish. High ceilings, crystal chandeliers, gold fixtures, rose-colored furniture, and enough plants to make a greenhouse jealous. Pictures of Richie with all kinds of music royalty hung up in every available space.

We pass three bedrooms, one with a double door and a gold lion painting.

Must be the master bedroom.

"Right in here," Derrick says, making a sharp left into the pink-and-leopard office. On the wall is a giant framed black-and-white photo of a black woman, her back to us, pouring out water from a metal pitcher from one hand, in the other a plastic jug.

I read the script underneath: She saw him disappear by the river. They asked her to tell what happened, only to discount her memory.

The arresting simplicity draws me in by the collar. So many messages, so gripping, and so . . . spot on.

"It's called *Waterbearer* by Lorna Simpson. I think my mom studied her in college or something. She loves art. Got stuff all over the house, but this one is my favorite."

"Why?"

He shrugs. "I mean, I ain't a black woman or nothing, but I guess I kinda get it. No one ever believes y'all."

A nerve is plucked like a violin string, the note ringing in my ear.

"Hey, you want to watch a movie or something?" I ask, bouncing on the balls of my feet.

"Sure! We can catch up on some *Love and Hip Hop.*"

"Cool!"

We kick it in his giant movie-theater-style den, complete with a large projector screen and reclining leather seats. I wait at least fifteen minutes before standing up.

"Uh, bathroom? Lady part problems."

His eyes widen. "Ohhhhh sure, straight down the hall."

In the bathroom, I turn on the faucet, crack the door open and creep past the den, using the plants as cover. I race down the hall, into the master bedroom, and trip over a tiger rug, stubbing my toe on a step stool.

"Shit," I whisper, biting a fist to suck in the pain, then hobble into the walk-in closet. Need to move fast.

I dig through the drawers, through all his pants pockets, blazers, shoes, socks, then move to the wife's side of the closet, her pants, her millions of shoes, her jewelry box. Nothing.

Derrick's voice booms behind me. "Yo, Chant!"

I whip around with a yelp. The room is empty, door still shut. I'm alone. Am I hearing things?

"Intercom system on the wall," he says, his voice muffled with static. "Press talk."

Intercom? I scan and rush across the room, to a box by the door, still gripping one of his mom's sweaters. Holding my breath, I stab the talk button and croak out a "Hello?"

Silence. More silence. Wait, can he tell I'm answering from his parents' room? Is he coming to look for me? Oh God . . .

"Hey, my bad," Derrick says. "Pops just text me, trying to roll through. Anyway, gonna order some Chinese food. You want anything?"

My brain clicks through its frozen gears. "Um, yeah. Shrimp lo mein. Please?"

"You ok? Need anything?"

"I'm good," I squeak, heart thumping. "Be right there."

Knees giving out, I collapse against the wall. Chinese food will buy me at least three extra minutes. The watch has to be here.

But what if his dad drops by?

Quickly, I rummage through hampers, dressers, and suitcases. Just as I'm about to give up, I spot another set of drawers by the nightstand. First one, papers. Second one, boxers. I scoop them to the side, finger flicking against something hard. I yank the drawer out farther.

Korey's watch ticks back at me.

With a tissue off the nightstand, I grab the watch just as the door swings open.

"What are you doing?"

Derrick's mouth hangs open, stunned to silence, and I'm momentarily relieved it's him and not Richie. He stares at the watch dangling in my hand, then at me.

"Derrick . . . it's not what you think . . ."

As I explain everything, the color drains from his face. He blinks twice and shakes his head.

"Nah. Pops and Korey . . . they've known each other forever. Korey is like a little brother to him! He wouldn't do that."

"He would for Jessica. He would do anything for her. You told me that."

A coating of realization melts into his skin, weighing him down. He leans on the door for support.

"Look," he mumbles. "I don't want to call the cops . . . so I think you should just leave whatever it is you found and go."

"But, Derrick, I *need* this watch. I need to prove that it wasn't me!"

"So you're gonna set up my *pops* instead?"

"No, no. Not set up . . . I saw Korey wearing it."

His face darkens. "And no one is going to believe you."

Cold sweat trickles down my back. "Derrick, I thought you were my friend."

"Put the watch down, Enchanted," he says, his voice clipped. "Even if you did take it, it wouldn't be enough to save you. He can just say Korey gave it to him. He was with him that day—easy alibi."

The key to freedom ticks in my hand.

"But I . . ."

"It's over, Enchanted. Don't pull my pops down with you."

In an instant, I know: no matter what I say, Derrick will always pick his father over me. I drop the watch. Along with my hopes.

"He's still my dad," he says to the floor as I pass. "Wouldn't you do anything to save your family?"

I give him one last look before heading out.

Derrick. Another apple that doesn't fall far from the tree.

## Chapter 84

# HOW TO WATCH THE SUN RISE

### AN OPEN LETTER FROM KA

The man publicly known as Korey Fields sold twenty million albums, toured around the world, and accumulated hundreds of millions of plays on radio and streaming services. During his rise to superstardom, he was also sued by at least four women for sexual misconduct, statutory rape, aggravated assault, unlawful restraint, and providing illegal drugs to minors in at least three different states.

We call on corporations with ties to Korey Fields's estate to insist on protecting and believing black women by proceeding with the investigation into his illegal actions. Together, let's end the devaluing of black girls and women.

We stand with Enchanted Jones and all the other women who have been assaulted by Korey Fields.

If you have been a victim of Korey Fields's abuse, please reach out to our organization. You are not alone.

—Korey Anonymous

Grandma always told me the sun rises in the east, sets in the west. I settled on a bench by the East River, thinking I would watch the sun rise. But the direction on the river isn't quite right. Still, it's a nice place to be during my last night/morning of freedom.

Mom must be worried sick, and Daddy is probably combing the streets looking for me, their phone calls endless. But I needed a moment to think. To be still. To read that open letter over and over. *I'm not alone*, it says. There were others.

Except I'm the only one going to prison. For something I didn't do, and there is nothing I can do about it. And how is it even possible for there to be so many? Korey couldn't have been in love with all of them. He couldn't have treated us all the same.

Could he?

I pull the crinkled note from my wallet.

*Meet at 421 Broadway for a KA meeting. Friday,*
*10 a.m. There are others.*
*You're not alone.*

• • •

Keeping my hoodie up, I enter a run-down office building in the thick of Chinatown, among the fruit stands and meat markets, and check the time. My phone is at five percent.

Ten a.m. The plan was to be at the police station two hours ago. But if I walk into that station, who knows if I'll ever know the full story. I have to take this last chance. Maybe someone has information on Jessica or Richie. Something that can help me.

The hallway is full of trash bags and dusty, discarded office furniture. The door to suite 8M squeaks as I shove it open. The room is dank and dark, blinds shut tight.

"You came!"

The woman who snuck up on me at the press conference is different today. Or maybe just herself—long blond streaky hair, tattoos up her arms, and a lip piercing.

"Yeah. But I can't stay long," I say, weary. "I . . . have to turn myself in today."

She nods. "I heard. I'm Cindy. Nice to officially meet you. This is Dawn, one of our private investigators."

Dawn is a cinnamon-skinned woman with thin bronze dreads, muscles pulsing through her forearms.

"Nice to meet you, Enchanted."

There is a scattering of about six women standing around the conference room, drinking coffee, nibbling on donut holes. Their chatter ceases the moment I pull back my hoodie.

"Oh, this isn't everyone, if that's what you're thinking,"

Dawn says. "Some people couldn't make it to New York. Some were just plain scared."

"They're still scared of Korey?"

"Not just of Korey. Of the systems surrounding him too. Most are still coping with the effects from their trauma. Depression, anxiety, paranoia, insomnia, even delusions." Cindy leads me to the coffee table. "We've been working with the girls for over a year. Please, help yourself! We're about to get started."

The stares are soul piercing.

I fix myself some tea to calm my nerves, something Grandma would do. Peppermint with honey.

"Hey."

Her steps are so silent, just like back in the house. A quiet baby mouse.

"Amber?"

Amber nods, then hugs me. A weak hug, eyes somber and sunken. She's lost weight, and her once bountiful hair has thinned with bald patches in the front.

"You OK?" she asks.

"Um, yeah. I guess," I mutter, the cup hot in my hand. "How are you?"

She shrugs. "I'm . . . staying with a friend. My mom won't let me come home yet. Said I wanted to be grown, so I better stay grown."

"When did you leave?"

"I didn't," she says, voice drifting. "But Jessica was never gonna let me stay."

• • •

"Thank you all for coming," Cindy announces, standing at the head of the square conference table, her back to the door. "I know this is difficult and triggering. We appreciate your bravery."

Eyes bounce around, all measuring one another, looking for the common thread.

"We just want to reiterate: what happens in this room, stays in this room," Dawn warns. "We picked this secure location to keep you all safe."

Next, we each take turns introducing ourselves, and Cindy brings us up to speed on the ongoing investigation into Korey. An investigation that started long before I even met him.

"Now that he's dead, what happens?" a woman named Lily asks.

Cindy sighs, tapping her pen on the table.

"Well, it's not the preferred outcome. We would rather have had a conviction. Still, we have our voices to shed light, and urge prosecutors to continue the investigation."

"Yeah, and no one is going to believes us," a woman named Robyn scoffs. "This is pointless now."

"Raising your voice is never pointless! We can still go after his estate and the label. Sue them for damages and hold them accountable. People on their staff knew what Korey was doing, aided and abetted. That shouldn't go unchecked."

"You mean they knew his preference for little girls," Lily corrects, snark mixing with her perfume.

"Aight, I'm just gonna say it," a woman named Dione says,

turning to me. "I was surprised as hell he chose YOU. He usually likes girls with long, pretty hair."

The other women nod, their hair flowing down to their shoulder blades. Not a short cut in the room.

"And you sang with him . . . like, onstage."

"She has an amazing voice," Amber says, eyes on the floor.

"Oh, so I don't?" Lily snaps.

"Easy, Lily," Dawn warns. "No one said that."

"They said you had a breakdown," Dione says. "Which, I don't blame you. Not after living in that house. But I mean, did you really have to kill him?"

My blood turns cold. "I didn't."

The room mutters.

"It's crazy that he was still doing it," a woman named Tessa says. "Still chasing after young girls. Even after the settlements."

"Why did you settle?" Amber asks.

She shrugs. "Lawyers said there wouldn't have been a chance in hell of a conviction. The best thing I could do was take care of myself. And he blackballed me. No managers, agents, or producers would touch me. My career was over before it started."

"I settled too," Dione says. "Detectives tried calling me an uncooperative witness and dropped the investigation all because I had the flu and couldn't make an interview. Real talk, I was scared. All those death threats and phone calls."

"I honestly thought settling meant he would've learned his lesson, you know?" Tessa shakes her head. "But I think that just gave him more power. Like, he realized he could get away with it and wanted it even more."

"My mom got a letter with these . . . pictures Korey had taken of me," Robyn says, blinking back tears. "Said, if I didn't shut up, they'd release the photos."

"He was threatening you," Cindy says. "It's witness intimidation tactics. To scare victims and silence survivors so they won't come forward."

"I know I was with him the longest," Dione mutters. "Five years."

"When was it over for you?" Lily asks.

Dione glances into her cup, her face ashen. "When he choked me until I passed out."

No one gasped. No one except me. It's like they were all too familiar with his dark side, which makes me realize . . . I only touched the surface of it.

"And you weren't the longest. That goes to that she-devil, Jessica."

The room nods in agreement.

"Anyone know what her deal is?" I ask, fishing for more info.

Dione shrugs. "Bitch is like a locked fortress. All I know is that she's been in the game for a minute."

"Then how old is she?"

Everyone shrugs.

"For all we know, she's a damn vampire."

The image of Korey and Jessica at that Grammys party pops into my head. My knuckles whiten as I grip the table.

"Hey, does anyone recognize the girl in the sex tape?" Tessa asks.

"She looks like Enchanted," Lily quips.

I shake my head. "It's isn't me."

The room stares, some crossing their arms.

"I swear, it's not," I add.

"Does it matter?" Dione scoffs. "It could've been any of us. That creep was always recording. He recorded us having sex, recorded me using the bathroom. Hell, surprised only one of those tapes showed up."

"He recorded when we had sex with . . . other women," Tessa says, her voice quivering with shame.

Lily chuckles. "He recorded me using a nanny cam. You know, one of them bears you hide in a baby's room? Couldn't believe it. I had no clue!"

A . . . nanny cam?

The cup of tea slips out of my hands, crashing on the floor.

"Enchanted," Cindy says. "You OK?"

I push up from the table, heart racing. "I—I have to go."

Cindy frowns. "Go? We just started."

"I'm . . . I'm sorry."

Behind me, I hear Lily mumble the word *liar.*

The sun blinds me as I rush out the building, heading for the uptown train, using my last two percent to make a call.

"Enchanted!" Mr. Pulley exclaims, his voice a low whisper. "Where are you? Everyone is looking for you. We were supposed to be at the station three hours ago."

"Mr. Pulley, did anyone check the security footage? Korey

had cameras all over the house in Atlanta. Probably did in his condo, too."

He sighs, a door closing in the background. "Yes, they checked them. But the system was turned off. Sometime before ten."

Jessica. She's the only one who would know how and have the access. She also knew when I was going to be there. She practically sent me into the lion's den.

"Did they recover any cameras or anything from his room?"

"Nothing. That's the first thing they would've looked for."

That means it's still there . . .

"Enchanted, why don't you come in," Mr. Pulley suggests, his voice soft. "We'll talk about all of this in person. Everyone is really worried about you. It's not safe for you to be alone."

No way I can go in now. Not when I know exactly what will save me.

A hand grabs me, pulling me out of the flow of walking traffic. I cry out but freeze.

"Enchanted!" Mr. Pulley yells over the line. "Are you OK? Talk to me?"

I can't talk. I can barely breathe.

Her hair is in a sloppy bun, tucked neatly under her hoodie. The same one I have on.

"Hey," she says in a sheepish voice.

Gab.

# Chapter 85
## REUNITED

Gab parks behind a construction dumpster not far from KA. We sit, sobbing until the windows fog.

"I'm sorry! I'm so, so sorry, Chant!"

I clutch her, afraid she'll disappear again, baffled by the relief.

"I've been calling and texting," I whimper, wiping tears away.

Gab checks the rearview, keeping her hoodie pulled up tight. "I changed my number," she says, glancing over her shoulder twice. "They were coming after me."

"Who?"

"Korey Fields. And his peoples or whatever."

"What?"

Gab shrinks in her seat, checking behind her again. "I came to your show in Connecticut," she says, meeting my eye. "I mean, yeah, I was ignoring you, but Jay convinced me to stop being petty. It was going to be a surprise."

"You were there? Why didn't you—"

She holds a hand up. "Let me finish. I got there late, made it to VIP with the pass you left, but when I walked in . . . I saw you passed out on the sofa. I literally could not wake you. Whatever you had . . . I don't know, but I wasn't going to leave you like that. Was gonna drag you out of there if I had to. But then Korey got up in my face. Said if I touched you, he'd kill me! I tried calling the cops, but then this crazy big guy broke my phone. So I ran, and the big guy followed me to my car. Told me if I told anyone what I saw tonight, he'd kill me."

My fingers lock tight against my chest.

"Then what happened?"

"It was like, a real nightmare. I don't know how they got my phone number, but they kept calling me, saying if I went to the police or told anybody what I saw, they would kill me AND Jay. It was scary, like they knew everything about me!"

"Think that's my fault," I confess. "I told Korey about you two."

Gab sighs. "Yeah, I figured. After they got to Jay, then they called my dad."

"OMG! What happened?"

"They told him that I was still seeing Jay and lying about it. My dad flipped and took me out of Parkwood. Said he wasn't paying all this money to send me to school to be some slut for a college kid."

Tears fill her eyes. She wipes them on her hoodie.

"Gab, I'm so sorry."

She waves her hand. "It's fine. Anyway, I kept quiet, because I didn't want those assholes to fuck with my life any more than they did. Changed my number and promised to keep my mouth shut. Then I saw you on the news. The way that lady attacked you . . . felt like it was all my fault. If I never convinced you to audition . . . you would've never met that monster."

"It's not your fault. None of it!"

She takes a deep breath. "Still, I couldn't let you think . . . you were alone."

"Thanks."

She nods as another question hits me.

"Hey, how'd you know where to find me?"

"That open letter! I reached out to them, told them everything. They said that you might come, so I hid outside to make sure you weren't followed."

"Followed?"

"They know they did wrong, Chant. They wouldn't be trying this hard to shut me up if they didn't."

Gabriela looks like she hasn't slept in days. Maybe months. She coughs out a laugh. "Jay told me you came by his job."

"Yeah, he played it off good," I chuckle.

"He was just trying to protect me. That guy, I swear it's stupid the way he loves me."

A tinge of jealousy bites my stomach. "I wish . . ."

"Don't say it. He wasn't worth it. He tried to separate us! All that 'Bright Eyes' bullshit . . ."

I blink. "What did you say?"

She cocks her head to the side. "What?"

A fog lifts and sharp clarity crashes into me. I press into the door.

"You're not real."

"What?"

"Oh God," I mumble. "Oh God!"

I swing open the door, stumbling away from the car.

"Chant! Where are you going?"

My thoughts spin counter clockwise.

Gab isn't real. There is no Gab. I'm imagining this. I'm losing it just like Grandma. Why now? Why?

A hand grabs my hoodie, yanking me back.

"Don't touch me," I scream, swinging. "Get off me!"

"The hell? What's gotten into you?"

Gab yokes my sleeve, eyes scanning the street. "Where are you going? Get back in the car! What if someone sees you?"

Even dressed down, Gab is gorgeous. Somehow, my mind made up the very opposite of myself. Everything I feared that I'm not.

I shove her away, crying. "You're not real!"

"What are you talking about? Of course I'm real!"

"No one knew Korey called me Bright Eyes. I never told anyone that! Not even you."

Gab frowns, flabbergasted, then lets out a chuckle before pinching my arm with a twist.

"Ow," I shriek. "What the fuck?"

"Is that real enough for you?"

The sting burns. But can people who imagine other people FEEL them?

Gab measures my silence, rolling her eyes. "Oh my God! Are you serious? Korey called *all* his girls Bright Eyes. It said so in that report about Candy. Didn't you read it?"

My knees jerk to flee but then I remember the woman who tried to kill me onstage. The wig, the way she called me Bright Eyes . . . she was one of us, another girl.

Damn, was anything we had real?

She shakes her head. "What's gotten into you?"

"The cops told me . . . they said . . ."

"And you believed them?"

My shoulders slump. If Gab is real . . . that means everything that happened was real. He took me from my family and friends, he took my freedom, he took my heart, he took my *songs*! Hot anger flashes through me.

"I didn't kill Korey," I say, hard. "You believe me, right?"

"Of course!"

"OK. I have an idea. But I'm going to need your help. And your car."

She smirks. "As long as I don't get killed, I'm down for whatever."

# Chapter 86
## GROUP CHAT

*W&W Squad (w/o the Jones sisters)*

Aisha: **Y'all seen that open letter? Signed by the victims.**

Sean: **So it wasn't just Enchanted? There were others.**

Aisha: **Has anyone heard from her yet?**

Malika: **No.**

Sean: **Nah.**

Aisha: **Her parents are freaking out. I can't believe she ran away.**

Sean: **I don't know. What if she didn't run away?**

There's some loyal fans out there. She could've been kidnapped.

Aisha: I feel awful.

Sean: Me too.

Malika: I don't. She murdered Korey Fields. We have a murderer in our damn Will and Willow chapter! Everyone is gonna know about us.

Sean: It ain't about US or you. You'd murder him too if he touched you. Wouldn't you?

Aisha: Did you actually READ that open letter? We gotta help her.

Sean: How?

Aisha: Maybe we can get a chain going with the other chapters. Ask around. Prove that he got, like, a pattern of doing fucked up shit.

Sean: I met this chick from the Atlanta chapter who said Korey used to hang out around her high school and pick up girls.

Malika: What? Why didn't you say anything?

Sean: IDK. Didn't seem important!

Aisha: Oh God! This girl from the Charlotte chapter told me the same thing. Thought she was just making it up to get closer to Enchanted!

Malika: So he's hanging around high schools? That's . . . nasty.

Aisha: We gotta tell someone!

Sean: Yo I'm telling my dad right now.

Aisha: We need to be looking for her! She's family!

Sean: **Word!**

Aisha: **I'm calling Shea! Maybe we can get other chapters to go out and search for her if we tell them the whole story.**

Malika: **I feel so fucked up.**

Sean: **Ain't your fault. We all thought the same thing!**

Creighton: **YOOOOO!**

Sean: **Yo, where you been?**

Creighton: **You know how they were saying she was crazy and shit?**

Aisha: **Yeah.**

Creighton: **I think I found her friend.**

Malika: **What are you talking about?**

Creighton: **That friend . . . Gabriela or something like that. I think I found her!**

Aisha: **Where!**

Creighton: **At the White Plains Galleria. Except her name ain't Gabriela.**

# Chapter 87
## HOW TO GUT A FISH

Outside the building is a mountain of flowers, teddy bears, posters, and candles, stretching from the door to the corner, a whole city block. Police barricades surround the entrance. Someone set up a Bluetooth speaker playing a steady stream of Korey's music. A few loyal fans camp on the curb, still teary-eyed.

Deep in the shadows across the street, I watch three officers patrol the quiet block. Through the glass doors, at the front desk, two doormen sit in their black-and-gold uniforms. I recognize them.

I wonder if they'll recognize me.

Down the block, a car whips around the corner, swerving, its wheels screeching before crashing directly into the barricade memorial, the bears cushioning the wall.

Fans are up on their feet, shouting questions. The officers run over.

Gab rolls down her window, flailing her arms.

"Help! Help, please."

One of the doormen steps outside, holding the door open to peer down the block, as the other doorman makes a call.

That's when I sprint across the street, hop over the fence, and slide past, grabbing the keycard hanging on his belt.

"Hey! Hey! Stop!"

Stunned, the other doorman stumbles to his feet, but I've already raced past him.

"Hey! Over here!" The doorman screams outside, trying to flag the cops down.

Running down the hall, I pass the first set of elevators, as doorman number two gives chase.

"Stop right there!"

Walkie static sings. "All units . . . suspect on premises!"

I slip on the marble tile, knee connecting with the floor, the pain a sucker punch. I swipe the keycard and enter the pool room.

"Hey! Hey!" doorman number two yells. I can feel him on my heels as my run becomes a limp.

I duck, stepping right then left, a quick dance.

"AHHHH!" He tumbles into the pool.

I hobble through the next door, to the elevator near the back entrance. The one Korey took me down during our swim lesson.

Keycard swipe. Up to the twelfth floor, the studio.

The elevator opens and I run through the back hallway to a door leading to the penthouse.

Locked.

"Shit," I mutter, racing to the front desk, and glance at the elevator floor indicator. It's still sitting in the lobby. But within seconds, it starts making its way up.

Second floor.

There are a dozen desk drawers. A key has to be somewhere. Frantically, I rummage.

Fourth floor.

My knee is throbbing. Still no key. Desperate to pry the door open, I grab a pair of scissors.

Fifth floor.

The bloodred light on floor five almost makes my heart stop. I rush into the dark studio, the place reeking of our memories. More drawers. Nothing but papers.

Sixth floor.

"Come on, come on," I whimper, clawing through stacks of music sheets. I rip the drawers out, tossing them onto the floor.

Eighth floor.

Stuck to the bottom of the last drawer is a gray key fob.

Tenth Floor.

Swipe.

I burst into the penthouse, release the breath I've been

holding just as keys jingle at the front door. More walkie static.

"Shit . . ." I gasp, and slice through the caution tape, jumping over police markers . . . Melissa still on the floor where I left her.

The front door flies open.

"Freeze!"

"She's got a knife!"

I slam the bedroom door behind me, clutching the scissors to my chest. Throat burning, lungs fried.

"All units, suspect has locked herself in her room!"

The room smells stale. The blood has dried light pink on the walls. The largest puddle near the bed, spilled buckets of beet juice.

Pounding on the door. More voices.

Flounder is on the dresser, the exact spot Korey placed him, untouched and unbothered.

I flip him over and stab his underbelly, but there's already a hole. One I never noticed before.

The door flings open right as I grab a handful of Flounder guts.

"On the ground! On the ground now!"

"Drop your weapon!"

And inside the fluff of fish guts . . . is a camera.

# *Chapter 88*

## STATE YOUR NAME FOR THE RECORD

*Transcript—June 10*

**Gabriela Garcia:** Am I free to go yet?

**Detective Fletcher:** Hang on, now. Why doesn't anyone at your school remember you?

**Gabriela:** I don't know. Ask them.

**Fletcher:** And what's the story behind your name again?

**Gabriela:** OK, fine. My full name is Olivia Gabriela Garcia-Hill. Growing up, I always went by Gabby Garcia. But when I enrolled at Parkwood, my dad wanted me to use a nice white name at a white school. So, I went by Olivia Hill . . . to everyone but Chanty.

**Fletcher:** And you never told Enchanted? Thought you two were best friends?

**Gabriela:** I don't know, guess I was . . . embarrassed that I let my dad, who was barely around, talk me into being something that I'm not while Enchanted was all super talented, had this amazing family, and wasn't afraid to be herself.

**Fletcher:** Why'd you wait to come forward?

**Gabriela:** Like all the other girls, I was scared. And it's not like you instantly believe us. When we say, 'Hey, I was raped,' you say, 'Are you sure?' Way to make us feel safe, Mr. Officer.

**Fletcher:** But you weren't reporting a rape.

**Gabriela:** Last time I checked, it wasn't legal to seduce an underage girl.

**Fletcher:** That's not what I . . . I mean.

**Gabriela:** It's just interesting how you assume a girl is crazy rather than believing her the first time she tells you something. Enchanted is, what, your sixteenth victim? It took sixteen girls to tell you something, and she had to risk her life to prove you idiots wrong.

**Fletcher:** She had multiple opportunities to

report her abuse. To walk away from her
mistreatment. She could've come to us.

**Gabriela:** OK, what if it was me? What if I came
in here, said my name is Olivia Hill and told
you about Korey? You'd hear my name, look at
my white skin, never expecting I'm a Latina,
and he'd be in lockup within hours. But a black
girl like Enchanted, she didn't stand a chance.
I see that now, and here I am, putting my white
name to good use to tell you you're all a bunch
of assholes.

**Fletcher:** This isn't about race. This is about
the truth!

**Gabriela:** The truth? Ha! It's funny the crazy
lengths y'all go through to disprove a black
girl rather than just taking her word for
it. Enchanted didn't deserve this. You made
her question her sanity. Made her family and
friends question her sanity. You're just as bad
as Korey with your brainwashing bullshit.

**Fletcher:** Whatever you say. It still doesn't
explain how she saw Korey onstage with her at
the talent showcase.

# *Chapter 89*

## PRINCESSES MUST SAVE THEMSELVES

Flounder recorded seventy-five minutes of footage. Positioned toward the bed, there was a crystal-clear view of Korey punching me in the face, then Richie opening the penthouse door from the studio . . . using the key fob Jessica gave him. Its battery died right as Richie shoved the knife into Korey's chest.

Richie was arrested. So was a thirty-five-year-old Jessica.

With all the bad press and Korey's obsession with me spiraling, a scorned Jessica saw the perfect opportunity to kill the man who broke his promise of stardom, pinning it on the girl who took her place. The murder would also guarantee Richie's documentary would be an instant hit. They planned to live happily ever after in the Hollywood Hills, managing Korey's estate. But once caught, Jessica sang like a humpback.

Love is complicated.

Will and Willow collected names and stories from several girls nationally who claimed they'd been with Korey Fields. With most of the black parents being wealthy and well connected, it added fuel to the fire of a growing case.

A box of Korey Fields's digital memory cards was recovered in the home he shared with his wife. There were dozens of them. Dozens of girls he recorded over his entire career.

Not nearly the number who have come forward.

# Chapter 90
## THE TRUTH

Even though it's summer, I feel like spring.

I feel like a plant being brought back to life, blooming and growing. The smell of sweet flowers, fresh earth, and new beginnings mixed with lemon icy and the fierce love of a mother and father.

More women come forward. KA moves to ban Korey Fields's music across all platforms. Radios refuse to play him, and debates carry on over social media. Or so I've heard.

Mr. Pulley didn't have to fight too hard to cancel my contract with the label. They quietly let it go, sending along a sizable check to cover any inconveniences. It helps to keep Shea in school and in Will and Willow. I won't be going back.

I plan to pursue music full-time, since I'm free, full, and whole.

"Bloop! Another girl came forward," Gabriela says, nose in her phone. "Second girl this week."

Gabriela and I share a veggie plate on my porch as the Littles play in the front yard. Last time I'll see her for the next few weeks. Planning to spend the summer with Grandma in Far Rockaway, to find my voice and return to the sea where I belong before Louie releases my EP in the fall.

"Good. Maybe someone will come forward soon so everyone can stop thinking it was me in the stupid video."

Gab puts down her phone. "Girl."

"What?"

She gives me a sharp glare. "Why are you still lying? You know it was you."

We hold a stare, Gab emboldened and I . . . resolved. Because if I keep denying the memory, it'll make it untrue.

Works for Grandma.

"It's not me," I say matter-of-factly and gaze into my cup of beet juice. I remember the blood . . .

I remember waking up to the sound of Korey screaming . . . the heavy footsteps as a man ran by my head.

I remember peering up from the floor, the room hazy, the taste of purple drink still on my tongue . . . seeing Korey on the bed, bleeding everywhere.

I remember him stretching and reaching for the knife lying between us.

I remember the fear, painted in memories, ripping through me . . . knowing if he reached that knife, he would kill me.

I remember wobbling to my feet, grabbing the knife, and plunging it into his chest.

I remember collapsing on the floor, covered in beet juice, and for the first time since I met him, feeling truly safe, before the world went black . . .

"Chanty, look at me!" Destiny says, calling me back as she attempts a cartwheel.

"Good job," I cheer, and take a sip of beet juice.

Stuff is better than I thought.

# AUTHOR'S NOTE

My first boyfriend was twenty-two years old; I was fifteen. The greatest secret I ever kept. It was exciting and invigorating to be considered so beautiful and adultlike. Everything a teen girl dreams of being seen as. But ultimately, I knew it wasn't right—the sneaking around, the lying. Still, at that age, I should not have been the first to come to that conclusion. Although, I did go to a predominately white high school in Westchester and was in Jack and Jill, I want to be clear: This book is completely a work of fiction.

If you've read *Allegedly* or *Monday's Not Coming*, you already know this book was inspired by a case . . . but this book is not about R. Kelly, nor is it a recount of his allegations.

This book is about the abuse of power. It's about the pattern of excusing grown men for their behavior while faulting young girls for their missteps.

It's about the blatant criticism of girls who were victims of manipulation. It's about holding the right person accountable for the crime he committed. It's about corporations attempting to silence victims and continuing to profit off the very monster they helped create.

About the individuals who were meant to protect and serve never believing victims in their moments of bravery. It's about girls trying to defend themselves against the world and the possibility of similar situations happening to anyone . . . even to girls from two-parent households.

This book is not about R. Kelly. It's about adults who know the difference between right and wrong. Because no matter where you stand on the issue . . . *he* **knew better.**

It is possible to have a loving relationship full of mutual respect and good intentions, like Gabriela's. But if you ever feel you are in a situation like Enchanted, where you're being used, threatened, sexually coerced, or you simply feel uncomfortable, please seek help right away. Tell your parents, one of your friend's parents, a trusted teacher, or a relative.

## RESOURCES

National Domestic Violence Hotline
www.thehotline.org
1-800-799-7233
The Hotline is the only 24/7 center in the nation that has access to service providers and shelters across the U.S.

National Sexual Violence Resource Center
www.nsvrc.org
"Our staff collects and disseminates a wide range of resources on sexual violence including statistics, research, position statements, statutes, training curricula, prevention initiatives, and program information. With these resources, we assist coalitions, advocates, and others interested in understanding and eliminating sexual violence."

RAINN
www.rainn.org
"RAINN (Rape, Abuse & Incest National Network) is the nation's largest anti-sexual violence organization. RAINN created and

operates the National Sexual Assault Hotline (800.656.HOPE, online.rainn.org y rainn.org/es) in partnership with more than 1,000 local sexual assault service providers across the country and operates the DoD Safe Helpline for the Department of Defense. RAINN also carries out programs to prevent sexual violence, help survivors, and ensure that perpetrators are brought to justice."

## ME TOO

metoomvmt.org

"The 'Me Too' movement supports survivors of sexual violence and their allies by connecting survivors to resources, offering community organizing resources, pursuing a 'me too' policy platform, and gathering sexual violence researchers and research. 'Me Too' movement work is a blend of grassroots organizing to interrupt sexual violence and digital community building to connect survivors to resources."

# ACKNOWLEDGMENTS

First, I want to apologize to my family for learning about my high school double life with the rest of the world. LOL! Thank you for understanding and continuing to be immensely proud of me. To my grandma, I wish you were still here just so I can apologize again. To my Jack and Jill family, I gave you all a hard time, but real talk, you saved me.

But really, this book is all Stephanie Jones's fault. There I was, minding my business and she just had to jump in my text and put the idea in my head. Mrs. Jones, I am so grateful for our budding friendship and cannot wait to see your books on the shelves one day!

To my beta readers, sensitivity readers, and blurbers . . . this wasn't an easy book to write and it definitely wasn't an easy one to read. I had so many doubts and insecurities, and I second-guessed myself the entire way. But you each took the time to respond to my questions and to hold me in my most vulnerable state. Thank you.

To Rachelle Baker, this cover . . . EPIC!! Thank you a million times over.

Huge shout-out to the publicity, marketing, School and Library, and design teams at HarperCollins. You all stepped up in a major way to support this book, and I'm excited to continue working together.

To Ben Rosenthal and Katherine Tegen, you continue to support every wild (read: insane) book idea I've had, without hesitation. I'm super grateful you took a chance on me when others wouldn't. We make an excellent team.

Tanu Srivastava, you were the MVP during the Covid pandemic

getting this book through its final days before print. I appreciate you!

Natalie Lakosil, the fact that I could sit on the beach and have a conference call with you in the middle of the work week is the best example of how you've changed my life for the better.

I feel like I should thank my therapist . . . because without her, I would not have been able to reconcile what happened to me and see that I am not my mistakes. So thank you for being so brilliant.

Proverbs 3:5–6 . . . Amen.

Last . . . MUTE MUTHERF*CKING R. KELLY!!!! www.muterkelly.org.